Joan Lingard writes for both adults and children. Her best known work for young people includes her much-acclaimed Ulster quintet, about the Protestant girl Sadie and the Catholic boy Kevin, and the 'Maggie' quartet, which she adapted for television.

Joan Lingard grew up in Belfast where she lived from the ages of two to eighteen. She lives now in Edinburgh with her Canadian husband and spends a certain amount of time every year in Canada. She has three daughters.

Also by Joan Lingard in Pan Books

Reasonable Doubts
The Second Flowering of Emily Mountjoy

Joan Lingard

Sisters by Rite

Pan Books
London, Sydney and Auckland

First published in Great Britain in 1984
by Hamish Hamilton Ltd

This edition published in 1989 by Pan Books Ltd,
Cavaye Place, London SW10 9PG

9 8 7 6 5 4 3 2 1

ISBN 0 330 30959 5

Phototypeset by Input Typesetting Ltd, London
Printed and bound in Great Britain by
Courier International Ltd, Tiptree, Essex

The author and publishers are grateful to the Society
of Authors, as the literary representative of the
Estate of John Masefield, for the quotation from *Cargoes*

for
three sisters by right:
Kersten, Bridget
and Jenny

1970

A man was shot dead in East Belfast earlier this evening. Mr Sam McGill, who was a member of the B Specials until they were disbanded last year, had gone to answer the door . . .

'Sam McGill?' said Aunt Belle.

The shooting was witnessed by his mother who was standing in the hallway behind him . . .

'That couldn't be Rosie's Uncle Sam, could it?'

The news reader's face dissolved to let the camera pan down a street of small red-brick semi-detached houses.

'It is,' said I and went closer to the television screen as if I could move into the street with the camera. A huddle of women stood outside Number Three. They looked familiar though I didn't recognize anyone. I couldn't see Rosie either. But it was unlikely that she would be standing at the gate. She would be somewhere inside the house behind the drawn blinds. She would be with her mother and grandmother and Uncle Billy.

Uncle Billy and Uncle Sam. In their church-going Lodge-going suits, their hair slicked down with Brilliantine. Once upon a time the suits had been for dancehall-going too. Rosie and I used to like walking the uncles to the bus stop on a Saturday night. 'Have a good time,' we would yell after them as they rolled away to the delights of the Floral Hall where coloured lights revolved and girls wore white high-heeled sandals and smelled of *Lily of the Valley* and *Midnight in Paris*. Everybody loved Saturday night. Except us left behind on the dead pavement. But our time would come, said the uncles, and it did, and by then theirs had passed.

'He had a girl for a while,' I said.

'Who, dear?' said Aunt Belle.

'Rosie's Uncle Sam.'

She'd had legs like pencils and been known as Magenta Lily. But in the end he'd stayed with his mother for he'd known when he was well off. And now he was dead, shot through his navy-blue suit, his white starched shirt, and his heart. He was soft-hearted, said his mother, wouldn't hurt a fly. Soft-headed, said some. As children we hung around him, Rosie and I, for his smile was easy and in his pocket he kept sugar mice and jelly babies. But he was led by the nose by his brother Billy, there was no question about that. Now if it had been him who had been shot one could have understood it. *He* was the hard man.

The women at the gate were being interviewed. Nudging forward, looking into the camera's eye rather than that of the interviewer, they told everything and nothing. *I heard this noise . . . And then.. When I looked I saw Mr McGill lying sprawled across the doorstep all doubled up like . . .*

'Terrible, isn't it?' said Aunt Belle, 'to think–'

The camera inched over and the door of Number Seven came into view.

'There's your old house, Cora!'

The camera swung even wider and came to rest on unlucky Number Thirteen. Teresa's house. Teresa and Rosie and I: three little pretty maids living in a row, as my mother sometimes called us, though Rosie was by far the prettiest and I was not pretty at all. Blood sisters, in spite of the problems that stood in our way. Or only one problem really.

'Such a quiet street it was,' said Aunt Belle. 'You could hardly credit, could you – something like that happening there?'

I extinguished the picture. The news reader had moved on anyway, to give details of other deaths in other countries. I didn't want to argue with Aunt Belle. I didn't want to have to say that I could credit it, all too easily. She said she'd make some tea, I looked as if I could do with a cup. On her way to the kitchen she touched me on the shoulder.

I reached for the telephone, drew back. Should I? Or

not? I fingered the scar on my wrist watching it turn white and then flush pink again as I released the pressure. I remembered the blood welling up out of the gash and Teresa crying, 'Cora's bleeding to death. Holy Mother of God save us!' Her appeal had been heard then, when we were only nine years old, but another nine years further on and the same cry was left hanging on the wind. Memories were beginning to come, thick and fast, like mist rolling in from the sea, threatening to choke me, but impossible to push back. I had been wrong to think there was a choice. I picked up the receiver.

The man of the house answered, the only man left in the house now. 'Who? For dear sake! It's been a long time . . .'

I had just returned from abroad, I said, and heard the news. We agreed that it was dreadful. We spoke for a few minutes, about violence and death and the dark days that walked upon the land of Ulster and then he called Rosie. 'It's Cora. Calling from London.'

'Cora?' Rosie burst into tears. When she could speak, she said, 'You couldn't come over could you? I know it's a lot to ask but I need you. There's another complication, you see, which I can't talk about now. Teresa's back by the way. She rang me briefly . . .'

When Aunt Belle returned with the tea I told her I was going to Belfast the next day.

'Are you sure you want to, dear? With all that going on? You haven't been back for years after all.'

'Seventeen. It was 1953 when we left, if you remember?'

But my memories were going to go back even further, to 1944, the year that Teresa's family came to live in the street.

ONE

'There's no mistaking what they are,' said Rosie's grandmother, who had come out to the gate – or to where the gate had been before they took it away for scrap iron – to watch the unloading five doors down.

Everything coming out of the maw of the pantechnicon looked chipped. The removal men were taking this into account and paying little attention to the pleas of the stout woman with the baby on her hip or of the red-faced man who was leaping about like a half-strangled hen, his arms outstretched to catch tilting furniture. A lanky boy and a girl of about our age were helping carry while various other black-haired children hung about getting in the way.

'The first ones intil' the street,' said Mrs Meneely, Rosie's mother, who accompanied *her* mother most places.

'And they won't be the last, Ina, you can bet your boots on that! Once they get a foot in–'

'Why your boots?' I asked.

'You ask far too many questions, girl!'

Rosie and I sidled off the wall.

'And where do you think you're going, Margaret Rose?'

'Just down to Cora's, Gran.'

Granny McGill gave us a look that told us to watch ourselves and to go so far and no further. Rosie and I would always want to go further but on this occasion only went as far as my house which, being Number Seven (oh lucky us!), was nearer to Thirteen. Neither Rosie nor I would have fancied living at such an unlucky number, though my mother said there was no such thing as luck. Any more than there was sin, disease or death.

The girl of our age had her eye on us and not on the

box she was carrying. It slipped down her thigh. 'For God's sake, Teresa, watch what you're doing!' cried the father. 'Your mother's best chinie's in that.'

Rosie began to giggle and then so did I since we did everything together. Convulsions overwhelmed us. Hands clutching our mouths, we ran round the side of my house and into the kitchen where my mother was making a chocolate cake with dried eggs and liquid paraffin.

'What's got into you two?'

'There's a bunch of RCs moving into Number Thirteen,' said Rosie between eruptions of giggling. 'You should see their stuff. All holes and things. And the kids stink.' She pinched the end of her nose. That was a lie, or was as far as Rosie was concerned, for we hadn't got close enough to tell. I was anxious about truth, having been brought up to be. But I knew too that Rosie was almost certainly right. So, had she lied or not?

'They're God's children, just the same as we are,' said my mother, which was what we expected her to say. 'Why not go in to the fire, girls? It's getting cold out.'

But the street drew us back. The afternoon light was dwindling, the pavement icing over. Our breath puffed white into the air. We skated up and down making a slide whilst keeping an eye on the new arrivals. Mrs McGill and Mrs Meneely had given up and gone in. The last stained mattress was carried from the van and the men fastened the big back doors and palmed their hands off on their aprons.

'*There was an old woman,*' chanted Rosie, '*who lived in a shoe.*'

'*Who had so many children . . .* '

So many children, so many children . . .

My mother rapped on the front room window.

'Let's go for a dander,' said Rosie.

Arms linked, we sauntered down the street. Lights blazed in every room of Number Thirteen.

'They'll need to get those windows covered before dark,' said Rosie whose Uncle Billy was an Air Raid Warden and considered it his duty to patrol the street nightly looking for cracks of light. He'd even been in a few times to tick off my mother, though with her he was not as sharp. 'Unless they're wanting to give the place away to the Gerries. Come to think of it, they might just.'

I couldn't see why, not our particular street. There was nothing special about it unless you counted Uncle Billy who was something important in his Loyal Orange Lodge. My mother was not inclined to count that. And my father? He was in a Prisoner-of-War Camp in the Far East. He'd been captured by the Japanese at the fall of Hong Kong. When war broke out in 1939 he was one of the first to volunteer. He was always a restless man, said my mother, after he'd gone. There had been no need for him to go, there being no conscription in Northern Ireland throughout the war. Before it, he'd been a toothbrush salesman for the whole of Ireland, North and South. He was fed up with toothbrushes, I remember him saying, as he stood in front of the fire wearing his creaking new uniform. The relics of his former life reposed in the shed at the side of the house. Rosie and I played with the samples, boxed in their narrow coffins, imagining them to be everything from bars of gold to sticks of dynamite.

'Anyway,' I said, 'it's a long time since the Gerries have been over our way.'

'You never know though do you but?'

At the bottom of the street we turned and came back up again. The pantechnicon had gone and the red-faced man was pinning sacking over the windows of Number Thirteen. From inside the house came the sound of Geraldo and His Orchestra and the squalling of small children.

'Teresa,' said Rosie, trying out the name. 'I suppose she's called after some saint or other. They're keen on saints. They light smelly candles to them.'

We proceeded to the McGills.

They were gathered round the table in the back living room drinking cups of dark tea: Uncle Billy, Uncle Sam, Mrs Meneely and Granny McGill. Although she was known as Granny there was nothing of the little old woman about her with bent back and wispy hair; she was tall and had shoulders as broad as a man's and hands almost as wide as her sons'. At that time she was in her mid-fifties, and vigorous with it. Much more vigorous than her daughter. Though that wouldn't have been difficult. Mrs Meneely was fond of her bed. There was no Mr Meneely: he'd died before Rosie was born. Slipped and fell when he was running for a tramcar, cracked his skull. Running away from his mother-in-law, said some. My mother said I shouldn't listen to malicious gossip. That was Error talking. But whenever I fell, which I seemed to do regularly, and saw the pavement coming up to meet me, I thought of Rosie's father and his skull cracking open, like an egg.

Rosie was much better informed about death than I: she knew about last gasps and last words and last wills and testaments. My mother said death did not exist: one passed on to a better life. She said I should not listen to Rosie's talk about undertakers and funerals. She said that if I believed in God I would have life everlasting. Never die? said Rosie. The place would be stuffed to bursting if that was the case. You'd be standing five deep on the pavement. When I walked home alone at dusk I curled my shoulders inwards and glanced about wondering if unseen people brushed against me.

Grandfather McGill's life was almost at an end. He was lying upstairs dying. It was a fact, said Rosie, and there was no use my mother saying he wasn't for the doctor had told them so. Only the day before he'd said it wouldn't be long now.

The McGills were discussing the new occupants of Number Thirteen.

'It'll be the ruination of the street,' said Uncle Billy. 'Imagine – Taigs!'

'Maybe they won't stay long,' I said. 'They might not like it.'

'Aye, they might not, Cora.' Uncle Billy gave me a nod of approval.

'I just hope there'll be no trouble that's all,' said Granny McGill.

'Why would there be?' I asked.

'You can't blame people for having strong feelings can you?'

I supposed not, though I was not sure.

'Their ways are not our ways, know what I mean?' I didn't, but knew that I was not meant to say so. 'And they wouldn't want us in their streets, would they?'

'The devil they wouldn't,' said Uncle Billy.

'Like should stick with like,' said Granny McGill. 'That way there's less trouble.'

'I can't get over the Flemings selling to them but,' said Mrs Meneely.

'They'll not be bothered will they, as long as they've got their dough?'

We heard a dull thud overhead.

'Sounds like the ould fella's fallen outa bed,' said Uncle Sam.

'He will try and sit up,' said Uncle Billy.

'Away on up and see, Sam,' said his mother.

Sam went up and was back down in a minute scarcely able to speak.

'He's dead,' he stuttered.

Rosie turned to give me a look of triumph.

George William McGill had been one of the quarter of a million Ulstermen who had queued at the City Hall in 1913 to sign the Solemn League and Covenant against Home Rule. He had signed in his own blood. Opened up a vein and dipped the pen in, said Rosie. He'd been a founder member of the Ulster Volunteer Force and had helped run guns and ammunition into the port of Larne in April 1914. What a night that was! Behind the drawn blinds his cronies reminisced, recalling how they'd outwitted police and army and taught them not to poke their noses into business that was too dangerous for them. Boys a dear, those were the days, when the Volunteers had been ready to fight to keep their rights and defend the faith!

'I'd prefer you *not* to go into the McGills just now,' said my mother who was reading about Life in *Science and Health with Key to the Scriptures* by Mary Baker Eddy.

But I slipped away as soon as I could and hurried up the street to the house with the shrouded windows and the black taffeta bow tied to the door knocker. All the houses had their front blinds drawn but one. Too much to expect any sign of decency from a crowd like that, said Granny McGill. But I didn't think they had blinds to draw. Earlier that day I'd seen the lanky boy washing *Taigs Go Home* off their side wall.

Upstairs in the McGills' best bedroom lay the old man, his chest festooned with medals and his liver-spotted hands awkwardly crossed. Rosie took me up to see him. We whispered. 'He's cold if you touch him.' 'Is that a fact?' I did not dare touch. It was difficult to believe he had ever been alive. We vacated the room to let the men of the Lodge file past to pay their last respects.

Downstairs in the scullery the kettle steamed continuously; neighbours handed in sponge cakes, flies' cemeteries and German biscuits. My mother donated the chocolate cake but declined the offer of a last look at the old man saying she preferred to remember him as he had been in life. I thought he looked better dead, with the fierce look gone and all the lines straightened out.

Only members of the family were admitted for the funeral service itself. Rosie's Aunt Gertrude came and Uncle Jack, and cousins Clark and Deanna. Deanna bounced her ringlets at me over the fur collar of her new coat as she went up the path. Uncles arrived from Ballymena and cousins from Magherafelt. And outside in the street the Orangemen waited, dark-suited, bowler-hatted, and sashed.

I, too, waited, and when I saw how they were having to manoeuvre the coffin to get it out of the front door I covered my eyes with my hands. 'It's all right, love,' said Mrs Robinson who lived at Number Eleven. I couldn't bear the thought that they were tilting him forward, that his face was being crushed against the lid. But in the next moment they had him righted again and were raising him shoulder high.

The old Volunteer was borne by his two sons and two nephews. They set off on the long haul to the cemetery at Dundonald. I mingled with the following crowd and went with them as far as Ballyhackamore where they put him into the hearse. I walked back with Mrs Robinson and she told me about some of the funerals she had seen. Women didn't go to the graveyard. They stayed at home to prepare the funeral feast.

And what a feast the McGills were making! Hams were on the boil on the old gas cooker, a large piece of beef was spluttering in the oven sending out a smell that made you feel daft for a taste of it, jellies were sitting on the window sills to cool, cakes of every colour lay on the big scrubbed kitchen table. There was no shortage of food in the McGills' house in spite of rationing. No dried eggs or liquid paraffin for them. They could get what they wanted on the black market which was thought fair game by everybody but my mother. A butcher who lived in the street made a fortune during the war selling chickens to American soldiers and shortly after VE day was able to move out to a big house up the Malone Road. They came back to visit from time to time in a long sleek black car, he with a fat cigar clamped between his newly gilded teeth, she wrapped in mink, with lips and nails tipped shocking pink. Granny McGill considered they'd gone above themselves and when they rang her bell she'd stand like a statue behind the lace curtains until they'd driven off. Even when they lived in the street she thought them vulgar with their tasselled blinds, mauve window surrounds and pink door with a plastic rose showing behind the glass panel. My mother always let them in, of course.

But on the night of the funeral the butcher and his wife jammed into the McGills' along with everybody else. Rosie and I sat astride the back of the settee. People squatted on the stairs and stood in the narrow hall. They ate and drank (ginger beer and lemonade – the McGills were strictly teetotal, which was one of the few things about them that my mother approved of) and sang. They sang the songs their fathers had sung. *Dolly's Brae, The Ould Orange Flute* and *The Sash*.

Here am I a loyal Orangeman, just come across the sea,
For singing and for dancing I hope that I'll please thee,
I can sing and dance with any man, as I did in days of yore
. . .

I could sing and dance with any man too. *And on the Twelfth I long to wear the sash my father wore.* The melodies were lively and tuneful and set your feet a-tapping and after all the tearful sighs of earlier in the day it was good to see people smiling and laughing again. I knew that if my mother could have seen and heard me she would not have laughed. *It's ould but it's beautiful, it's colours they are fine . . .*

While we were singing Orange songs my mother was drinking tea in the RCs' kitchen. They were called Lavery, she found out. Rosie and I didn't pass up the opportunity to refer to them as the 'Lavvies' thereafter, which, predictably, sent us into paroxysms of laughter. My mother had taken them a round of soda bread and some angel cakes. The lot was gone before she'd finished her second cup of tea.

'Are they starved?' I wanted to know and was sure that Rosie would want to know it too.

'Hardly that. It's just that they don't get many treats since there are so many of them. Too many. However.'

And in the years that followed more were to be born.

'The eldest's eleven, that's Gerard. He seems a bright lad. And then there's Teresa, she's nine–'

'Same as me.'

My mother nodded. 'And then there's Brian and Bridie and Michael and Mary. Nice looking family. They just need a good wash and brush up.'

'And what about Mr Lavery?'

About him she was less enthusiastic, though admitted she had no call to be, even if he did seem a bit excitable and she couldn't help wondering about his red face. But he did work for his living, he had a job in a greengrocer's shop on the other side of town, so Granny McGill wouldn't be able to call him work-shy. She claimed most RCs wouldn't do a hand's turn to save themselves.

'Do you know, Cora,' said my mother, 'someone put a banger through the Laverys' letter box last night? It just missed wee Mary.'

'It couldn't have been the McGills. They were busy with the funeral.'

'I never said it was, dear. I certainly *hope* it wasn't. But the Laverys have as much right in this street as anyone else. And they need support. And so,' she went on, becoming brisk, 'I've asked Teresa to tea tomorrow afternoon.'

On the stroke of five, when I would rather have curled up in the old leather armchair with my library book, or listened to the wireless, Teresa arrived. She had had her face washed and her tangle of hair reduced to some sort of order. She looked wary, and ready to cut and run.

'This is Cora, dear,' said my mother, dragging us together. 'I hope you'll be good little friends.'

Fat chance, thought I. She had already caused trouble between Rosie and me. 'You're not having a Mick to tea are you?' Rosie had been outraged but less, I knew, by the fact that I was going to take tea with a follower of the Church of Rome than that that follower was the same age as us. In plain words, she was jealous. We seldom used plain words with one another; we favoured finery, duplicity, and exaggeration.

I asked Teresa if she'd like to listen to *Children's Hour*?

'Don't mind.' She lifted one sharp-pointed shoulder. She was wearing a summer dress which was too tight and too short. She kept tugging at it as if she needed more room to breathe.

My mother quizzed her gently over tea and we found out that the Laverys had lived up the Falls. (That den of iniquity! Wait till I told Rosie! And then I remembered that we weren't speaking.) An aunt of Mr Lavery's had died and left him some money so Mrs Lavery had decided they should use it to move into a better district.

'To give us more chance,' said Teresa.

Of what? I wondered.

When we'd finished eating my mother said, 'Now off you go and play and I'll do the dishes.'

I took Teresa out to see the toothbrush samples. The shed was roomy and held house and garden tools as well, and a battered suitcase full of dressing-up clothes. I loved being in there at night with the light sending funny shadows over the rough wood walls. This was my magic place: it became, in turn, an ark made of gopher wood, Ali Baba's cave, Toad Hall, Wonderland. 'And through the looking-glass we go!' I cried as I swung open the door and ushered Teresa in. She gave me an odd look. She stood on one leg with the other twisted round it so that she looked like some sort of bird, a young crane perhaps, and her head drooped as if it wanted a wing to hide under. Her teeth chittered.

I took an old tartan travelling rug and wrapped it round her shoulders. Now she had turned into the Indian squaw in my Geography book at school. 'Curiouser and curiouser,' I said. She gazed blankly at me. 'Me Hiawatha.' Batting my fingers against my lips I made a waw-waw sound. Still she looked blank, but when I suggested we play at shops she came to life. I let her be the shopkeeper. She was good at it, moved straight into the part without hesitation and put on a voice that had me doubled up in stitches. *Sassitches are tarrible scarce so they are right now but I'll oblige you with a half poun' if you don't let on to that wumman down the street...*

We were holding our sides with laughter when the door scraped open and Rosie put her head in.

'You should be ashamed of yourself so you should, Cora Caldwell, playing shops with a dirty Fenian lavvy brush!' She faced Teresa. 'If I'd a penny do you know what I'd do? I'd buy a rope and hang the Pope and let King Billy through!'

The travelling rug was flung aside, and in one wild leap Teresa was across the floor and had hold of Rosie's fair curls. Rosie screamed and took a handful of Teresa's black ones. They held tight. They let their voices soar.

Before long my mother arrived on a peace mission. 'Girls, girls . . .' She forced them apart, kept them firmly at bay. They snarled and spat and aimed kicks behind her back. I could tell that she was Knowing the Truth about them, reciting inside her head that they were God's children made in God's image. Heaving and panting, they subsided. Teresa's dress was torn from shoulder to waist. Spittle ran down Rosie's cheek. My mother took their hands and let them into the house. I straightened the toothbrushes, put out the light and went in after them.

They sat one on either side of the fireplace scowling down at their laps while my mother read to them from her book with the gold cross and crown on the cover. ' "*Divine love always has met and always will meet every human need . . .*" ' Her voice, soft and gentle, flowed on, mingling with the soothing crackle of the fire, and gradually the scowls faded and the lines were straightened out just as they had been on the ould fella's face after death. She read for a long time and when she closed the book she said, 'Be at peace with one another, children. There is enough violence in the world as it is.' Then she made us cocoa and jam sandwiches with Veda bread and went upstairs to find an old dress of mine for Teresa.

Next day at school Rosie said, 'Your mother's a queer turn so she is.' No queerer than her lot with their Orange singing! 'Oh, all right, Cora, I wasn't meaning nothing.' We were friends again, promenading round the playground, arms linked, sharing our playpieces.

After school we went for a walk down the main road, past the Roman Catholic church. As we approached the gate Rosie stopped to shake a stone out of her shoe.

'Look in, Cora, look in!'

I looked. There was nothing much to see except the gloomy grey building so unlike the white and bright one I went to on Sundays on the corner of University Avenue. I loved that place: it was light inside, and warm, and it had a blue ceiling and a green carpet. And everybody smiled. You couldn't imagine anyone smiling inside that grey church. They'd be crossing themselves and dipping their fingers in dirty water and praying to graven images. It gave us a thrill just to stand there staring, for when we were younger we had never dared do it. 'Look away!'

Granny McGill would command as she hurried us past, and a feeling of terror would seize me until we were safely by. Look away, she would say too, if we saw nuns, usually in pairs, or a priest, coming towards us. From beneath my lashes I would squint at the long swirling black skirts and ugly black shoes. The Roman church was black and dirty, said Granny McGill.

'That's your friend's church.'

'It's not my fault.' I felt miserable. 'It's my mother who wants me to be friendly with her.'

'I don't see why we shouldn't,' said Rosie. I stared at her. 'It could be good crack.' She smiled. She loved the hint of danger.

Before we had time to move on we were swept up by Aunt Gertrude and taken along to Uncle Sam's shop. She was going to collect a pair of black courts which he'd been re-soling.

'You shouldn't hang about there, girls.'

'A nun might get us and eat us for dinner you mean?' Rosie's face was innocent. It was easy for her to look like an angel.

Uncle Sam's face shone when he saw her. 'How're you the day then, Princess?' He had his hand in his pocket and was pulling out a bag of cinnamon balls. We sucked the stingy hard sweets letting them bulge out our cheeks whilst Aunt Gertrude inspected her shoes. Uncle Sam's handiwork was first class; he enjoyed his trade, handled the shoes lovingly. I was never sure whether I liked his shop or not: it was so poky and dark and the smells so overpowering that I wanted out not long after I was in.

Satisfied, Aunt Gertrude took away her shoes and Uncle Sam put his arms round us.

'And how're my wee girls then? My two wee sweethearts.' He cuddled us close to his leather apron. 'Will I take youse to the pictures on Friday night then?'

Rosie and I would have sold our souls, had we been asked to, to go to the pictures. Please, please! we clamoured. We were crazy about Deanna Durbin, Shirley Temple and Esther Williams. The men who squired them we cared less about. We wanted to be like the women, made over in their images, and were certain that we would be, one of these days. Somewhere over the rainbow, bluebirds flew; so if birds could fly over the rainbow, why then, oh why couldn't we? We planned to go to Hollywood the minute we left school.

On Friday night we went to the Astoria Picture House with Uncle Sam. He had a bar of chocolate in one pocket and a poke of liquorice all-sorts in the other and when he wasn't dishing out the sweets he was holding our hands. And after we'd stood like soldiers to sing *God Save the King* he took us upstairs to the café and bought us ice cream in silver dishes. Such heavenly delights. We swooned with contentment, just like they did on the movie screen.

TWO

The dark evenings suited the flowering of our friendship with Teresa Lavery. Daylight waned before tea-time. After tea we gathered in our shed, Teresa usually arriving last, tapping before she opened the door and poking her head in to make sure that everything was all right.

'Come in and shut the door up quick!' Rosie would cry. 'We're playing at German spies. I'm going to be the spy. *Heil Hitler*!'

My mother would give me lemonade and biscuits to take out, and three cups. She didn't ask if the McGills knew that we were now a threesome but said that Mrs Lavery was delighted that Teresa had made some nice wee friends. '*She* doesn't mind Teresa mixing with Protestants.'

When I passed the information on to Rosie she said, 'That's because Mrs Lavery'll be thinking Teresa'll get us to turn. But we won't turn, will we?'

'Never!' I didn't in the least fancy mixing with nuns in black skirts and standing in a cupboard telling my secrets to a priest behind a grill. Rosie said you had to strip naked, but I wasn't sure whether to believe that or not.

'You never know, *we* might just get Teresa to turn.'

'Protestant you mean?'

'Well, not that thing you go to.'

We had an argument then. 'Have it your way,' said Rosie when I wouldn't give ground, but she wouldn't really accept that Christian Scientists were Protestants. 'You're dead ignorant so you are, Cora Caldwell. There's heathens as well. What about Indians and Japs and Rebecca Cohen? She's a Jew. If it weren't for the Jews there wouldn't be a war on. My granny told me.'

'They started it, you mean?'

Rosie nodded. 'And they don't eat pigs and they do funny things to boys. Something dirty.' She began to giggle.

'Tell me!'

I had to push her head first into the dressing-up suitcase before she did. It was another of Rosie's stories that I found difficult to believe. 'It'd be sore. And it'd bleed.' It was true though, swore Rosie: it was the Bible that told them to do it. But what about Protestant boys then? Why not them? We tried to find the passage in the Bible but it proved impossible. 'There's too much of it and it's too wee print,' said Rosie, shutting it in disgust.

We consulted Teresa.

'But what's it for like?' she asked. She had brothers, we had thought she might know. It was a mystery that exercised our imaginations for a long time. Rosie dared me to ask Rebecca Cohen but I hadn't the nerve. She was four years older and eyed us as if we were worms when she swanned past, her head held high at the end of her long slender neck.

'Do you like being an RC, Teresa?' asked Rosie.

'It's all right.' The wary look was back in Teresa's eye.

'Our church is really nicer, you know. You don't have to tell your sins to nobody. You can do what you like.'

'But God'd know, wouldn't he?'

'I'm not so sure about that. He must have an awful lot of big sinners to keep his eye on. People like Hitler and Lord Haw-Haw. I don't suppose you're a big sinner are you, Teresa Lavery?'

Rosie jumped as someone rapped on the door at the back of her head. Uncle Billy's voice rang out.

'You're showing a light in there, girls!'

She was up on her feet quickly and had her face pressed against the door. 'A light, Uncle Billy? Surely not.'

I pushed Teresa into a corner and threw dressing-up clothes over her.

'There's a slit, Margaret Rose. That's all it takes. Better open up and let me see if the door's fitting properly.'

We put out the light and opened up. His torch light

shone between his shipyard boots. Raising the torch, he fanned the shed in the way that searchlights raked the sky when they were looking for enemy aircraft; he picked out the tools and the toothbrushes and bundles of clothes. I heard the inward rush of Rosie's breath and then the outward flow of it as he turned to give his attention to the window, which was covered with black-out material, and to the door, which he admitted seemed to fit well enough, although he thought we would do well to put a curtain at the back of it when we had the light on. You couldn't be too careful, the enemy was everywhere, crafty devils that they were, and the North of Ireland had more than their fair share of them. They came across the border of course, from the Free State.

'Down there they want the Gerries to win. Oh aye, it's a fact. The Gerries promised they'd give them Ulster if they bate us. That'd be the day! But you girls must do your bit and all! And remember that walls have ears and the enemy's queer and sleekit. Take that new lot down the road. Who knows why *they*'ve come here!'

He moved out on to the path. 'Your mother in, Cora? I'll just take a wee look in on her while I'm here.'

As we closed the door the clothes in the corner stirred. Wait! we cautioned. We listened to the sound of Uncle Billy's feet clumping round to the front door.

Teresa's black head sprang up.

'Now don't take on, Teresa,' said Rosie. 'He didn't mean nothing by it. It's just his way of talking.'

Normally fairly quiet, Teresa's whole body shook when her temper rose. 'We're not German spies! We're not, I tell you! My da's never set eyes on a Gerry in his whole life except at the pictures.'

It was all right, we told her, we knew he was innocent too. We calmed her down and gave her the last of the lemonade.

'That was a close one, wasn't it?' Rosie grinned. 'We'll need to watch so we will. We'll put a blanket over the door and you stay at the back of the shed always, Teresa, with a few clothes handy. We'll just have to be prepared.'

'Would you get into trouble if he caught you?'

'I might. But who cares about that? We're allies aren't we?'

We nodded solemnly.

'We should swear it in blood. Like they did at the Covenant.'

'But I don't know if I feel like opening up a vein, Rosie.' I was bad with blood, always had to look away. Teresa had one leg twisted round the other and her head was beginning to droop.

We wouldn't have to open veins, said Rosie, as we weren't going to write our names or anything, just smear our blood together. The idea still made me feel queasy but there was no holding Rosie back once she had an idea wedged in her mind. She searched the shed for a suitable cutting instrument and decided on the hedge-clippers. She wiped the rust off on her skirt.

'Where'll we do it?' Teresa was staring at her skinny arms and legs. They didn't look too promising for spare blood. My arms were plumper and whiter. I had the white skin of a pale redhead.

'The wrist's the best. I'll go first.'

Rosie held the clippers over her left wrist and then quickly nipped the skin. A small trickle of red emerged. 'See! Quick now before it dries up! You next, Teresa.'

In spite of the droopy head Teresa too acted boldly and made it seem like no bother at all, though I noticed that she bit her bottom lip hard when she swung the clippers downward.

Now it was my turn.

'There,' said Rosie, drawing a line on the inside of my wrist with her finger.

Only half looking, I plunged the points of the clippers in. Blood spurted out.

'You're full of blood,' cried Rosie. 'Wrists together now!'

They rubbed their wrists against mine and our blood mingled. So blood sisters we became from that moment on. It was just like signing at the City Hall, said Rosie. I couldn't take my eyes off my wrist. Blood was continuing to well up and ooze over my hand.

'Open the door!' I was gasping.

'Cora's bleeding to death,' cried Teresa. 'Holy Mother of God save us!'

The air revived me a little. I could feel the warm wet blood flowing down my fingers and dripping on to my leg.

'I'll take you in.' Rosie put her arm round my waist. 'We'll say you slipped. You away on home now, Teresa. Run, for dear sake! Don't stand there gawping like an eejit.'

Rosie brought me into the living room where her uncle and my mother were drinking cups of tea. Uncle Billy leapt up at once saying oh my God what in hell's name had we been up to and he'd better run like blazes and fetch the doctor. My mother said calmly that we had no need of a doctor and I would be perfectly all right in a minute.

'Lie down on the sofa, dear.'

I fell down. My mother and Uncle Billy lifted me on to the settee and Rosie ran to fetch towels from the bathroom. They laid my gory wrist on top of them. I had to turn my head away.

Uncle Billy and my mother faced one another across me.

'You're crazy, woman! She could die.'

'She is God's child. Made in his own image. How then could she die?'

'I know all that but I'm getting the doctor and I don't bloody well care what you say!'

Rosie stood at the back of the sofa, her face the colour of semolina. My head was floating, my thoughts spinning. When I closed my eyes I saw fountains of blood spurting and wanted to scream, but could not. I felt the coolness of my mother's fingers against my temple. Her lips were moving.

And then Uncle Billy was back with a man in a bowler hat. I could not place him for he wore no sash and he sang no song. He carried a black bag in his hand. My mother and Uncle Billy were arguing but I could not hear what they said. I saw him push my mother, she staggered sideways, the room tilted and I lost consciousness.

Hours later, I awakened in a high, narrow bed; I had tubes in my arm and a bottle of red liquid hanging overhead. Beside me sat my mother reading from the book with the gold cross and crown.

'Cora, thank God! How are you, love?'

'Fine.' My voice croaked like a frog's.

'I knew you would be. I never doubted it.'

'I saved your life for you I did, young lady,' said Uncle Billy.

I didn't know whether to say thank you or not, so kept quiet. My wrist was hidden under a thick bandage which I wanted never to have to take off. I shuddered at the thought of seeing the scar again. Rosie had said it would be there for ever and ever.

'Sit down, dear, you're still looking peaky,' said Uncle Sam. 'Ina, away and make her a wee cup of tea.'

They fussed about me and Aunt Gertrude and Deanna, who had dropped in, kept stretching their necks to take a look at my wrist.

'You're mother's a good woman, Cora,' said Granny McGill, 'but sorely misguided.'

'She has faith,' I said feebly, wanting to defend her more strongly but unsure how to do it. 'Old Mr McGill signed his name in blood to defend *his* faith.'

'That was a different matter entirely.'

'You're right there, Ma,' said Uncle Billy. 'He was defending our whole Protestant heritage and our right to remain loyal to our King and country.'

'Hear, hear!' cried Uncle Sam.

'I see Mrs Lavery's expecting again,' said Aunt Gertrude to Mrs Meneely who was edging her way back into the room with the teapot. 'Poor woman. It's desperate the way they have to go on having those children.'

'Do they have to have them?' I asked.

Rosie and Deanna gave me looks that said how can you be *that* stupid? I seemed to have great gaps in my knowledge which no one else had, and that worried me. I did not always trust Rosie's explanations.

'The priest makes them,' said Deanna, bouncing her ringlets.

'Deanna's right,' said her mother. 'Well, it's another one for them, isn't it?'

'They'll be swamping us soon,' said Mrs Meneely, lifting a chocolate-coated marshmallow with her free hand. She watched the chocolate crack as she bit into it. She loved sweet things. Her hips were spreading, visibly, it seemed to me as I watched, and her breasts bounced like soft balloons. As the years went by the dimples deepened in her fingers and wrists and her eyes receded.

'That's what they're after of course,' said Uncle Billy, 'outnumbering us.'

'Why don't you and Uncle Sam have a whole lot of children then?' said Rosie. 'And swamp *them*?'

Deanna snickered.

'None of your cheek now, Margaret Rose,' said her grandmother.

'What's cheeky about that?'

Rosie and I were hastily sent up to Ballyhackamore for a message at Mrs McCurdy's. Whilst she was rummaging through her boxes looking for pink knicker elastic Teresa came in. We didn't dare communicate with her except by rolling our eyes and jerking our heads. Mrs McCurdy had a tongue the length of the Newtonards Road on her. 'What's got into you the day, Rosie Meneely?' she demanded as she measured off the elastic along the edge of the counter. 'You'd think you'd got St Vitus Dance.' Rosie put on her innocent look and handed over the money and then we went outside where we hung about. We excelled at loitering with or without intent.

When Teresa came out of the shop we let her set off first and walked two steps behind.

'Ma said to ask youse if you'd like to come to tea tomorrow?' she said over her shoulder.

'Both of us?' I asked.

Teresa nodded. 'But I don't suppose you'd be able to, would you, Rosie?'

'No,' said Rosie sadly. Her daring would not extend that far. She was jealous of me going though, wanted to see the inside of the Laverys' house for herself, and was in a bad mood with me for the whole of the following day at school. She had three chocolate digestives for her playpiece and wouldn't give me one. I promised I'd tell her *everything* about the Laverys but we both knew it wouldn't be the same. 'You'll probably get stale bread and marge,' she said as a parting shot. 'We're having a fry – rashers and eggs and potato bread and tomatoes and sausages as thick as your arm.'

Teresa had made a sponge cake which had collapsed in the middle.

'You'd think it'd been dive-bombed,' said Gerard Lavery.

It was the first time I'd been close enough to hear him speak. He had eyes like Teresa's, dark, and watchful, until he laughed and forgot himself, in the way that she did. She made a fist and lunged at him, missing, and made him laugh now.

'You're not getting any for that.' But she relented and he had the thickest piece on the plate. He was her favourite sibling. She was always cracking him up, telling us he was the brainiest boy in the school. That might not mean much though, said Rosie (to me) not in *that* school. But he was going to sit for a secondary school scholarship and wanted to be a surgeon when he grew up. Teresa said he loved the sight of blood.

During the meal Mrs Lavery sat by the fire smoking and reading *Woman's Own* which my mother passed on to her. She liked the stories. When the noise got too hectic she glanced up and said, 'Give over, youse lot, can I not get a minute's peace?' The bump in her stomach was rounding out. I thought of the priest coming in to see how it was getting on and nodding his head with approval. My eyes kept sliding to the mantelpiece to the picture of the Virgin Mary wearing a halo or to the side wall where Jesus hung from a wooden cross. The sight of the crumpled body hurt my eyes. You could see the agony in the arms and legs. When I told Rosie about it she said it was disgusting to have a thing like that in your house, not that we should hold it against Teresa since she didn't know any better.

'Want to play cards, Gerard?' said Teresa.

'I'll give you a couple of hands.'

We threw the dishes into the sink on top of the others that were already there. Teresa said she'd do them all after. We played whist at the kitchen table and Gerard won every game but one which I took.

'That was good playing,' he said, making me feel like Shirley Temple. 'Would you like to learn sevens?'

He played with us until it was time for me to go.

'Leave her home now, Gerard,' said Mrs Lavery, ignoring my objection that it was only two doors up. 'You never know who's about on these dark nights.' And in spite of my protest I was not averse to the idea of having Gerard Lavery walk me home. It would be something else to tell Rosie.

'See you tomorrow,' said Teresa, her hands in the sink.

I bumped against Gerard in the backyard and felt the warmth of his hand as it curled round my wrist. He guided me on to the path, then released me. I had my fingers tightly crossed that we wouldn't meet Uncle Billy on patrol.

'Dead dark isn't it?' I said, feeling I ought to make conversation.

'It is that,' he agreed.

A light was coming bobbing towards us. I got ready to run. Then the man behind the torch coughed.

'Is that you, Da?' called out Gerard.

'Aye, is that you, Gerard lad?' The light jerked closer and came to a halt in front of our feet. 'And who's the wee girlfriend you have with you?'

'It's Teresa's friend from Number Seven,' said Gerard and I thought his voice sounded cold, not at all like it had been when we were playing cards.

'The wee sandy Prod?' The light travelled up my body.

'Cheerio,' I said quickly before it would reach my face and darted up the path to my house. 'I can't stick Mr Lavery,' I told my mother.

'He's not bothered you, has he?' she asked sharply.
'No.'
'Are you sure? You can never be certain with men . . . You must watch them, Cora.'
I promised that I would.
But she did not tell me what to watch.

In June the Allied troops landed in France. 'It'll soon be all over bar the shouting,' said Uncle Billy, though there were to be many more dark weeks and months ahead before Hitler was properly on the run. '*Run rabbit, run rabbit,*' sang Rosie and I as we pranced up the street. There was still not much sign of the Japanese running. I was finding it more and more difficult to remember my father. In the photograph on the mantelpiece he looked stiff and strange and his gaze went past me when I tried to catch his eye. My mother read out only parts of his letters to me – 'Daddy wants to know how you're doing at school, says you must be big now, sends his love' – and after she'd refolded the letter she would go straight to Mary Baker Eddy. Once, when I sneaked a look, I saw that his writing was all higgledy-piggledy.
At Christmas Aunt Belle's letter said she would be coming home on leave in a few week's time and she had a notion to go to Dublin.
'Dublin,' mused my mother. 'I think you and I might go with her, Cora.'
Dublin. Sin city! Sodom, Gomorrah, Rome, Dublin. There wasn't much to choose among them, if you could believe Uncle Billy.
'You wouldn't catch *me* going there,' said Rosie. My mother had offered to take her but the McGills wouldn't consider it. 'It's full of German spies,' said Rosie, 'and you'll trip over priests and nuns on every corner and the shawlies have about fifty-five children each and they *smell*.'
I promised I'd bring her back a gigantic box of milk chocolates with hard centres. Not much was rationed in the South, except for clothes and tea. Tea was the great thing. Tea unlocked the magic gates. 'Now you take a

good few quarters with you,' said Mrs Jamieson from down the street. She went to Dublin regularly, knew all the ins and outs. 'And pack your case light on the way down, maybe put in an old jersey or two that you can throw out and take a few old labels from Cleavers and the like with you.'

Aunt Belle arrived wearing her ATS uniform, with her hair rolled up like a sausage under her cap, and carrying a kitbag. She was fizzing with excitement. She threw her cap up in the air and tugged at the sausage roll. Hairpins winged in all directions. She had just got engaged to a really nice bloke, a corporal in the Signals, and they were going to get married as soon as the war was over which everybody said couldn't be long now.

'*We're going to hang out the washing on the Siegfried line,*' sang Rosie and I.

Aunt Belle thought she would buy her engagement ring in Dublin. Len had told her she should just go ahead.

The black-shawled women were waiting for us at Amiens Street station. They must have smelt our tea for they advanced with outstretched arms and soon had us encircled. The shrilling of their voices and the stench of their bodies made me step back. Rosie had been right about the children too: they did seem to have dozens of them, in their arms, under their shawls, behind their heels. Fingers grazed my coat and one old woman, toothless, dirt embedded in the lines of her face, touched my cheek and said what a pretty girl I was. I was both fascinated and repelled. But I warmed to the compliment, for it was seldom that I was told I was pretty. I was too gawky and too freckled for that. I smiled at the old woman and she squawked, 'Pretty girl, pretty girl,' and came closer so that her smell invaded my nostrils and I wanted to shove her away. And then I was ashamed for I had been taught to love my neighbour. I pushed my way out of the gaggle.

Aunt Belle auctioned the tea for clothing coupons and the shawlies scattered to seek fresh prey. They moved like a flock of rooks across the station floor. My mother said something about the Roman Church having a lot to answer for. I tugged at her hand.

We stepped into the streets of Dublin. The bright lights astounded me.

'It's like daytime.'

'This is what it'll be like in Belfast,' said Aunt Belle 'when the lights come on again.'

But I knew that it could never be quite like this. There was an excitement about the city that made me want to skip. The streets swarmed with people who looked as if they were enjoying themselves. Pub doors swung open spilling out light and noise. The restaurants were busy, the shop windows full. I was enthralled.

I told Rosie that I was going to live in Dublin when I grew up.

'But what about the nuns and priests?'

I hadn't noticed that many.

'Not noticed them? You must need glasses, Cora Caldwell!'

There had been so many other things to do, I retorted, like eating knickerbocker glories in Cafolas, drinking tea in Bewley's Oriental Tea Room, shopping in O'Connell Street, walking in the Phoenix Park, taking the tram to Dun Laighoaire and walking along the sea front; and there had been so many other things to look at, like chocolates piled up on shop counters, pounds and pounds of them, and silk stockings and diamond rings.

Aunt Belle bought a diamond ring putting every penny she had left into it, and a few of my mother's as well. 'Go on, Belle, it suits your finger! And you only get engaged once.' How true that turned out to be. The diamond sparkled on Aunt Belle's fourth finger. The jeweller told us it was a bargain and would cost two if not three times as much in the North. That decided it.

The night before we came home we sat in our hotel room sewing labels from Robinson and Cleaver's and Anderson and MacAuley's into our new clothes. My mother sprinkled a little talcum powder over them, so that the materials wouldn't look so new. 'There now!' She admired a green corduroy dress she'd bought for me. 'You'd never know, would you?'

I was surprised by her – *breaking the law* – but said

nothing. There was much that I did not understand in adult behaviour and awaited the day when it would become clear to me.

And now for the ring. Where was that to be put? My mother had an idea: we would bury it inside a quarter pound of butter. Mrs Jamieson had told us that you could bring in one or two small things if you declared them. It was the big stuff they were after.

The compartment was crowded going back. Nobody was saying much or reading the newspapers and magazines they held in front of them. Smugglers the lot of them, I decided, eyeing the bags and suitcases on the racks over their heads. The woman opposite me kept wiping her forehead and the man in the corner had a shifty eye that moved from Aunt Belle to my mother and back again. The customs had their spies everywhere, Mrs Jamieson had warned us.

The train halted at the Free State border. The customs here weren't really interested, we could be taking half of Dublin back with us as far as they were concerned, as long as we had paid for it. We rumbled across no man's land to the British post.

Now, the atmosphere changed. All was hustle and bustle as passengers got up to take down their luggage. The woman opposite stood on my new sandals and didn't even say she was sorry. People were talking loudly in the corridor.

'They're on the war path,' said a man in a checked suit, putting his head in.

I saw a customs' man go by with a fur coat over his arm. Mrs Jamieson had told us perturbing tales of how, if they suspected you, they took you into sheds and stripped the clothes off you. How could I ever stand naked in front of a man? I whispered in my mother's ear.

'Don't be silly, dear.' Unlike everyone else, she was smiling. And Knowing the Truth no doubt, but what the suitable truth would be in this situation I could not imagine. Surely God couldn't approve of us smuggling?

'Right then.' The men were at the door. I didn't like the look of the thin faces under the peaked hats and knew there was going to be trouble. My mother continued to smile and Aunt Belle said, 'Certainly, Officer,' when she was asked to open her case. He ran his fingers through her silk underwear and I felt sick. 'Where did you get this lot?' He looked at the utility labels which she had sewn in so carefully the night before. 'Don't make me laugh!' Nothing would make him laugh, I decided. He lifted the honeymoon camiknickers and petticoats and stuffed them into the sack he was carrying. He allowed me to keep my dress and sandals although I didn't think he was fooled. There wasn't much room left in his bag anyway.

My mother, who had also been told by Mrs Jamieson that it was good tactics to declare something, offered the information that she had half pound of cheese, a quarter of butter and a box of chocolates, already opened.

'You're not allowed to import foodstuffs into the United Kingdom, madam.' He held out his hand.

My mother faltered, my aunt held her breath. I saw her hold it: her rib cage froze.

'You can't take the butter,' I cried. 'You can't!'

'Cora!' said my mother.

'And why not, miss?'

'You just can't.' My voice faded to a squeak inside me.

'Is there something special about the butter?'

'No. It's just that – I'm very fond – desperately fond – of butter. If you could put a buttercup under my chin you would see how fond.' I felt my temperature rising.

'Cora dear,' said my mother, more softly this time.

'I'm sorry, miss, but the law's the law.' His hand came out for the butter. Perhaps he was fond of it too, would take it home to his wife for tea and she would cut into it and find Aunt Belle's ring and her eyes would shine, like the diamond itself. We watched as his fingers curled round the packet and then rested for a moment, as if he were in two minds, but in the next instant his hand was in motion again swinging up and over the bag and opening like the jaws of a crane to release its prey.

We travelled the rest of the way back to Belfast in silence. Aunt Belle was brave; she didn't cry or let anyone in the compartment know what a terrible thing had happened to her. I watched the countryside rushing by and the long trail of smoke the train was leaving behind and ate chocolate after chocolate from the opened box until my mother removed them saying I would be sick. I looked at her in surprise but she didn't seem to have realized what she had said.

Aunt Belle never did get married. Len was sent to France and killed by a stray bullet just five days before the war in Europe ended. It was as if losing the ring like that had brought her bad luck. My mother said that was nonsense.

'If you ask me,' said Rosie, 'it was because it was a Papist ring.'

Another possibility occurred to me: that Aunt Belle was being punished for doing wrong. My mother did not like that theory either. She said that God was a good God, merciful and forgiving.

'You worry about things too much, Cora love. Why is it that you cannot just accept?'

THREE

Victory in Europe! It had come in spite of terror and the road *had* been long and hard, but without victory, we knew – since we had been told – there would be no survival. Waving our Union Jacks we danced around the City Hall and watched the older girls being kissed by American soldiers who had lost their pork-pie hats in the scrum. So the lights came on again in Belfast though were to go out some three months later in a place called Hiroshima. And on the twelfth of July the Orange Walks were started up once again.

'*On the green grassy slopes of the Boyne*,' sang Uncle Sam, as he shaved with an open razor, mirror propped above the scullery sink. 'Ah hello, there, Cora girl! You're up early. Grand morning isn't it?'

> *'Where the Orangemen with William did join,*
> *And fought for our glorious deliverance*
> *On the green grassy slopes of the Boyne.'*

I watched the suds sliding along the silver blade and Uncle Sam's neck emerging clean as a baby's.

'Are you coming with us to the "Field"?' I shook my head. 'Ach sure, why not?'

'I'm not allowed.'

'Will I've a word with your mother?'

'It wouldn't do any good.'

'But it's the first parade for six years!'

I knew that, oh how I knew it! For days now I had heard about nothing else from Rosie and for nights now had heard the banging of the Lambeg drums in the distance.

'That was one good thing about the war,' said my mother, 'those things were banned.'

Uncle Sam went back to his singing.

The smell of frying sausages was making my mouth run. Mrs McGill and Mrs Meneely were in the kitchen packing up the picnic. They gave me a sausage and a few potato crisps with a wee blue bag of coarse salt. Granny McGill said my mother's head was full of right queer notions.

'Sure what harm would it do you to come? The children all have a great time running races and that, don't they, Ina?'

Munching, slightly comforted by the taste of the salty crisps and the warm sausage that had burst between my teeth, I went upstairs to the bedroom which Rosie shared with her mother. She was sitting on the double bed with her blue taffeta skirts spread round her like a fan and she had one knee pulled up so that she could fasten her blue satin shoe. I dropped down beside her like a sack of potatoes. 'Watch!' she cried. Lifting my feet, I stared mournfully at my stained gym shoes.

'How do I look?' said Rosie.

'Great.' I began to pick at the edge of a scab under my right knee.

'You're not even looking.'

'I am.' Still picking, wincing a little from the pain, I chanted, '*My name is Shirley Temple and I've got curly hair, but I'm not able to do the Betty Grable–*' She pushed me but when I tried to push her back she screamed. 'Keep your pus-y hands off me, rotten old Apple Core! Granny'll have your guts for garters if you tear my dress.'

It had cost fifteen shillings for the material and ten to be made up and hours of agony at the dressmaker's. Mrs Seddon was a wee woman, not much bigger than us, but she could stick in pins with great ferocity if you didn't stand still.

'You can come on the "Walk" when you're older and your mother can't stop you.'

'I wouldn't come if you paid me. Stupid old Orange

parade with stupid old Orange men and stupid old drums banging–'

I shifted to get out of her reach but was not quick enough; she punched me on the right shoulder. I lunged back, caught hold of her hair. She screamed between her teeth keeping the sound down.

'We're off,' called Uncle Billy from below.

We ran to the top of the stairs to see him and Uncle Sam leave the house. Their navy-blue suits had been pressed until they looked like new, there was not a speck of dust on their bowler hats and their orange collarettes gleamed in the dim light of the hall.

'You're two fine looking men,' said their mother, giving their shoulders a last brush off.

'See you later!' cried Rosie.

'See you, Princess!' said Uncle Sam.

I walked up the street with Rosie and her mother and grandmother feeling a terrible dowd in my old cotton dress and no bow in my hair. Rosie's head was ribboned in red, white and blue. She swanked up the road, ignoring warnings not to get too worked up or else she'd be sick long before they ever got to Finaghy.

At the main road we joined Aunt Gertrude and Deanna who waved us in to the space they'd kept beside them. Deanna, all in white, trimmed with fur, looked like a dandelion clock. She and Rosie eyed one another's outfits. I saw Rosie's lip curl.

Union Jacks hung from upper windows; red, white and blue bunting linked the lamp-posts. In her window Mrs McCurdy had a big bunch of Sweet William and a faded Coronation picture of the King and Queen. The butcher had a portrait of the King propped against a carcass of lamb.

The sound of music was in the air, rousing, stamping music that set the blood tingling and the feet jumping. In my excitement I stood on one of Rosie's satin shoes. She lifted it to strike me on the shin but was impeded by her mother who caught her by the ankle and, spitting on her hanky, did what she could to scrub out the offensive marks.

They were coming! I stood in the gutter and leant out from the waist to get a better view. Rosie forgot her scuffed shoe. First came the huge banner of the Lodge carried aloft by Uncle Billy and Uncle Sam and two other stout-armed men. Four small boys held on to its tasselled stays for dear life in case the wind would take a swipe at it. The hand-painted picture of the man in the plumed hat and the white horse rippled. LONG LIVE KING BILLY, the slogan said above it. And THIS WE WILL MAINTAIN, underneath. We waved and we cheered. The uncles never looked sideways. The drum major drew level dazzling our eyes as he tossed his baton high over his head, twirled it behind his back, and now he was turning himself round and round, and all the while the baton was on the go, whirling, birling, rising, falling. And then the drummer with his drum so large I was amazed he could get his arms right round it. And what a sight it was all decorated in scarlet, orange and gold! I longed to play a Lambeg drum. The band followed tootling on their flutes and banging on their drums. Deanna's father was playing the trumpet just like Louis Armstrong. Deanna waved frantically and got her fur-fringed bolero in a twist.

'Sure isn't this just good fun, Cora?' said Mrs Meneely. 'I don't know what your mother could object to. Plenty RCs come out to watch and all.'

At last came the dark-suited men of the Lodge walking two abreast, their arms swinging, their feet moving in time (more or less) to the music. Some of them carried rolled black umbrellas like lances in front of them. I glanced up at the sky but there was no sign of rain. It was tradition, said Granny McGill, to remind you of the days when the Orangemen had had to defend themselves with whatever came to hand.

Rosie and her family had to wait for a car which would pick them up and take them to the 'Field' where they would eat, drink and be merry, play games and listen to speeches. I left them and ran beside the uncles' Lodge for a long way going quite close to the city centre which I was not allowed to do alone. When I tired I turned and walked the other way. Wave after wave of men passed me with banners, fifes and drums. I enjoyed the pictures on the banners which depicted scenes from Irish history (Prods triumphing of course) and some from English such as a turbanned black man giving a box of jewels to Queen Victoria and her Albert. I didn't understand the caption: THE SECRET OF ENGLAND'S GREATNESS. The slogans bemused me. TRUST IN GOD AND KEEP YOUR POWDER DRY. CEMENTED WITH LOVE. NO SURRENDER. I knew that one well enough and knew what it meant.

The marching men would never surrender, nor tire either. They wouldn't need to for they hadn't even started on the parade proper, were only on their way to the rallying point at Carlisle Circus where they would meet up with Lodges from all over the city and province. They looked as if they could have walked the length of Ireland.

And now the men were behind me. The sound of the music was diminishing. Rosie and Deanna waved from the rear window of a car. Walking backwards, I watched the flip-flap of their hands working like frantic windscreen wipers. Then they, too, were gone.

In the streets behind the main road it was like Sunday. A piece of rope dangled from the lamp-post at the corner of our street. Putting the loop under my bottom I swung idly to and fro wondering how to fill the long hours before Rosie would come back and tell me everything. Teresa had gone to stay with an aunt on the Falls for a few days.

We hadn't seen as much of Teresa since summer had come in. The evenings being long and light, people tended to potter in their gardens and backyards or stand on the pavement having a crack with neighbours. Every now and then my mother asked Teresa to tea and we would play up in my bedroom but Rosie didn't come on those occasions.

I went on swinging until I began to feel sick then decided to go for a walk along the railway path. You could gather wild flowers on the bank and with a bit of luck I'd see a train or two go by headed for the sea at Bangor or Donaghadee.

I picked a big bunch of grasses and pink and blue flowers. A pair of lovers passed murmuring into one another's hair. They didn't see me. Then came two men with lean whippets who did. One was Mr Robinson from two doors down. He was not an Orangeman. His wife said he was a good Protestant but he had no time for all that carry on. Anyway, he was too busy racing his dogs. He said I shouldn't be hanging about down here on my own. But it was daytime, I protested. That was all very well, he said, but a girl of my age shouldn't go about alone; I was getting big now. And don't be going on the track, he cautioned, before continuing along the path with his friend, their skinny dogs hugging their heels. I hated the thinness of the animals' shanks.

A girl of my age. Ten, soon to be eleven. I was considered big for my age. Some said I looked more like twelve, or thirteen. Pulling back my shoulders and pushing out my rib cage, I imagined myself to be like Rebecca Cohen whose bosoms were round and whose skin was smooth and brown and whose eyes were the colour of hazel-nuts in October. When Rosie wanted to be nasty to me she said I had eyes like gooseberries and that my freckles looked like chicken shit.

I climbed up the bank to the wire fence that ran along the top and looked down at the railway lines. Until Mr Robinson had put the idea into my head it had never occurred to me to set foot on them, but now that it had I found it irresistible. I needed something to throw back at Rosie in return for all those races she would have won and all those Orange boys with their sleek hair who would have hung around her open-mouthed.

In a second I was over the fence and sliding down the bank on the other side. I stepped on to the track and stood between two sleepers with my legs wide apart and my hands on my hips. A strange calm came over me. I listened for the sound of a train, half hoping half fearing, and heard only the thump of my heart.

'Hey, get off there!'

Quickly, I turned, not knowing from where the voice had come, not waiting to find out. My turn was too swift, I caught my toe on the edge of a sleeper and went sprawling. My head struck an iron joint and I saw stars or thought I did in true comic book manner, though it didn't seem very funny to me, not at the time, only later when I was recounting the tale to Rosie. She asked me if I remembered the picture we'd once seen in which a girl was tied to a sleeper and a train was coming? I *had* remembered the girl as I lay half-stunned on the track and I remembered too the yowl of the train as it sped closer and closer and how Rosie and I had clung to one another hardly daring to look.

No train came along the line then, only Gerard Lavery whose voice it was that had called to me. I tried to rise. He picked me up and carried me over to the bank where I sat blinking in the sunshine. He let me be for a few minutes until my eyes had focussed again and my heart had stopped pumping so hard, then he said, 'Let's take a look at that head.' He put his hand on my temple. 'You're going to have a nasty bump there in the morning by the looks of it. You've got a high forehead haven't you? Must be brainy. Put a cold cloth against it when you get in.'

'All right,' I said meekly. I felt very meek. Was it possible that one day I might inherit the earth? How could anyone inherit the earth? The whole earth? My mother had said that was what Hitler had wanted to do: he had thought he was God. But he was dead now. And the people of Europe were free.

'Are you all right?' Gerard was frowning at me.

'Yes, thank you.'

'You seem to be accident prone.'

'How do you mean like?'

'Well, you do have a lot of accidents, don't you? Cutting your wrist and that?'

When I told my mother what he'd said she said that was Error talking, trying to worm its way in, and I most certainly was *not* accident prone and should not listen to the likes of Gerard Lavery who, whilst he might be a nice enough boy, did not think as we did. He did not know the *real* truth about man; he worshipped graven images and wanted to be a doctor when he grew up. He had won the scholarship into a Catholic boys' secondary school.

I mentioned the scholarship while we sat on the bank and said I was pleased for him. He shrugged. He was sitting with his legs bent and his bony elbows resting on the knobbles of his knees. He seemed to be all points and bony projectures.

'Aren't you pleased?'

'I'm not taking it up. We can't afford the uniform.'

'But that's not fair!'

He had nothing to say to that.

'But what'll you do?'

'Stay on at the public elementary of course. Till I'm fourteen.'

'And then?'

'Get a job, I suppose.'

I felt a vibration in the bank. 'Something's coming!'

We heard a high shrill whistle and then the rumble of a train which grew louder and louder until it deafened our ears and there was the engine and now the carriages rushing past filled with passengers bound for the pleasures of the seaside. Usually Rosie and I waved at trains but today I did not sensing that Gerard would think it foolish to wave at strangers.

How quiet the world seemed when the train had gone by. I ventured to say so and he smiled. 'Come on and I'll give you a hand up.'

I scrambled up the bank and he helped me over the fence but when I tried to stand on the path my head swam and I staggered. He steadied me.

'I think I'd better give you a piggy back.' He bent over and I grasped his shoulders. With a shrug he hoisted me up. His smell was strange to me and his hands, under my knees, felt rough, like fine sandpaper, and warm, almost hot. If Rosie could have seen me she'd have wet her knickers. The thought nearly made me wet mine. I giggled nervously. 'Hold tight now!' he commanded and I did, all the way along the path and through the streets, hypnotized by the sight of his black hair curling so close to my face and by the feel of his hands on my legs. I felt as if I was moving through a dream.

When we reached the corner of our street he stopped and my head jerked forward sending my chin into the midst of those curls. 'I think I'd better leave you off here.' He leant over and with reluctance I slid down his back on to the pavement. I thanked him.

'Remember – a cold cloth now!'

I ran home to ask my mother if we could buy a uniform for Gerard Lavery so that he could go to St Malachi's.

'We couldn't do that, I'm afraid, dear. Apart from anything else, I haven't got the money to spare. And besides, the uniform would only be the start of it for Gerard. There'd be all sorts of other extras, bus fares and so on . . .'

I consulted Rosie and she agreed that we should help him since he was Teresa's brother and she was our blood sister. 'Though that doesn't make him our blood brother. He couldn't ever be that since he's an RC.' When I reminded her that Teresa was too, she said, 'But Teresa's different. Exceptions prove the rule, my granny says.' I wondered if Granny McGill had any exceptions to her rules? I'd have been really interested to know. 'Stop going off the subject, Cora!' said Rosie. 'You've an awful habit–' Of wandering. Yes, I knew that. I found that one thought led to another and in school whenever we undertook any activity like reading round the class I could never keep the place and was usually chastized by a swish of the cane against my legs. 'Gerard Lavery, Cora!' Rosie reminded me. And his uniform. What were we to do about it? What could we do? I suggested we take round a collection box the way we did for other charities. 'But would people give for Gerard Lavery's uniform?' said Rosie. 'It's not like going round for the worn-out horses.' We'd collected for them last winter. 'We could say we're collecting for the Red Cross,' I said. 'It's almost true after all – they help the poor too, don't they?'

We made holes in two old tobacco tins and stuck red crosses on them.

'It'll be good crack anyway,' said Rosie.

We went further out of town, to Knock, where we were not known, and tapped on doors of more opulent semi-detached houses than ours, and even detached ones. I let Rosie lead the way up the long drives. Some of the women turned us away as if we were suspicious characters and watched our departure from behind their curtains but others smiled and asked us into the kitchen and gave us chocolate biscuits and said how nice it was that we should give our time to collect for good causes. Pennies and threepenny bits and even sixpences dropped through the crude slots. One woman who was lonely gave us a florin which Rosie bit on when we got home to make sure it was real. We had to hear all about the woman's loneliness to get it but we didn't mind; we sat in her front room in the depths of chintz settee and told her how sorry we were that her husband was dead and her mother was senile and her son had married a nasty-minded girl who was dead mean to her. 'Come back,' she said, 'come again,' but we didn't. We were afraid to in case we'd be rumbled.

We counted our loot in my shed. One pound sixteen shillings and eleven pence. It was a lot of money. But was it enough for a uniform? Blazers were dear, said Rosie, whose cousin Clark was about to go up to secondary school. 'And then he'd need underpants and things.' But he'd have those anyway, I objected. 'He might not,' said Rosie knowingly. We decided that I should pass the money over to Teresa and ask her to give it to Gerard. I wrote a note saying: *From wellwishers. If this is not enough for a uniform more will be forthcoming.*

'Where do you get all those funny words from?'

I didn't know: they just came into my head. She attributed them to the book by the American woman which we read from daily and she might have been right for it was full of long words. Though I did read a lot of other books too.

When Teresa came in later I gave her the envelope. She fingered it and frowned. 'Is it money, Cora?'

'Just give it to Gerard and don't let on who gave it to you. Promise!' I made her cross her heart and hope to die. It was not a pledge *she* would be able to take lightly.

Ten minutes after she'd gone home our door bell rang. My mother went to answer it. I was upstairs writing in my diary.

'Cora, it's Gerard Lavery – to see you.' She sounded surprised.

A blush flamed my cheeks. I rubbed talcum powder into them and brushed my hair and straightened my dress which had got twisted from lying on the bed. 'Cora!' 'I'm coming.' I went down to meet him.

My mother had gone back into the living room but had left the door ajar. Gerard stood on the front doorstep with not a hint of a smile on his face and his hands behind his back.

'Hello,' I said.

He pushed the envelope into my hands and walked away.

FOUR

We had talked for so long about what we would do when my father came home from the war that when, suddenly, a telegram announced his imminent arrival, I felt as if we were waiting for a stranger. And perhaps my mother did too. She got Mrs Jamieson to perm her hair and cut out a new dress for herself on the sitting room floor.

He came into our house on a late summer's day, a tall emaciated man with yellow skin and a sandy moustache, wearing crumpled civilian clothes and walking with two sticks. My mother read to him the passage in the Bible where Jesus tells the bedridden man to take up his bed and walk. My father threw away his crutches and fell down in the yard. Patience, Desmond, counselled my mother; he must not lose heart. She continued to read to him daily from the Bible, and from 'Science and Health'. *When we come to have more faith in the truth of being than we have in error, more faith in Spirit than in matter, more faith in living than in dying, more faith in God than in man, then no material suppositions can prevent us from healing the sick and destroying error.*

'Faith, Cora, that is the thing, eh?' He stood by the front room window propped between his crutches watching the street. His disability had not curbed his restlessness. 'You're a good little Christian Scientist, aren't you?'

I supposed I was: I went willingly to Sunday School and said my prayers and when I bumped my head or barked my shin I declared that there was no sensation in matter. The pain usually went away quickly. I intended, when I was twelve, to become a member of the First Church of Christ Scientist, Boston, Massachusetts; and when the time came I did, and for the next four years was a passionate adherent, reading the Lesson Sermon daily, bidding Satan to get behind me when his shadow crept into view. In those years I had no doubts and wished that Rosie could know 'Science' too, for her not knowing was the only thing that came between us. Teresa I could not expect to share my religion: her own was too powerful. But Rosie was not religious, ever; she went to church because if she did not her granny and her uncles would have thrown tantrums.

At the Wednesday evening testimony meetings in our church my father listened intently and one evening, assisted by the guiding hand of my mother under his elbow, rose to his feet. I felt sick with nerves for him as his voice began to fumble for words, but once he had the first two or three out he steadied and spoke quietly but easily. He told how in the beginning, when he had first been wounded, he had almost lost faith in God, but since coming home, gradually, with the help of his dear wife and other good friends in the church he had refound it, and with the refinding of his faith so the pain in his leg had grown less and each day he walked a little better. ' "All things are possible to him who loves God." I am confident that with God's help I shall walk again unaided. I give thanks to our Lord Jesus Christ and to our leader Mary Baker Eddy . . .'

After the service, people clustered round him in the foyer congratulating him. ' "Thy faith hath made thee whole," Desmond,' said Mrs Hastings-Smith, a Christian Science practitioner and a friend of my mother's who was to play a considerable part in my life. He managed to walk down the church steps unaided and got without wincing into Mrs Hastings-Smith's old Lagonda – she often gave us a lift home – but when he came into the house he was grey and exhausted and the next day his limp seemed more pronounced and he chewed the corner of his lip distorting the shape of his moustache.

My mother was not deterred. She admitted defeat on nothing that I knew of, and the reassurance she offered was immense: her calm words quelled rising tides of sickness and fear, dispelled doubts, and gave confidence. Since my father was not fit enough to go back to his old job we had only his war pension to live on, but that she managed well, making do and mending, ekeing out and wasting nothing. She read to us about the loaves and fishes.

But there was little left for extras and when, at the end of the school year, I won a scholarship to a girls' fee-paying school, my first thought was the uniform. Would we be able to afford it? I was mindful of Gerard Lavery's fate every time I saw him pass on the grocer's bicycle or heard him push the newspaper through our letter box on his morning paper round. That dull thud on the mat made my heart drop.

Rosie was going to the fee-paying school too, but as a paying pupil, and she already had her uniform which she wore in the street during the holidays. That was not very sensible, said my mother, who was doing sums on the backs of envelopes. Billy McGill had been promoted to foreman and Sam was doing all right in the shop trading in a few things other than shoe repairs so there was never any question of Rosie not getting what she wanted. But I need not have worried for Mrs Hastings-Smith insisted on kitting me out.

'You see,' said my mother, 'God always provides,' and I wished he could have provided for Gerard too. Teresa was not going on to secondary school either. She said she didn't care but I saw the way she eyed my green tunic and blazer.

I had to go and show my uniform to my fairy god-mother. She lived out of town. We went on the bus, my mother and I, and spent the afternoon with Mrs Hastings-Smith in her beautiful old Georgian house. Everything in Hastings Court was ancient and falling into tatters but I fell in love with it at once, the way I had with Dublin. This was what I'd always dreamed of: a house with a wall round it and a garden like a park and an orchard full of gnarled trees that seemed to hug secrets to their branches, and in the house itself room after room to wander through filled with treasures of the Occident and Orient. Mr Hastings-Smith, long since passed on, had travelled to the ends of the earth, as I planned to do one day. With Rosie and Teresa. I talked about it to them and drew verbal pictures of all the exciting places we would go to. Tibet and the Yukon, Samoa and Samarkand, Nineveh and distant Ophir. We could bring back apes and peacocks, as well as sandalwood, cedarwood and sweet white wine. But what would we do with peacocks and apes? objected Rosie. *Do* with them? Such a question could not be answered. Should not be asked. '*Rowing home to haven in sunny Palestine,*' I murmured. I would not even have minded a dirty British coaster with a salt-caked smoke stack. Maps drove me crazy, even the sight of a foreign postage stamp made my blood tingle. I ached at the thought of the time I must wait before I could set out. Why did one grow so slowly? At night in bed I travelled up the Nile to the Sphinx and across the Arabian Sea to reach the shores of India. Sometimes I travelled in the company of Gerard Lavery. I came to know him well in those dreams which I wove before falling asleep. He would be a good traveller, tireless, bewitched by everything he saw, not wanting like Rosie to know every two minutes when we were going to stop for a rest. She had to have ten stops to get up Cave Hill and after that she would need the toilet.

My mother and I had tea with Mrs Hastings-Smith in the conservatory. 'So much nicer to be amongst the plants in summertime I always think,' she said. Most of them were tinged with brown at the edges or else spotted. They crowded against the glass as if they were desperate to get out. A sill full of geraniums was doing well though, their blooms sizzling red or pink or coolly white. The sun beat in on us, the atmosphere was jungle-like. We might have been up the Amazon. The thought sustained me. When Mrs Hastings-Smith saw me sweating so profusely she suggested I remove my blazer and tie. Now I could enjoy myself fully. I loved the tea in the thin cups, not caring that they were cracked, and the thin sandwiches with a sliver of cucumber nestling in the middle, and the thin almond cakes served on a tarnished silver salver. Everything was thin except Mrs Hastings-Smith who, I presumed, ate more heartily at other times. A woman who was neither young nor old and whose name was Marcellina waited on us in a black dress and off-white apron.

'*Marcellina*?' Rosie interrupted me in the middle of my report. 'Sounds like a saint's name. She must be a Mick. Fancy having a Mick living in your house!'

'Come back whenever you like,' Mrs Hastings-Smith had said, and I intended to. My mother thought she might want for company at times. Her only son Bertrand was manager of a tea plantation in India. He sat, bristling with ginger moustaches, in a silver frame (tarnished of course) on top of the grand piano. 'And bring a little friend if you wish,' she had added.

I was torn as to whether to take Rosie or not: I longed to show her everything, to fling open doors and reveal treasures from China and Japan, to tell her how Bertrand rode a jewelled elephant in the mountains of Assam, yet I did not want her to be a part of it. Before I knew it Mrs Hastings-Smith would be buying *her* party dresses and silver shoes. One Saturday afternoon when I'd been invited to Hastings Court and Rosie was going to Deanna's birthday party where there were to be ten kinds of sandwiches and six kinds of cake, I asked Teresa to come. Mrs Lavery was dubious. 'A big house in the country? Are you sure now she wouldn't mind our Teresa coming?' I reassured her, Teresa's hair was brushed until she yelled, and we set off, pleased with ourselves at being allowed to go alone on the bus out of town.

Marcellina had provided thicker sandwiches and a cake solid with moist red cherries, which disappointed me a little, but I soon recovered to enjoy the tea in a different way.

'Play in the garden, girls,' said Mrs Hastings-Smith. 'Feel free . . .'

We ran between the trees in the parkland holding our arms out wide pretending to be aeroplanes, we picked green apples in the orchard throwing them into the long grass after the first mouthful, we found an old coach-house which we swept out and played at houses in.

'Stay the night,' said Mrs Hastings-Smith. 'Why not? There are so many beds. Isn't there someone you can send a message by?'

Mrs Robinson had a telephone. I rang her and she fetched my mother who had no objections. She said she would speak to Mrs Lavery.

'Is it on?' asked Teresa, who had the fingers of both hands crossed. She had never spent a night away from home except with her aunt on the Falls.

'It is!'

At bedtime Marcellina gave us cocoa and doughnuts in the kitchen. On the back wall hung a picture of Jesus with a halo at the back of his head.

'Will you be coming to Mass with me in the morning, Teresa?' she asked. So they had recognized one another.

'If you like.'

'Your mammy'd want you to go, wouldn't she?'

Teresa and I were given a large double bed in a room with pink satin wallpaper. There were some dark marks on the walls which felt damp when you touched them. The bed felt a bit cold and damp too to begin with and we didn't like the darkness when Marcellina put out the light. I was used to sleeping with my door open and the landing light on. We cuddled up together in the centre of the bed and talked until our throats grated. We vowed we'd be friends for ever and ever. I wished Teresa could come to the new school with Rosie and me, then life would be perfect. Should I speak to Mrs Hastings-Smith? 'I don't see what she'd want to do a thing like that for.' 'She seems to like you.' 'But paying . . . Anyway, it's a school for Protestants isn't it?' I thought they would take her if she wanted to come. Teresa considered, decided better not; she wasn't sure her Father Flynn would like it.

At last, exhausted, we fell asleep and did not stir until we felt Marcellina's heavy hand ruffling the bedclothes and heard her deep voice telling us it was time to stir our lazy bones. Teresa got up to wash her face in cold water from a china bowl. I saw her shoulders quiver.

'Could I come, Marcellina?' I asked. 'Please!'

'Your mammy wouldn't mind?'

No, not at all, I assured her, and Teresa said that my mother had nothing against anybody or anything, which was not quite true, but I was not in a mood for establishing truth this morning. I was too excited at the prospect that lay ahead. For I could see that Marcellina was going to say yes.

I had to promise not to tell Madam. 'Cross my heart.' As I made the sign of the cross my heart fluttered. I thought I could smell incense already.

We walked through a quiet lane to the church. Dew spangled the hedgerows. Birds shrilled in the high trees. We wore headscarves tied by Marcellina in stout knots under our chins. I heard the bell tolling ahead and felt my knees begin to quake.

The church was bigger than I'd expected and the steps leading up to it were thick with people. Two nuns swept past us, their black skirts eddying, their crosses swinging. 'Come on then,' said Marcellina and led the way.

I thought my legs would buckle under me as I followed her thick red ones upward. Teresa took my hand. At the door I faltered. 'There's nothing to it,' said Teresa. 'I don't think I'd better,' I said and turning, went stumbling back down the steps breaking up the ranks of people who looked at me as if I were demented. And perhaps I was a little.

'You needn't have been afraid,' said Teresa kindly, when she came back. 'Nobody'd have bothered you.'

But when I said she could come with me to my church if she wanted, she said she wouldn't dare. 'Ma'd kill me. Anyway, we're not allowed.'

Rosie said it was mean of me to take Teresa out to Hastings Court before I had taken her. 'I suppose she's your best friend now is she?' I denied it. 'See if I care, rotten old Apple Core. Core, core, core! Friendly with a lavvy brush, a lavvy brush!'

We made up in time to start our new school together and on the first day walked sedately down the hill, side by side in our uniforms. Gerard Lavery passed us going home from his paper round. He ran his eyes over us but only nodded in response to my bright 'Good morning!'

'Fancy letting him put his hands under your legs when he gave you that piggy back! A Fenian!'

'There was nothing else I could do. I was injured.'

'I thought you weren't meant to get injured if you're a Christian Scientist!' Even on our way to a new school we could not resist trying to score one another off.

We joined the streams of green girls going through the gateway. We quietened. I wished that I, too, had worn my blazer during the holidays so that it would not look so split new. Rosie had her beret on at a jaunty angle and swung her arms as she walked.

Thus began our secondary education. We became proficient at Latin which was compulsory and relentlessly taught by the headmistress, Miss Lightbody, herself; at curling one another's hair with the crucible tongs in the room that held a few bunsen burners and one or two other bits of rusted equipment and was known as the science 'lab'; at cleaning mice droppings from the baking boards in the domestic science room which had once been a stable and still smelled like one; and we developed a passion for hockey. On dank afternoons we chased a barely discernible ball up and down a muddy, uneven field. Even the hockey pitch was substandard.

The school was bursting out of the seams of the old house it occupied and for the first year our form was taught in the local Presbyterian church hall. It was the ruination of us. Since the teachers – some not as fast on their feet as they needed to be – took a few minutes to walk between the school and the church we spent a substantial amount of time unsupervised. We turned into tearaways (though that was not a word in use then), if not all twenty-four of us, then a significant proportion. Enough to be a disruptive force. Rosie and I had a natural tendency towards disruption and soon had ganged up with half a dozen others of similar bent. We went through the connecting door into the church and took turns to climb up into the pulpit and deliver sermons. *Dearly beloved . . . Oh come all ye faithful . . .* The congregation turned somersaults in the aisles displaying green knickers. We went out to the shops which was not permitted. We played football in the church garden. We walked round the edge of a static water tank that had been left over from the war, with our arms stretched out like tightrope walkers. We pretended we were circus performers. Deirdre Fish was ringmaster.

'We bring you straight from Billy Smart's Circus – the most daring tightrope walker in the length and breadth of Ireland – Miss Cora Caldwell!'

'Hip, hip!' cried Rosie.

I wobbled, lost balance and fell in. Accident prone! I remembered Gerard Lavery's voice as I waded through the filthy water to the edge where a forest of hands waited to haul me in. Rosie held her nose with her free hand.

Miss McCloy, the mathematics teacher, was standing on the corner watching us. 'Follow me, girls.'

'*Fall in and follow me,*' sang Rosie under her breath. It was all right for her, well relatively all right; compared to me, that was. I glowered at her.

'Really, Cora, I am surprised at *you,*' said Miss Lightbody. Did she mean because I looked as if I wouldn't get into trouble or because I was at the school on a scholarship? I stood before her with water running down on to the moth-eaten half-moon rug looking longingly at the hissing gas fire whose heat she blocked. She had lifted her skirt and was warming her knees. 'You girls will have to mend your ways or else leave the school.'

Expulsion! That was what she threatened us with. We stood in a line staring at our shoes. I would never be able to face my mother and father if that were to happen and then there was Mrs Hastings-Smith . . . My uniform was no longer so shining and so bright. We were dismissed to think over our sins, and I to get dried off by the housekeeper.

'Ach they'd never expel us,' said Patsy McKenna, as we walked up the hill. 'There's too many of us. They wouldn't be left with enough pupils in our form.'

'They need the fees,' said Deirdre Fish, whose father was an accountant in the Northern Ireland Civil Service. High up, she said. Close to the PM. I saw him seated on high like an archangel in one of Teresa's holy books. In Christian Science we didn't believe in angels, not with wings on anyway.

'They look as if they need every shilling they can get their hands on,' said Rosie.

But they might not need me, I thought miserably. I brought in no shillings.

'Come on, let's go and have an ice,' said Eithne Potter, putting her arm through mine. 'I'll buy you one, Cora.' I already owed her a penny halfpenny. Her father was a bank manager.

We stood on the corner sucking ice cream cones and reviewing our situation. A familiar looking figure pushing a pram was coming down the hill towards us.

'There's Teresa.' I poked Rosie in the back.

Rosie turned about and began to talk to Angela Simpson. 'Did you see the Corpse's face? Suffering duck! I thought I was going to die so I did.'

I said hello to Teresa who seemed too embarrassed to reply. She bent over the pram to wipe the baby's nose.

'Who on earth was that?' asked Dierdre after they'd gone.

'She's a friend of ours. Isn't she, Rosie?'

'You're thick with her all right. Even though she's a Pape.'

'You shouldn't say Pape, Rosie,' said Susan Orr, whose father was a minister of the Church of Ireland. 'They're Roman Catholics.'

It was almost dark and rain was spattering our faces. My teeth were rattling. I am not going to get a cold, I told myself; *I am not.* We parted for the night and went our separate ways. Rosie and I had a row on the way home. I told her she had betrayed Teresa. And loyalty was one of the most important things in life: we were always being told so, at school and at the Girl Guides. 'And we're blood sisters!' Rosie denied her betrayal claiming that she had been talking to Angela and hadn't seen Teresa going by. 'And that's the truth, Cora Caldwell. I *didn't* see her. And you are the one who is lie-telling when you say that I did.'

I had a headache when I got in, a real hot throbbing one. My mother laid her cool fingers against my forehead and slowly the ache subsided. I told her about the static water tank and the uniform and Rosie Meneely whom I hated. I wept. My father, looking distressed, limped from the room. It will all pass, said my mother, and of course it did.

Next morning Rosie called for me and said she was sorry. She was sorry too about Teresa and was going to give her her blue bangle to make up for it. 'I'm a right eejit at times, Cora, I don't know why it is. It just seems to come over me, the way Ma's nerves do.'

We linked arms.

And we were not expelled that day or any other, though I always considered it was a miracle that we were not. At the end of the year we were moved out of the church hall and back into the main building where the scope for disruption was not so great.

In history we learned about the disruption of the monasteries during the reign of Henry the Eighth but not a word did we learn about the disruption there had been in Ireland in the early part of our own century. It was Gerard Lavery who first told me about the 1916 Easter Rising in Dublin but that was not until some time later.

In the summer of 1947, aged fourteen, he left school and went to work full-time for Mr MacMahon.

'Earning peanuts he is,' said Mrs Lavery. 'And yon old skinflint MacMahon wouldn't so much as give you the free sniff of a quarter of tea.' She was expecting again, having miscarried six months previously. Teresa spent as much time at home as she did at school, a practice which brought the attendance officer and the priest chapping at the door, though Father Flynn knew the score and only made a few noises before accepting a cup of tea. Mrs Lavery said beggars couldn't be choosers and lit another Woodbine. She needed something to keep her going.

What kept him going, said Gerard, was the thought that he wouldn't have to deliver groceries all his life. He still intended to be a doctor and worked at nights on the kitchen table. I helped him with Latin but kept thinking there must be something else I could do. I decided to talk to Mrs Hastings-Smith.

And so Gerard went to work at Hastings Court where he earned twice as much as he had as a delivery boy and where he got peace in the evenings to work at his books. He lived in during the week and came home on Sundays.

Teresa and I went out on the bus to visit him one Saturday. We heard him whistling as we walked down through the orchard. He was clipping the hawthorn hedge that ran round the back of it. His face seemed fuller already and his skin was browning.

'So you're liking it then, are you?' said Teresa. We followed him along the hedge watching the snip of the shears.

'It's great. Marcellina feeds me till I'm nearly fit to bust. And she–' he nodded his head towards the house '–lets me use the books in the library. She says I should work for Matric,' he said over his shoulder to me.

'So you should then. But she wouldn't want you to do medicine, you know.' I hadn't told her that bit about him, only that he was a keen scholar and wanted to get on in life.

'She said it wouldn't worry her. Each till his own.'

We helped tidy up the fallen branches and then raked leaves from the lawn until we were called in for tea by Mrs Hastings-Smith. Afterwards, when Teresa had gone off to have a crack with Marcellina in the kitchen, I took another stroll around the grounds and came upon Gerard washing the Lagonda outside the coach-house.

'It's a beaut. She says when I'm seventeen I can get to drive it. She's a great woman. I'm right grateful to you, you know, Cora.' For a moment he looked awkward. He ducked his head and rubbed the car bonnet vigorously with the chammy.

'That's all right.' I smiled into the golden autumn sun even though I knew that all it would do for me would be to bring out more chicken shit. 'Did you ever fancy going up the Amazon?'

'The Amazon? No, I can't say as I ever thought of it exactly.'

But if he did think of it would he fancy it? I gave him time to consider and he thought that he might. I told him I'd just been reading a book about a man called Colonel Fawcett who'd gone up the Amazon and disappeared. (So what? Rosie had said when I told her; lots of people must disappear all the time, everywhere, never mind up the Amazon.) To Gerard I confided that it was my ambition to go on an expedition, when I was older, to look for Colonel Fawcett. He did not ask why; he said, 'That could be exciting right enough.'

That night I dreamt I was paddling up the Amazon in a canoe with Gerard Lavery. The sun glittered on the water, the foliage was densely green, edged here and there with brown, and sometimes spotted, and bright flowers blossomed above our heads, sizzling red and pink and coolly white.

FIVE

The words which my mother read daily aloud appeared to have some effect on my father's state of health: his leg improved, though not sufficiently to enable him to be employed again as a commercial traveller – that required mobility and stamina – but he did manage to get a job selling socks and ties in the men's section of the Bank Buildings department store. At school I was vague as to what he did emphasizing rather his glorious war record. In private Rosie called me a liar but I maintained that he had been a hero. Not getting medals didn't prove anything.

'But what's the point in getting medals then?' asked Rosie. 'If it doesn't prove anything?'

Teresa who had been half-listening while she turned over the pages of *Woman's Own* said, 'Do they mind like – the girls at school – if your father sells ties?' Hers sold cabbages. At least we presumed he did: all we knew of his activities was hearsay. He left the street early in the morning to go to market and came back late in the evening. When the pub was shut, said Granny McGill: it was a wonder he had the energy to father all those children.

'Of course they mind,' said Rosie. '*Their* fathers are bank managers and civil servants.'

She had told them that her Uncle William was a manager in the shipbuilding business. She made it sound as if Harland and Woolfs would collapse without him. Uncle Sam she never mentioned. Though the girls all took their shoes to him to be mended.

'Rosie's uncles are awful,' Dierdre Fish said to me after

she had been to tea at the McGills. 'The shoemaker one kept touching me.' She shivered.

It was just Uncle Sam's way, I wanted to tell her but didn't, for I knew she wouldn't understand; he liked touching people. His hands were soft and gentle in spite of the leather he handled, whereas Uncle Billy's were hard. Sometimes Uncle Billy would splay his fingers to show us the breadth of their span. He'd make a shadow with them on the wall. 'Billy should've played the piano,' said his mother, but they didn't make me think of music. They reminded me of a picture I'd seen of a bird of prey with wings stretched wide, hovering.

Uncle Billy and Uncle Sam. In their church-going Lodge-going dancehall-going clothes. For they did go to dances in spite of their mother's disapproval, at least for a few years, whilst they were still in their twenties. And from time to time 'walked out' with girls. Rosie and I liked to watch them setting out for the Floral Hall with their collars crisp and white and their handkerchiefs showing just the right amount in their top pockets. They'd be joking with one another. 'You're a right looking toff the night, Sam.' 'The girls'll not be able to take their eyes off you, Billy.' In the years before we went to secondary school we'd walk with them to the main road and wait until the trolley bus came. We wished we could go with them. How we wished it! They promised they'd take us when we were bigger. How big? They held their hands a foot above our heads. We protested and they lowered them a little. They laughed. We liked them in this mood better than their Lodge-going one. And then the trolley bus would come swooshing in to stop packed with people on a Saturday night out. 'Have a good time,' we'd yelled after them as they rolled away to the magical delights of the Floral Hall where coloured lights revolved and the girls wore high-heeled sandals and smelled of *Lily of the Valley* and *Midnight in Paris*. We would go there, too, one of these days.

We no longer walked the uncles to the bus stop. 'Getting too big for that eh?' said Uncle Sam as he ducked in front of the mirror combing the Brilliantine into his hair.

'It's just that we're too busy,' said Rosie. 'Going to tea and things.'

We went to tea with Deirdre Fish. The Fishes lived in a quiet, tree-lined road of detached houses where everyone had cars and telephones and nobody wrote on the walls or drew hopscotch marks on the pavement. As we turned into it we paid attention to where we put our feet and pulled our shoulders back.

'I'll bet you won't find any Papes living here,' said Rosie, but she was wrong, for the Fishes' next door neighbours were Catholics. He was a professor at Queen's University.

'They're very nice people,' said Deirdre, sounding like her mother whom we had met briefly and who had looked over the tops of our heads as she spoke to us. We thought it must be something to do with watching her deportment. Deirdre led us upstairs to her bedroom which would have been good enough for Shirley Temple. Rosie said so.

'My name is Shirley Temple
And I've got curly hair
But I'm not able to do the Betty Grable
For my name is Shirley Temple and I've got skirts up there!'

Rosie flicked her skirt up over her bottom as if she were doing the can-can and winked.

'I've never heard that before, Rosie.' Deirdre giggled.

Rosie was good at making the girls laugh. She was always ready to coarsen her accent and be outrageous.

Deirdre had a brother called Hugo. Rosie, when she was thirteen going on fourteen, batted her eyelashes at Hugo Fish. In school Deirdre passed notes slipping them from the end of a ruler over my head on to Rosie's desk. *Hugo loves you. Hugo wants to press you to his heart.* Between the rows of pegs in the cloakroom Deirdre and Rosie shared secrets.

Rosie began to go to the Fishes for tea more often, and without me.

'She's a right nice girl that Deirdre,' said Mrs Meneely. Deirdre had brought Turkish delight when she came to tea. 'A real little lady. But no side with her. She and Margaret Rose seem to get on really well.'

'Thick as thieves,' said Granny McGill with satisfaction.

'I dunno,' said Uncle Billy. 'She looks a bit fast to me.'

Fast? The women were shocked. 'She's from a very good family, Billy,' said Mrs Meneely. 'They tell me her uncle's a cabinet minister,' said Granny McGill.

'Hugo Fish is ghastly,' I said to Teresa. 'He's got spots on the back of his neck and his hands sweat.' I had had to dance with him at Deirdre's party knowing full well that he had not wanted to dance with me. He'd been given a push in the back by Rosie who had wanted to tango with his friend Randolph.

Gerard's skin was brown and unspotted, and his hands firm and dry. I could still remember the feel of them when he'd carried me home from the railway track, or convinced myself that I could. Now Rosie and Deirdre walked on the railway path with Hugo and someone called Quentin. Rosie said I would faint if I knew what they got up to. 'They wouldn't get up to *that,* would they?' Teresa was horrified. 'Who knows?' said I who did not know exactly what *that* was. My mother did not believe in discussing anything to do with bodily functions – there was no sensation in matter after all – and I never heard the word sex mentioned in our house. I learned more about that side of life (Mrs Meneely's terminology) from Mrs Robinson at Number Eleven.

I often talked to her as she stood at her gate, and sometimes she'd ask me in, when the children were asleep. Her husband, he who walked the whippets, was either at the dog track or working night shift at the docks where he was something to do with security. It was no life, said Mrs Robinson, being stuck in every evening after working your fingers to the bone all day. She used to enjoy a night out, at the pictures, or the dancing, or just going for a drink in a cocktail lounge. 'You'd never know who you'd meet.' She shook her lion mane's shock of hair the colour of a daffodil. 'Those were the days.' The good-time days long gone never to be had again. 'Don't you be in any hurry to get yourself shackled, Cora. A bunch of roses and a white dress and after that what have you got?' A lifetime of drudgery. I could have put the words into her mouth but did not.

Her good times did not need to be over, I told her; I would baby-sit and she could go out, to a cocktail lounge or a dancehall, or anywhere she wished. She did the roots of her hair, squeezed her body into a lilac taffeta dress and her feet into a pair of high-heeled silver sandals and set off for the Floral Hall. I imagined the lights revolving over her brilliant hair and shiny body.

Half-way through the evening Mrs Lavery came in to borrow a quarter of tea. Her man had a desperate thirst on him and she'd clean forgotten to buy tea that day and now Mrs MacAteer was shut. 'Mrs Robinson won't mind lending me a quarter. She knows I'll pay her back in the morning. We often help one another out.'

She stayed to smoke a cigarette – one of Mrs Robinson's Woodbines that were lying on the mantelpiece – and I said that it was nice for Mrs Robinson to get out for a change.

'Aye it's good to get out, Cora, you're right there. A woman sees too much of the inside of a house so she does. Watch that you don't get a ring put on your finger till you've lived a bit, girl.'

Two warnings from two different women.

I would watch, I told her, although at nights I dreamt of walking down the aisle on her son's arm. The aisle of a Protestant church, not a Catholic one. I could not let a priest or the smell of incense into my dream.

Mrs Robinson came back from the Floral Hall smelling of drink and with a love bite on her neck. At least I presumed it was a love bite, never having seen one before. Rosie talked about them, considered them romantic; I was less sure. I thought it would be like having a vampire suck blood out of your neck.

'Did you have a good time, Mrs Robinson?' I was

desperate to know all the details and not just have them hinted at, the way that Rosie did.

'Great, love. Feel ten years younger. Don't be letting on to your mother where I've been though, will you? She's a good woman but she doesn't understand everything. Just say I went to visit my sister up the Ormeau Road if anyone wants to know.'

I asked if she had seen Rosie's uncles at the Floral Hall.

'Billy and Sam? No, not them.' She laughed. 'Don't know as I'd fancy dancing with either of them.'

'Oh, why not?' I scented gossip.

'Wandering hands, that's their trouble. Gropers. Suppose I shouldn't grudge them, not really. It's all they've got after all. A wee bit of a feel. But that Billy McGill's so hypercritical with it – lecturing you about going to church or not showing a light for the Gerries and all the while his hand's wandering across your behind. Oh aye and a few other places as well if you'd let him. That black-out business was a right good excuse if you ask me. He was one person who wasn't so pleased to see the lights go on again.'

'I don't suppose he'd touch – well, every woman he called to see about the black-out?' I felt anxious.

'He'd have a go, love. So you watch him.'

When I went home I looked at my mother but could not imagine her with a man's hand on her behind. There were a lot of things I could not imagine. The act itself. How was it possible? I asked Rosie who laughed and said I was dead ignorant but did not enlighten me. I would never be able to do the act, I didn't have a hole inside me big enough. I wished I could ask Mrs Robinson but didn't want her to think me ignorant too.

But she told me things that no other woman in the street would have done. Most of the women were what Granny McGill called respectable, God-fearing women, keeping clean houses and bringing up their children in the expectation of them doing better than they had done in life.

'You're spending rather a lot of time at Mrs Robinson's, dear' said my mother, who did not care for her bleached hair or her chain-smoking. When my father chatted to Mrs Robinson on the pavement my mother would call him in to mend the iron or to give her a hand to carry the coal.

'Her sister's not well.' I did not tell a lie. 'She's got five children and her husband's no good. Mrs Robinson's really fond of her sister.' I was pious in my defence of her.

One night she brought back a man. He scuttled round the side of the house behind her and stayed in the backyard whilst, after a quick word to quieten the dogs, she came on in. I saw the man's shadow on the wall. He was wearing a longish coat and a trilby hat.

'I'll let you away now, Cora, and thanks very much again.'

I was disappointed for usually we had a cup of coffee and a blether. I wouldn't have minded if she'd brought the man in and we could all have had coffee together. She was moving around the living room plumping up the cushions on the sofa and humming under her breath. *We'll gather lilacs in the spring again. . .* She smoothed her hands over her hips. She avoided my eyes.

'Use the front door tonight, dear.'

I thought I heard her laugh as I walked up the street. I imagined her in love with the man, locked in close embrace on the sofa, ready to do the act.

And walk together down an English lane . . .

'I was just coming for you,' said my father, who was standing at our door. 'Your mother was getting worried.'

Next morning, Mrs Robinson had a black eye. 'You can never tell with men, Cora.' But why had he done it? 'Some men get excited and a bit violent. They need it to get worked up.' I could still not understand, but she would say no more about it. She was cheerful and undeterred by the injury, however, and when her eye healed she was ready to taste the delights of the Floral Hall again.

'Have a good time,' I called after her. I always seemed to be calling that after other people. Rosie's uncles. Rosie herself. One day it would be my turn to have a good time. Skirting the greyhounds which were tied up in the yard (I hated the way their long wet noses tried to poke up my skirt), I went into the garden and hung up the washing that was lying in the zinc bath. As I was propping up the line with the pole, Teresa came out of her back door. We gossiped over the fence. She told me about a Georgette Heyer novel she was reading. I asked about Gerard. He was in great form, she said, didn't come home much though, even at week-ends, he was so busy with his books. Someone called: she had to go.

I retreated inside, to lie on the sofa and imagine myself floating around the Floral Hall in the arms of Gerard Lavery. Then I imagined myself lying on the sofa in his arms and my face grew hot and my body trembled. I was sure he would never black my eyes.

Mrs Robinson came back with a different man that night. At least I presumed he was different from the last one. This one came straight in with her, did not wait in the backyard for the coast to be cleared. They were both what Granny McGill would have called the worse for wear. Stotious, in fact. They were supporting one another and laughing like drains and clutching at one another's clothing. The V-neck of the taffeta dress suddenly ripped to the waist and the breasts which had been straining behind the bodice burst forth in joyous release. He had both his hands on them. They were the biggest breasts I had ever seen, and perhaps that he had too for he didn't seem to be able,to get over them.

'Wait now, Eric,' Mrs Robinson was saying, trying to take hold of his hands, and all the while they were laughing and grappling, a bit like two kids about to fight. 'Wait till the girl's out the door.'

I told Rosie about Mrs Robinson and her fancy man: I couldn't resist it. I was tired of Rosie and Deirdre Fish and their secrets and the way they thought they knew everything to do with men and sex. Sex! There, I had used the word. 'That's what they were going to do – sex! They were all excited, Rosie.' Even as I was telling her, I suspected it would be a mistake, and it was, for she told Deanna whom she liked to tell shocking things to, and Deanna who was a natural born tale-teller told her mother who told her father who told Mr Robinson who beat up his wife and gave her more than one black eye to contend with this time. Her good times came to an end for once and for all. She looked mournfully at me as I sloped past. She had thought she could trust me.

'I told you not to tell!' I was furious with Rosie.

'You shouldn't have told me then should you. It was your fault in the first place. Anyway, Mrs Robinson's a bad woman, she probably deserved all she got.'

'Look who's talking! You go along the railway path don't you – with Hugo Fish and Randolph and anyone else you can get your hands on?'

Two years earlier, she would have mauled me; now, we had passed the stage of physical violence, more or less. How dare I suggest that *she*–? When she got her breath back she laid into me. I was jealous, I couldn't get anyone to go along the railway path with, not even Eithne Potter's brother who was half-witted and no one else would touch with a barge pole. I retaliated: she was just saying that because I wasn't fast, like her. We were like bloodhounds after one another, remembering the scent of battle from former years and wanting to taste blood again. Teresa, looking on, was troubled, and implored us to stop. We would not stop until we had said everything that we had stored up. Words flew like darts finding targets.

'You're a prig.'

'You're a tart.'

'I hate you, Cora Caldwell!'

'I *despise* you, Rosie Meneely.' I often had the edge on her for nastiness.

Make up, make up! cried Teresa, dragging us together, as my mother had done to her and Rosie years before. She turned over the wrist of my left hand so that the scar was exposed. 'You have to, you're blood sisters.'

'You shouldn't take on so, Teresa,' said Rosie, when we had made up. 'Quarrelling's not that serious. Lots of people do it.' She said her mother and father had fought; her father had been a wild, passionate man, a bit like Clark Gable in *Gone with the Wind*. I couldn't imagine Mrs Meneely married to Clark Gable, being carried up the stairs in his arms. The staircases in our houses were narrow and she was large, though perhaps she had eaten less when Mr Meneely was alive. Teresa said her parents seldom quarrelled, her father didn't like arguments and her mother was usually too tired. She and Rosie didn't need to ask if my parents quarrelled.

In school, when the lesson dragged, I thought about Gerard Lavery carrying me up the wide staircase in Hastings Court.

Rosie wrote notes, her fountain pen spluttering as she pushed it impatiently along, and flicked them through the air to Deirdre Fish. *He kisses divinely. With his mouth open. He is wild and passionate.*

That note was caught in mid-air by Miss McCloy who informed us that she had played cricket with her brothers as a child. We stared at her in disbelief. Impossible to imagine her wielding a cricket bat, or having ever been young. The staff were unmarried to a woman. Spinsters. On the shelf. Never been taken down and never would be now. A fate worse than death. Infinitely worse, said Deirdre Fish. Miss McCloy unfolded Rosie's note. Her mouth twitched. 'I think, Margaret, that perhaps your mother ought to see this.'

Mrs Meneely didn't know what to do, other than give Rosie a lecture on the inadvisability (using different words) of getting a reputation for being fast. 'You'll ruin your chances if you do that.' 'Don't be so old-fashioned, Mother,' said Rosie, which did not ease Mrs Meneely's anxiety. Reluctant to confide in her family who might stop Margaret Rose going to the Fishes' house again, Mrs Meneely came to consult my mother. The living room door closed at their backs reducing their voices to a murmur. I returned to my bedroom where Teresa was sitting on the bed.

'He kisses divinely,' I said and kissed her on the mouth.

'You're not meant to kiss girls.' Blushing, Teresa wiped her mouth with the back of her hand.

In Glenmachen woods we all kissed one another, I told her, when we went on Girl Guide hikes. When we went without our Guide captain, that was, unofficially, just the eight of us in the White Rose patrol. During the week we made confetti and on Saturdays, carrying our billy cans and staffs and the little pieces of chopped-up coloured paper in grocers' bags, set off for the woods. We conducted marriages, taking turn to be the minister, and subsequently moved on to divorces since it was boring to be married to one person for too long. Rosie and Deirdre had been 'married' for four weeks and were refusing to be divorced, thus disturbing the permutations.

'Divorce?' said Teresa. 'But that's a sin.'

'If I went to your church would I've to confess to getting married and divorced in the woods?'

'I'm not sure. I think so.'

'Would I be pardoned?'

Only if I were to promise to do it no more, it seemed. Well, I wouldn't have minded that, for the weddings, exciting at first, were beginning to bore me, especially since Rosie and Deirdre spent half the time rolling in the fallen leaves together and wouldn't take their turn at cooking the sausages or cleaning out the billy cans. The rest of us sat round the camp fire singing songs about coming round the mountain in silk pyjamas and cuckaburragh sitting in the old gum tree. *Merry, merry, king of the woods is he!*

'You might get a few Hail Marys,' said Teresa.

Hail Mary full of grace . . .

What a daft thing to have to say! I didn't say so as I didn't want to hurt Teresa's feelings.

'I bet you don't have many sins to confess.'

'Oh, but I do!'

I couldn't believe it. 'You don't have much chance for sinning. You're either here or at your own house.'

'But you can sin anywhere, Cora. Inside your own head even.'

Yes, I did know that.

We heard a door opening below. I crept out on to the landing.

'Thanks very much, Mrs Caldwell, it's been a great help getting it off my chest. And I won't say nothing to my mother or Billy, like you say, but I'll take a stricter line with Margaret Rose from now on. She's a good girl really, she just gets carried away.'

In future when Margaret Rose went to the Fishes' she was to come home by eight.

'You can do a lot of kissing before eight,' said Rosie.

SIX

Uncle Sam had a girl called Lily. She was not an orange lily – she favoured pink: rose, sugar, and magenta. But most of all she favoured magenta. She was a very thin girl with legs like pencils, a very white skin and light frizzy hair held back from her low forehead by a pink Alice band. She kicked with the right foot of course, that went without saying, though her father, Rolly Jack, was not a Lodge man and her mother was an infrequent attender at church. They lived in a terraced straight-off-the-street house near the main road.

Lily worked in the baker's opposite Uncle Sam's shop. Often he would go in for a jam doughnut to have with his cup of tea mid-morning. They would have a bit of a crack, natural enough, about his liking for doughnuts and the weather and what was on at the Astoria Picture House. Lily was fond of the pictures, especially a good Western, which was Uncle Sam's own weakness. Hopalong Cassidy and a bag of liquorice allsorts, and they were prepared to let the rest of the world go by. Lily liked dancing at the Floral Hall too. So they had a lot in common, Uncle Sam and Lily; they started walking out together.

'He'll need to watch himself there,' said Aunt Gertrude. 'The way he's carrying on he'll be putting ideas intil her head.'

'She's got them already if you ask me,' said Mrs Meneely. 'She knows when she's on till a good thing.'

They often passed remarks about Lily in front of Uncle Sam but he never let on he heard. He would sit staring out of the window smiling to himself and then get up and go out.

'He's a changed man,' said Aunt Gertrude. She was in giving Mrs Meneely a home perm. The smell of the neutralizer was catching my nose. 'I see a difference on him from last year. Oh yes, indeed I do.'

'That wee girl's nothing but a scheming young hussy,' said Mrs Meneely. 'And common as all get out.'

'You're right there, Ina,' said Uncle Billy. 'And that Jack family is dead ignorant so it is.'

Granny McGill was saying nothing, as yet.

So absorbed were they in there watching of Sam and his Magenta Lily that they did not register anything important about the new people moving into Number Eleven. The Robinsons had moved out a month before, to some other part of the city, no one seemed to know where. Since that terrible night when Mr Robinson had beaten up Mrs Robinson and the dogs' protracted howls had set the street's teeth on edge and I had wept into my pillow until it was sodden, people had ceased going in and out of the house and she had ceased to stand at her gate. Her hair grew in lank and dark, her rolls of flesh expanded. She let herself go, as the women in the street described it. Let her self go? But where had it gone to? Up into the air like a spirit released from its body? But she'd stayed behind locked inside her solid prison of flesh. She looked totally dispirited. So when the Robinsons sold up I was relieved and felt mean about feeling that way, but now at least I could pass their gate without having that hot sour taste at the back of my throat.

The incomers were quiet, kept themselves to themselves. 'She seems a decent enough wee woman,' was Granny McGill's opinion after a brief exchange in the street. 'Mrs Gracey they call her. She's a welcome change after that other harridan, that's for sure.'

The Graceys had no children and both worked in the Civil Service. I wondered if they'd know Mr Fish. 'Hardly!' said Rosie. 'He's on the top rung.'

It was only when Mrs Meneely went to call with a sponge cake that she found out what they really were. The crucifix on the back wall was a dead giveaway.

'There was I drinking my tea when I happened to turn

my head and see this thing behind me! It gave me a right turn. I came away at a queer lick I can tell you!'

I suppressed a giggle.

'Graven images,' said Uncle Billy, frowning at me.

'That's the second lot intil the street then,' said Granny McGill, with what I thought sounded like satisfaction.

'Infiltration,' said Uncle Billy. 'I told you it would happen didn't I?'

'But it's four years since the Laverys came,' I said.

'They'll be pleased any road,' said Mrs Meneely.

But when Mrs Lavery called to borrow a bowlful of sugar she was told by Mrs Gracey in the nicest possible way that she and her husband didn't believe in borrowing and lending, it only led to trouble. Mrs Gracey also said in the nicest possible way that she would appreciate it if Mrs Lavery would see to it that her children's toys – a euphemism for the collection of old tyres, tin cans and cardboard boxes the younger ones played with – were not left on the pavement outside their house or in their driveway.

'Driveway!' said Teresa, her eyes sparking. It was she who had to superintend the clearance.

'I see he's got a car, that Gracey fella,' said Granny McGill. 'They say he's going to build a garage at the side of his house.'

'He's the type to get above himself if you ask me,' said Mrs Meneely.

'We'll just see where it gets him,' said Uncle Billy, splaying his fingers.

It was not long before TAIGS GO HOME appeared on the Graceys' side wall. Mr Gracey didn't wash it off, he took a walk up to the police station on the main road. Our local constable came round wanting to know if we'd any idea who'd been writing on the Gracey's wall. He said he didn't want any trouble. This had always been a quiet district and he'd prefer it to stay that way.

Mr Gracey cleaned his wall and nobody wrote on it again, not, I'm sure, because they were afraid of the constable but because it wasn't going to pay off. The Graceys were not going to be crushed by slogans.

For a week or two the McGills' attention was taken up by the goings on at Number Eleven and so Uncle Sam was left to rendezvous in peace with the light of his life. But Lily was not for hiding her light under any bushel, she wanted it to shine where it would be seen. She steered Uncle Sam determinedly in the direction of the street. Arm-in-arm, they strolled down one side and up the other, pausing every few yards to admire the roses and lupins in the front gardens, and when they passed the McGills' house she tucked her hand deeper into the crook of his arm and smiled up into his face. There was an air of defiance about the tilt of her nose, as if she were expecting opposition.

'The impudence of her!' said Mrs Meneely.

Uncle Sam and Lily were seen looking in a jeweller's shop window at Holywood Arches.

'Something'll have to be done, Ma,' said Aunt Gertrude.

Granny McGill was still saying nothing, as yet.

Rosie and Deanna planned what they would wear as bridesmaids. Rosie fancied sea green but Deanna said green was unlucky for a wedding.

'Not that it matters anyway,' said Rosie. 'Granny'll not let him marry her.'

'How can she stop him but?'

Rosie gave Deanna a look that would have withered the sturdiest orange lily.

The day came when Granny McGill did speak. Uncle Sam had come breezing in with smiles all over his face saying as innocently as anything that he'd like to bring Lily home to tea. Rosie and I were in the kitchen making toffee apples. We turned off the gas ring.

'I don't think that'd be suitable somehow, Sam.'

'But why not, Ma?'

Yes, why not? I, too, awaited the answer.

'She's not good enough for you, son, that's why not. What is she? A bakery assistant. You can do far better than that.'

What if he were to come in with a school teacher who

had her own car and a legacy in the bank? Would she give him her blessing then?

'But I'm only a shoemaker myself, Ma.'

'Deed you are not! You're a businessman and don't you forget it, like your father was before you. Aren't you set up in your own business?'

He could not deny it. He stood there leaning against the dresser fidgeting with his cuffs. I longed to tell him to cut and run, to get out, whilst the going was good, but the McGills would have killed me; all but Rosie, that was. I could feel her shifting about beside me.

'Granny,' she began.

'You stay out of this, Margaret Rose.' Mrs McGill looked back at her son. 'And what about her father? Would you want to saddle us with Rolly Jack for a relative, tell me that?'

'He's a decent enough man. It's not his fault that he's a semi-invalid and can't work.'

'Can't or won't?' She was used to the idea of Catholics not working but an idle Protestant did not fit in with her scheme of things. 'Everyone knows Rolly Jack's cough comes on when it suits him. When I passed him the other night in the street he was as full as a po. Didn't even know me. *And* his wife keeps a dirty house.'

'You've no call to say that!' Uncle Sam was actually getting worked up. I wanted to cheer. 'She may not be as tidy as you–'

'I'm not talking about tidy. I'm talking about dirt. *Dirt,* Sam.'

'But it's not her mother he's going to marry,' blurted out Rosie. 'Lily looks clean enough. Her overall's always spotless.'

'Who said anything about marry? And I've told *you* to hold your tongue already.'

Uncle Sam's face and neck were brick red right down to his too-tight collar. Recently he'd been putting on weight. Too many doughnuts and cream cakes. He put a finger inside the collar to ease it.

'I'm only wanting to bring her home to meet you, Ma.'

'That's the first step though isn't it?'

'Well, I'm certainly not going to bring her home if she won't be welcome.' He all but slammed the door as he went out.

Rosie and I escaped before we could be called back. We hurried after him.

'I think he should go ahead and marry her.'

'It's easy for you to say that, Cora. But they'd all be against him if he did.'

'He should just let them be then. If he loves her–'

Rosie, normally swayed by the word 'love', sighed.

Ahead, we saw Uncle Sam meeting up with his true love. We stationed ourselves behind a parked car. He was talking but she was clearly not pleased with what he was saying for she was tossing her frizzy head about and had her hands placed on her narrow hips so that she stood arms akimbo, the way her mother did when she gossiped on the doorstep. Uncle Sam's head now was dropping; lower and lower it went, until his chin seemed to disappear. Then Lily wheeled around on her high thin heels and wobbling a little in the effort to walk fast, left him. He went after her and they vanished down a side street so we were uncertain as to what the outcome was then. But we soon knew for the following evening she appeared in the street walking on the arm of Hughie Jamieson.

'Look at her!' said Granny McGill. 'A different man every day. I'm sure Mrs Jamieson won't be a bit pleased to see that. You're well out of it, Sam.'

Sam now was saying nothing.

But the next day I saw him having a long conversation with Lily across the counter in the baker's. He came out looking sad and leaving his doughnut behind. She didn't run after him with it.

When Rosie and I went in later to buy vanilla slices for her mother, Lily dropped the doughnut disdainfully into Rosie's hand and said in a put-on voice that her uncle had forgotten something. She was lucky – knowing Rosie – that she didn't get the doughnut back in her face. For a moment they faced one another. Looking at Lily's face, I realized that although I had been all for Uncle Sam marrying her, I didn't really like her. There was something mean about that pinched drawn-together mouth. She'd have squeezed the life out of Uncle Sam if she'd married him. One way or another, he was doomed.

'Come on, Cora,' said Rosie and on the way out, 'Common as dirt!' She dropped the doughnut on the doorstep.

The following summer Lily Jack married Hughie Jamieson and seven months later produced an eight-pound baby.

'See what a lucky escape you had, son. I told you she was no good.'

'It's true, Ma. I did right to listen to you.'

Lily was the last girl Sam McGill ever courted. He gradually dropped off going to the Floral Hall too. He continued to go to the pictures on a Friday night and he never missed a meeting at the Orange Hall. His face set in harder lines. He and Uncle Billy became 'confirmed bachelors'.

'You're too good to them, Ma, that's the trouble,' said Mrs Meneely.

'Aye, they know when they're well off right enough,' said Granny McGill.

So said Mrs Lavery, too, about her eldest son. 'He's on till a good thing – put on to it by you, Cora – and I don't blame him for staying out there at week-ends. He needs the peace and quiet to get stuck into his books.' She wanted him to stick in so that he would get on. In the Lavery house there was neither peace nor room for getting on. Teresa and Bridie slept in the front parlour and if Gerard came home he had to sleep there too. 'They're getting too big to have their brother in with them,' said Mrs Lavery. 'Father Flynn was just remarking on that the other day there. "I hope you're keeping them separate now," he said. It's easy for him to talk, mind.'

Father Flynn talked plenty when he came into the house. He dandled Peter and Paul on his knee and said what lovely babbies they were. He called Mrs Lavery a good Catholic mother and Teresa a good Catholic daughter. What did he say to Mrs Gracey when he called there? She was producing no children at all for the Catholic cause. How did she get away with it? Money, said Rosie; it was well known that priests could be bought if the price was right, even by murderers.

Father Flynn smiled at me and said, 'And how're you doing then, Cora girl? It must be grand for you having the Laverys as your friends. You'll be lonely on your own eh? It's not good to be an only child, for neither you nor your mother.' Why he should sound sad about that I could not understand for surely he would not wish for the proliferation of Christian Scientists? That would only work counter to his own campaign.

But as for being an only child, I didn't mind at all, perhaps I even preferred it, not that Father Flynn seemed to be able to understand that. I enjoyed the company of Teresa and Rosie but liked time on my own too, especially on going to bed. Teresa, dead beat (her own words), went out like a light, her consciousness extinguished. I wanted to hold on to mine as long as possible, for that spell between wakefulness and sleep seemed to belong more completely to me than any other of the day and night: it was a time and a space in which I could control my own destiny, be admired and successful, and reign supreme. Once I slept I lost that control and slid down into multi-coloured, fast-moving, turbulent dreams which swept me along rendering me in turn exhilarated, terrified, happy, sad, sometimes making me gasp for breath, sometimes, in a quiet stretch, lulling me, making me smile, before the current would carry me on again until, at last, I was washed up on the shore of morning. Washed-out. 'I fear she has too vivid an imagination,' I overheard my father say to my mother. My mother said, 'The imagination *should* be vivid, Desmond.' Negativism was alien to her. And he should not fear anything. Perfect love casteth out fear. *Perfect* love? How was that possible? The people I loved – my mother, father, Rosie, Teresa, even Gerard, even God, yes, even God – I also hated, at times. I despaired of reaching perfection.

I asked Father Flynn about the possibility of perfect love.

'God's love is perfect, Cora, for his children.'

'But often he lets terrible things happen to them.'

'He must punish them too though. Like a good mother punishes her children. To teach them to be good.'

'But she doesn't maim or kill them. If you're dead you can't learn anything from it.'

'Ah yes but, you see, it's more complicated than that – we cannot begin to understand God's design . . .' He began to slide away from me, to waffle, to fill his pipe, to let his eyes stray to a small child whom he might pick up, distract himself with. My mother said I should be watchful of him but I could not see how he could be harmful.

When we played the girls of the convent school at hockey we were watchful. 'The place smells,' whispered Deirdre as we were led down a pink-washed corridor by the captain of the convent hockey team. 'Incense,' said Rosie, her eyes bright. Her Uncle Billy hadn't been sure about her coming, not at all sure. But Rosie was not going to be left out. 'It's only to play hockey, Uncle Billy. We probably won't even see a nun.' But we did: two patrolled the perimeter of the pitch throughout the game. 'Putting the evil eye on us,' said Rosie with satisfaction.

Nuns were good and kind, said Teresa. She had thought she might like to be a nun herself but her mother wouldn't be able to manage without her. Rosie and I were horrified. Lock herself away? Shave her head? Never get married? Teresa wasn't sure if she wanted to get married.

'But you want to fall in love don't you?' said Rosie. 'And if you fall in love – *really* in love – you'd want to marry him, wouldn't you? Of course you would!'

Teresa loved love stories. Ethel M. Dell, Florency Barclay, Annie S. Swan. When she wanted a good read she would come along to our house and curl up in the corner of my bedroom. We went together to the public library which looked like an old shack and whose books were like something left over from Dickens' time with greasy spines and food-spattered pages. I turned the pages with a stiff post-card reading my way through splats of tomato sauce and egg yolk. But as I grew older my library books became cleaner. Readers of Jane Austen were less inclined to eat and read at the same time.

I tried to interest Teresa in Jane Austen – I was passionate about *Pride and Prejudice* and *Emma* – but she just laughed. 'Away you go, Cora!'

Rosie also preferred love stories. She and Teresa discussed the lovemaking of the sheik in Ethel M. Dell (not the physical details, only the romantic preliminaries) and both fell in love with the pansy-eyed Garth Dalmain in *The Rosary*. (Initially, Rosie would not open the book because of the title, but once that hurdle was cleared, she was hooked.)

Love – or talk of it – dominated the conversation of our fourteenth and fifteenth years. Rosie had forsaken Hugo and Randolph for Quentin who tangoed to perfection. *Jealousy! 'twas only through jealousy! our hearts were broken* . . . In my bedroom we practised the tango, the samba and the slow foxtrot. Slow, slow, quick, quick, slow. To the soporific voice of Victor Sylvester on the wireless. 'You should see the size of Quentin's bedroom', said Rosie as she steered Teresa between the foot of the bed and the chest of drawers. 'It's like a ballroom.' 'You've not been in his bedroom?' Teresa stumbled. 'Just to *see* it. He showed me it when his mother was out. Don't look so shocked, Teresa! You're a desperate wee prude at times so you are. No wonder the priest's proud of you!'

I tapped Rosie on the shoulder, to break it up.

'Girls,' called my mother from below, 'the ceiling's shaking.' It was cracked already, had been since 1940, when a bomb landed at the end of our road.

We dropped backwards on to the bed.

'Who do you love, Cora?' Rosie began to tickle me and Teresa attacked the other side. I doubled up screaming for mercy. 'Tell, tell!' they demanded, showing none.

I owned up to a passion for Carey Grant. My other I could not confess to.

'It's so nice for me to have young people around,' said Mrs Hastings-Smith on the way back to Hastings Court after church. She drove the Lagonda with what I could only think of as gay abandon, but she never as much as put a scratch on its side, though the country lanes were narrow and the hedgerows bushy. She patted the car's bonnet affectionately when we got out. 'Dear Bruno's car. Such a shame he passed on so soon.' I asked her what he had been like and she said, 'I forget now, dear. There must be a photograph of him around somewhere. In the library perhaps?' I wondered if she remembered what her son Bertrand looked like, apart from all those moustaches which must be frightful in the Indian heat. She had little to say of him. He might come back one day, she supposed; the house *was* his, after all. They had got their independence in India now of course, it was difficult to know . . .

After lunch, I wandered through the long corridors watched on either side by Mr Hastings-Smith's ancestors. Humourless-looking men all. I passed the loud-ticking ornate Grandfather clock, and the even more ornate Dutch ormulu cabinet. I passed the closed kitchen door behind which Marcellina and her not-so-young man tickled and slapped. I heard the soft smack of her hand and then her full-throated giggle. I listened to the howl of the wind and the rattle of rain on the cupola. I opened the library door.

My route had been deliberately circuitous for I had known that I would find Gerard sitting there, at the mahogany table, the lamp with its green silk shade casting its strange light over his opened books and his hands, and had wanted to delay the moment of finding him in order to enjoy it the more.

'Cora!' He turned, yawning, and pushed his chair back from the table, glad to stop for a while. I sat down beside him, looked at the books.

'History? Do you need that for medicine?'

'I've changed my mind about that. Are you surprised? It was getting too difficult trying to do physics and chemistry on my own and then I didn't have the right apparatus. Besides, I'm interested in history.'

'So what are you going to be now?'

'A lawyer. Does it sound a crazy idea to you?' He seemed anxious to know. To me the idea sounded marvellous, much better than being a doctor, for that had bothered me. I was a Christian Scientist after all and if he were to become a doctor I didn't see how he and I – He said, 'I want to be able to help my people, you see. They're ill done by, you know, Cora, the poor ones at any rate. They can't get jobs and houses, not as easy as Protestants can. We're second-class citizens. Are you aware of that?'

I was not sure: I had not thought about it, had not heard the term before.

'Then think!' he demanded, pulling his chair up closer to mine and looking into my face. Rain beat against the window shrouding us from the world outside. A shiver of pleasure ran up my spine and made my shoulders twitch.

'I suppose you are right,' I said after a moment though I had not done much thinking. I didn't know where to begin. Hesitantly, I said that I could see that his family was – well, not very well off. 'But there's eight of you, nearly nine.' I paused, embarrassed. 'I mean to say . . .' What did I mean to say? That if his mother had had fewer children they would have had a better chance in life?

'It's not just to do with children though, Cora. That's a moral issue, you see. Not political. The Oranges are always throwing our children in our face but that's not the nub of it.'

We could have argued about that, but I desisted, recognizing that there was truth in what he was saying. I knew that Uncle Billy was a top dog, and Mr Lavery an underdog, and that it was not due just to Billy McGill being one of a family of four and Mr Lavery one of ten. Or because Protestants worked harder – so it was said – than Catholics.

'Listen to this!' Gerard picked up a notebook close-packed with his own writing. '*Many in the audience employ Catholics, but I have not one about the house . . . Ninety-seven per cent of Roman Catholics are disloyal and disruptive . . . If we in Ulster allow Roman Catholics to work on our farms then we are traitors to Ulster*. Who said that?'

'I don't know.'

'Lord Brookeborough! *Our* Prime Minister!'

'And here's another Prime Minister, James Craig, for

you – *I prize the office of Grand Master of the Orange Institution of County Down far more than I do being Prime Minister. I have always said that I am an Orangeman first and a politician and a member of this Parliament afterwards.* He told that to the House of Commons. And they approved! How could Catholics trust men like that, ever?'

'I don't like Orangemen either,' I said feebly. He was on fire and there was I sitting like a jelly fish.

'I never said you did. I'm not attacking *you*.'

'I am a Protestant though, at least sort of, though not the kind the Orange Order approves of.'

'Not all Protestants are bad.' He grinned.

I relaxed, felt myself firming up inside. I told him he should become a Member of Parliament; he had the voice for it.

'There's small chance of getting in as a Nationalist MP. The way the constituencies are laid out you've no hope of overturning the Unionist vote. No, I'll go for the law and see what I can do that way.'

'You're for a United Ireland then?'

'Of course I am! We never should have been split in the first place . . .'

Nationalist talk. Fenian talk. My spine tingled again. Rosie would say I was a traitor for listening and her uncles, if they could have seen me, would have never let me cross their Loyalist doorstep again.

'And so the French and Irish troops, led by the Roman Catholic James the Second were beaten fair and square by the British and Dutch troops led by William, Prince of Orange, at the Battle of the Boyne.'

'Yes, I know all that.' I was slightly impatient; it was not what I'd asked.

'Orange societies were formed,' went on Uncle Billy, holding forth, ignoring my interruption, 'in order to assist the Williamite cause.'

'That was 1690.'

'In the eighteenth century attacks on Protestants and their property increased and after a skirmish known as the Battle of the Diamond, the Protestants reorganized for their defence into Orange Lodges and created the Orange Order.'

'Hallelujah!' said Rosie, without looking up from Ethel M. Dell.

'What did you say, Margaret Rose?'

'Nothing, Uncle Billy. I said nothing.'

'Now this was an organization dedicated to the defence of Protestantism and totally opposed to the spread of Roman Catholicism which was regarded – and still is regarded – as unscriptural in doctrine and superstitious in practice. Do I meet your points, Cora?' When he saw me slow to respond, he went on, 'The situation is no different today, make no mistake about that. If we give an inch, they'll take a mile. Would you fancy the rule of the priests, Cora?' Not particularly, I had to admit.

'The good Lord will look with favour on you, Mrs Lavery, you may take comfort from that.'

'But I have enough children, Father. Eight is enough.'

'It is God's will.'

'Or Patrick Lavery's.'

'What did you say, woman dear?'

'Nothing, Father, I said nothing.'

What could she say? The child was already there in her stomach, kicking, pushing his hands and legs out for anyone with sharp eyes to see.

'You're a good woman, Mrs Lavery. And a good Catholic.'

Oh yes, and a good mother. Amen to that.

She puffed her Woodbines when he had gone and rested her swollen feet on the fender. 'It's all right for him,' she said, but without ràncour. It was the lack of rancour that I could not understand.

'You can get torn apart when you have a baby,' said Rosie. 'Mrs Jamieson told me. She says you can split in two. She almost did, when she had her Hughie. His head was so big. Can't you feel what it'd be like – splitting?'

I could. Like an apple being halved. Uncle Billy could

break apples in two with his hands. I said, 'My mother says it's a natural process.'

'Your mother! Everything's natural for her except sickening and dying.'

'She said she was happy when I was born.'

'She didn't have another though did she?'

'But Teresa's mother's had eight. And she's still going about. So it can't be that bad.'

'She's had no choice though, has she, Teresa?'

Teresa would only shrug. She had left school and was working as tea girl in the office at the Rope Works. Everybody was friendly and she enjoyed the crack. Her mother was pleased too. 'At least it's a step up.' She herself had worked as a mill girl in a linen factory in York Street, going to work in clogs, head tied up in a turban. If Teresa were to stick in at the night school – which she was, doing book-keeping – then she might get a job eventually as a wages clerk. She was sharp at figures.

In the course of our school day we sweated over trigonometry, constructed Livy and followed the fortunes of Maria Teresa of Austria.

I raised my hand.

'Yes, Cora?' asked Miss Bell.

'Do you think the British should have executed the leaders of the Easter Rising?'

'The Easter Rising?' She looked back uncertainly at her notes. Her eyes leap-frogged up and down the lines.

'Yes, in Dublin. In 1916.'

'That has nothing to do with the succession of the Hapsburg Empire.'

'But don't you think they made a mistake – from their point of view? I mean, before it not all that many of the Irish people were for the Rising. But after they'd shot Clarke and MacDonagh and Pearse and–'

'I don't think there is any need to go raking up those old Troubles again, Cora.'

'Did you know they shot Connolly sitting in a chair? Because he couldn't stand up?'

'That is enough, Cora! You are wasting our time. We

must stick to the syllabus. Now then, girls, in 1745, Frederick the Second of Prussia . . .'

'Take Derry, Cora,' said Gerard. 'Two-thirds of the population is Catholic, right?'

'Is it?'

'Yes. You can take my word for it. Yet *two*-thirds of the corporation is Protestant.'

How could that be? I might well ask.

'You divide up the electoral districts so that some are large and some are small. The Catholics are bunched together, the Protestants are in the smaller wards.' Gerard spoke in simple terms so that I might understand. I got the picture.

'It's called gerrymandering. You might ask your Miss Bell what she thinks of that. And not *only* that – you don't get a vote unless you're a ratepayer. So not everyone gets a vote, and the higher your rates the more votes you get, since you have extra nominees for every ten pounds a year valuation after the first ten. So the better off you are the more votes you get. And which part of the population is the better off?'

That I could answer: my ignorance knew some bounds.

'No, no, Cora, look, you've got me wrong,' said Uncle Billy. 'I don't hate Catholics. It's just that I see how sorely misguided they are. My faith *means* something to me, just like your mother's means something to her. So why shouldn't I defend it? What's wrong in caring about your faith? That's what the Solemn League and Covenant was all about. That's what Ulster's all about. We'd have died rather than live under Catholic rule. This is a Protestant country and that's the way we intend to keep it.'

'No Pope here!' said Uncle Sam.

'You've said it, Sam,' said Granny McGill.

I retreated, at least in the meantime, to the issues of the accession of Maria Teresa to the Austro-Hungarian throne and to the causes of the American War of Independence. They were simpler, as far as I could see. The causes were dicated to us: one, two, three, four. And then the effects: one, two, three, four, five. Everything could be reduced to cause and effect. Opinions didn't come into it.

'History is facts,' said Miss Bell.

'Your Miss Bell wears blinkers,' said Gerard.

Did we not all? I wondered.

SEVEN

Rain was gouting down, spilling out of the gutters, leaking into the house in a score of places, plopping into well-placed buckets and basins. Gerard said he would leave me to the bus stop. He carried a striped golf umbrella like a canopy over our heads. We splashed through puddles bumping into one another in the dark until he told me to hang on to his arm for dear sake! My feet soaked up water like sponges but I did not care. I would have walked happily through the Red Sea beside him. Very happily. For we would have come then into the land of Egypt.

We had to wait at the bus stop. The country road was deserted. Gerard talked about the burning of the city of Cork by the Black and Tans in December 1920. Burnings, murders, reprisals. What a terrible past this country had had. And it was the near past, not two hundred or a hundred years ago. As I stood there shivering from the rain dripping down my neck and the thought of people screaming, trapped in raging fires, I never imagined that the past would catch up with the present again or that the present would slide back into the past. 'And when the whole place was alight,' said Gerard, 'they tried to stop the fire engines getting in. They even cut their hoses!'

The lights of the bus loomed up. Gerard stuck out his hand,

'See you next week!' He handed me up on to the step.

I sat on the empty back seat of the bus to discourage the yawning conductor from opening up a conversation. I wanted my thoughts to myself. The bus swooshed through the dark wet countryside of County Down and came into the dark wet Sunday night streets of Belfast.

My thoughts stayed with a flame-filled winter night in Cork.

It was still raining when I got off the bus. Outside Mrs McCurdy's shop the Salvation Army played and sang under black umbrellas. *Stand up, stand up for Jesus*...I skirted round them and headed for home.

On the corner of our street an ambulance turning fast made me take a step back on to the kerb. Its blue light was flashing. All the houses were lit up and Mrs Meneely and Mrs McGill were at their front room window. Oh God please God, I gabbled. I ran. Gulping for air, I came into our house. My father sat by the fire looking into it – thank God, for he had been coughing a lot lately, from the bottom of his lungs – and my mother at the table. She was reading aloud from '*Science and Health' with Key to the Scriptures*, '*God never endowed matter with power to disable life or to chill harmony with a long night of discord. Such a power, without the divine permission is inconceivable.*'

'What is it?'

'It's Mrs Lavery, dear.' My father chewed the edge of his moustache.

'She's in God's hands, dear.'

'Is she–?'

'No, love.'

Mrs Lavery gave birth to a boy that night, Anthony John, a lusty, demanding, aggressive child – oh yes the aggression was there early enough – and one hour later, she died. Or passed on. Or went to join her maker. Each to his own jargon. But one could not escape the bald truth, that Mrs Lavery lay cold and lifeless, gone from her husband and her children, in the form that they knew her. Wherever she was she was not with them. The children crept around looking stunned, Patrick Lavery sat in the kitchen with his hands laid flat on the table, tears coursing down his puffy cheeks. He wanted his wife and not this new bawling son. He had other sons. Gerard laid a hand on his shoulder. In her mother's chair Teresa rocked the new-born child.

Father Flynn was there to comfort them. 'It was God's will and one cannot reproach that. He saved the baby for he is pure and innocent. Your dear wife is with God now. She was a good mother and a good Catholic . . .'

'It's a scandal,' said Granny McGill, 'to let the poor woman die to bring yet another Lavery into the world. It's not as if there aren't enough of them as it is. And what are they all to do now, would you tell me?'

'See what I was meaning, Cora?' said Uncle Billy. 'About the power of the priests?'

'It's lucky you are, girls,' said Granny McGill, 'that you weren't born Roman Catholics.'

'You can say that again,' said Rosie, crossing herself.

'Don't do that, Margaret Rose!' said Uncle Billy. 'Not even as a joke.'

Teresa came to me in tears, fresh tears, different tears, which sprang from anger as well as from distress. 'The McGills are putting it about that our father asked for the baby's life to be saved before our mother's. But it isn't true. He didn't! You can ask him yourself.'

I didn't need to ask him and I told Rosie so. 'Maybe he did ask them to save Mrs Lavery,' she said, 'but how do you know the doctor paid any heed? He's a Catholic himself isn't he?'

How could one be sure of anything?

Only by having trust, said my mother, in life and in other people, but most of all in God.

The McGills sent a wreath, as did most people in the street, but did not go to the funeral. My father, a black band round his arm, and dragging his right foot, walked with the other mourners from the Catholic church to the cemetery. Gerard and his father carried the coffin on their shoulders, with two brothers of Mr Lavery's supporting it at the back. Gerard's face was set like stone.

After the procession passed me, I came home and wept. I sought out my mother and surprised her with a hug that half-strangled her.

Rosie and I discussed what we could do to help Teresa. Rosie's hands were tied, so to speak, by the fact that she was not supposed to be friendly with Teresa at all. The McGills knew that I was, though had no idea to what extent, and did not approve, but said they supposed that

that was my business, and my parents'. Moral support, said my mother, that was what Teresa would need more than anything else, and what Rosie and I were best fitted to give. She knew us too well to suggest anything domestic.

When the relatives had departed from the Lavery's, I went in. Bridie was washing nappies, Teresa struggling to feed Anthony John who golloped his bottle too fast and immediately threw it back up again, whereupon he roared with fury and waved his arms as if it were someone else who had deprived him. 'He's a stout lad,' said Father Flynn, chucking him under the chin on his way out.

In the living room Gerard was carpet-sweeping in an effort to remove the remains of the funeral feast. At the end of the week he would go back to Hastings Court.

Teresa was unable to return to her job and so gave up the promise of a career as a wages clerk. She had no choice, even I could see that, much as I protested and declared it wasn't fair. My father said that life was not fair, which was something my mother would never have admitted to. She had brought me up to expect equity (as well as freedom from sin, disease and death). Such high expectations to be raised on! No wonder I took a tumble at the end of my teens. Already I was suspecting the fallibility of my mother, though most of the time shied from facing up to it. And what about the infallibility of our leader Mary Baker Eddy? My father was uneasy at my murmurings; he wanted me to have faith. He said that life was better if one had beliefs, a creed to live by. Something to hold on to. 'One shouldn't deride that, Cora.' His leg seemed to have stiffened up again, with the onset of a new winter. I saw that he was ageing, whereas my mother showed few signs. Her face was as unlined as mine was.

My father hated his job in the Bank Buildings. Standing behind the counter all day having to be polite to every Tom, Dick and Harry, and every Tom, Dick and Harry's wife. He missed the open road. And he missed Ireland itself. 'It was great, Cora, driving west, drawing close to the mountains, smelling the ocean, stopping off at some wee place . . .' I understood his yearning completely. As the years passed, the list of places that I resolved to travel to grew longer.

'It seems,' I said to Rosie, 'that unless you're very determined you end up doing exactly the opposite of what you want to do in life.'

We agreed that we would not let it happen to us.

'The thing is,' I said, 'to know what you want.'

Rosie decided to train as a kindergarten teacher, teach for a year or two and then marry. Well of course marry. Not to was unthinkable. Be an old maid? Rosie said that it didn't do to wait too long either for then the field was reduced. The field? Was it a race then? Like the Grand National? First into the straight comes Rosie Meneely . . . 'Don't be silly, Cora! Why do you have to pick up on things so? No, but twenty-one or two would be a good age.' I would be that age by the time I finished university. 'That's all right then,' said Rosie. But I wouldn't want to get tied down before I'd had time to do anything else. Not unless (I said to myself) Gerard Lavery would wish to tie me down. 'What are you smiling for?' said Rosie. Nothing, I said, still smiling. Rosie wanted a man with money. 'Well, why not? It's nicer than no money. What does no money do for you? Look at the Laverys!' And she wanted a house like the Fishes'. What was the point in being uncomfortable if one didn't have to be? Deirdre Fish wanted the same things – more than that, expected them, so she didn't have to spell it out, about the money and the kind of house. Their conversation about the future depressed me. It seemed to me that they looked into long tunnels; well-carpeted, plush tunnels maybe, but tunnels nevertheless, in which one would long for fresh air and the sight of the sky overhead.

'You do have loopy ideas, Cora,' said Rosie. 'As for doing history – I'd die of boredom.' She did not believe me when I said that it need not be all causes, one, two, three, four, that it could be exciting. 'Exciting? I'd sign up for the mission hall first.'

For Teresa we saw no future, other than the present stretching on and on. By the time the children grew up she would be too old to marry, said Rosie. I thought, thinking of Mrs Lavery, that Teresa might be better off not marrying.

'But what else would she do when she was thirty? Go back to being a tea girl? And maybe she wouldn't have to have children if she played her cards right. Look at Mrs Gracey!'

Mrs Gracey had got promotion, to the rung above her husband – 'No good'll come of that,' said Granny McGill, who had definite ideas about a woman's place – and went to work dressed in a smart grey suit carrying a crocodile handbag. She was driven by her husband in their Morris Minor and sat in the front passenger seat waving to us, a bit like the Queen when she passed. For their holidays they went to the English Lake District. They had replaced the railings which were taken away during the war and closed their driveway off with a gate which was kept shut. Even Father Flynn hesitated before tampering with the latch.

On one occasion he came away with blood dripping from his thumb. He bound it up with his handkerchief. 'Tricky thing that. I can't seem to get the hang of it. And they weren't even in. They always seem to be out enjoying themselves,' he said sadly. He fell into step beside me. 'Going along to the Laverys' are you? I'll join you. I've a dry throat on me and there's always a bit of tea on the boil there. She's a grand wee mother is Teresa . . .'

Gerard also talked to me about Teresa. As the months went by Mr Lavery came home less and less – 'He can't face my mother not being there, I know that's what it is' – and Teresa had more and more responsibility. And more worries, for the children, particularly the boys, were wild and not very biddable. 'She doesn't complain much but she has it hard,' said Gerard. 'You'll stay friendly with her won't you, Cora?' But of course. Did he think I would not? 'No, not really. She needs you, you know.' My pleasure was almost as great as if he had said that he needed me, but I knew I could not expect him to say that even if it were true, for Rosie, whose advice I relied on in these matters, had told me that boys were often reluctant to express their feelings and guarded themselves in case you got ideas. In case they thought you thought they might want to marry you, she meant. I didn't really think that far ahead about Gerard and myself, at least not rationally, only as part of my daydreaming before I fell asleep, in the hope that I might carry him over into my dreams with me. Strangely, I seldom did. And when I did the dream was not always to my liking.

'Encourage Teresa to go on reading,' said Gerard. 'Bring her books from the library, talk to her about them. She needs something to lift her mind away from the house and the children.'

So I set about educating Teresa. 'But what's wrong with Ethel M. Dell?' 'Nothing – I suppose. But don't you find her books – well, flat?' 'I dunno. Sometimes, maybe. You can guess too easy what's coming.' 'Exactly!' I felt I'd triumphed already. 'Why don't you try this?' '*The Last September*?' It was set in Ireland, I explained, in the South, before partition. I watched her begin. 'It takes a while to get into it,' she complained. I urged her to stay with it, to give the words time to shape up in her head, and she did and, gradually, rejected her love stories for the denser, more resonant worlds of Elizabeth Bowen and Rosamund Lehmann. I had a list of other writers drawn up and envied her the pleasure of discovering them for the first time, I realized that I could influence people: I tasted power. The feeling made me glow. Was it wrong to feel like that? But I was influencing her for good, I told myself. Good? How did I know it was good? Or better than the other? In what way? The questions wriggled about in my mind like tadpoles swimming blindly up and down. And then I decided that the fact that *I* thought it was good was good enough.

I talked to Teresa about history too, and anthropology. I was reading Margaret Mead. And Freya Stark. 'It'd be great to travel,' said Teresa, 'but I don't suppose I ever will.' I protested. She mustn't limit herself. She would travel if she wanted to travel. We would go together to the Valley of the Assassins, and perhaps even take Rosie, although she would be bound to gripe about the lack of comfort. Walking twenty or more miles a day through bandit country and sleeping on the ground wouldn't be much in her line. Teresa said she wasn't sure if it would be in hers either. It would be, if she gave it a chance. 'The important thing is not to close your mind, Teresa.'

Her oldest brother's mind was far from closed. On Sundays, at Hastings Court, we sat at the table under the green lamp and worked at English, Latin and history. His progress was swift. I wondered if I should not become a teacher?

'Would you like to?'

'I wouldn't mind. But not all my pupils would be like you. Or Teresa,' I added hurriedly, feeling the beginnings of a blush. I blushed too easily and it infuriated me. And then I dropped my pen and bumped my head on the edge of the table as I went under to retrieve it.

'Are you all right?' He put his hand on my forehead and I trembled. I jerked my head back.

'I'm fine.'

'You're a great one for bumps on the head, aren't you?'

Whenever I came into too close contact with the opposite sex I felt my body seizing up. At dances – on the few occasions when a boy did ask me to dance – I trod on my partner's toes even though I could dance, if not divinely, at least competently, with Rosie and Teresa. I made gauche rejoinders to simple remarks.

We finally made it to the Floral Hall, Rosie and I. The lights spun, the girls tripped about on high high heels, the men stood around in their best suits. I had a sense of déja vu. The men were watching, weighing us up. It was just part of the form, said Rosie, impatient with me. 'Smile, for God's sake! Take that stupid frown off your face or you'll never get anywhere. How can you expect anyone to ask you to dance if you look like that?' I did not expect it, I started to tell her, but she was already looking past me smiling her brightest smile at the approaching man. He swept her off into the centre of the dance. Deirdre Fish was dancing, and Susan Orr, and Angela Simpson.

As they went round they lifted their hands from the men's shoulders to wave.

Eithne Potter and I stood bravely side by side until I suggested we went to the Ladies, the wallflowers' age-old retreat. We passed as much time as we could going to the toilet, washing our hands, combing our hair, re-adjusting our petticoats, and even talking animatedly to one another as if we were uninterested in what was going on around us. It never occurred to us to go home. That would have been to admit outright defeat.

'Oh well, shall we?' said Eithne, after someone had been sick in one of the basins.

As we went back into the hall a man stepped out in front of me and jerked his head to one side. If it had not been for the proffered hand I might have thought he had a nervous twitch. I accompanied him on to the floor. His head came half way up my chin. He looked creepy to me, he had eyes like a hooded crow, but I thought I should make an effort. Rosie said there was no point in coming if you weren't prepared to make an effort. Besides, I felt grateful to him for choosing me and putting me out of my misery. 'Good band, isn't it?' I said brightly. He grunted. 'I'm very fond of the foxtrot,' I said and smiled though he was not looking at my face. He didn't even grunt that time. Under my breath I sang, '*I don't like crapgames with barons and earls,*' and as I passed Deirdre Fish I waved to show that I was having a good time.

Suddenly, he pulled me up dead and dropped my hand. What was wrong? I was alarmed. Had I stood on his foot or did I have that dreadful odour? *That's why the lady is a tramp*. He was looking at the entrance, at a girl who had just come in. Without a word he left me and pushed through the dancers towards her. She was not even all that pretty. They seemed to know one another; she must have gone to the cloakroom and he had filled in the time by asking me to dance. People were bumping against me. Excusing myself and apologizing for getting in the way, I stumbled to the edge of the room. I sat down. Don't sit, Rosie had told me, that was fatal. The man and his girl glided by. He stared through me as if he had never seen me before and perhaps he had not, she flared her nostils and sent me a message that said hands off! My hands felt unclean from having touched him for those few rounds of the floor.

'What happened?' Eithne arrived breathless beside me.

'The next dance will be a Ladies Choice!' cried the Master of Ceremonies.

'Let's go,' I said.

We took the bus to the City Hall and from there walked the three miles home. In a chip shop on the Newtonards Road we bought chips and a poke of hot peas and vinegar. The food warmed our stomachs and cheered our hearts. When we had eaten them we linked arms and as we walked we sang. *I'm going to buy a paper doll that I can call my own . . .* The pubs were emptying and one or two men in flat caps swayed in front of us with suggestions but we had no real trouble. I came into the house with pink cheeks and bright eyes.

'You look as if you've been enjoying yourself,' said my mother with relief.

I vowed I would never go to a dance again. But of course I did. 'Oh come on! You can't stay in on Saturday night.' Rosie was impatient. *Everybody* loved Saturday night. The whole world. Even the Jews in Palestine? The Arabs on the shores of Araby? 'Oh shut up, Cora! But it'll be better next time, you'll see. You never know who you might meet.' Prince Charming himself? Perhaps glass slippers would be the answer? She said I was impossible. I propped up the wall at Albert White's, the Plaza, the Orpheus, and rugby club hops, and was persuaded to give the Floral Hall one more chance.

Rosie made me up for the occasion. She plastered my chicken shit with pancake make-up and decorated my eyes so that when I looked in the mirror I was startled.

'You don't make enough of yourself, Cora, that's your trouble.'

I slipped out of the house calling goodbye to my parents from the doorstep. Their desire for me to be successful would not go so far as to applaud me looking like a tart.

'Don't be ridiculous,' said Rosie on the bus. 'You

always exaggerate.' She had also sprayed gold dust on my hair. 'You look nothing like a tart. And just leave that top button of your blouse undone. You've got fantastic bosoms. Far better than mine.' But the size of one's bosom had nothing to do with it, as I had already observed.

Whether it was the gold dust or the decolleté we could not afterwards decide but no sooner had I set foot inside the dancehall than a partner claimed me. He was not four foot two fully extended either, he actually topped me by a good three inches. I could look up to him and when I did I saw that he was dark and quite handsome. 'Told you so didn't I?' said Rosie's triumphant look as we passed on the dance floor. She looked like I had felt when Teresa told me she wanted to read Jane Austen. My partner could tango too, and so, I discovered after the first round, could I. I relaxed and took a longer look at his face. He seemed all right! Nothing freakish or odd: he had two eyes, a nose and a mouth. He spoke with a Southern accent. And he made the running with the conversation. We went through the usual preliminaries about coming here often and where are you from and he told me he used to live in Dublin but was working in Belfast now as an engineer. 'And what about yourself?'

I told him I was a student – which was what Rosie had told me to say – and that I lived in East Belfast. It was all proving easy after all. At the end of the dance I said, 'Thanks very much' and sauntered back to my friends who swarmed round me buzzing with questions. I felt like flapping my hand at them. I kept my head away from theirs, allowed myself to remain aloof. A stunner, Cora! A real catch. Bit like Clarke Gable. *But I'm not able to do the Betty Grable . . .*

The drums rolled for the next dance. And there he was on the threshold of our beehive looking in. Deirdre Fish flashed a smile, Angela Simpson heaved a breast and the strap of her brassiére slipped down over her shoulder. But it was me he was looking at. 'Excuse me,' said I, and the girls broke up the cluster to allow me to emerge.

At the end of that dance he said, 'Let's have the next,' so I stayed with him. After the third he told me his name was Michael. 'Cora,' said I, and we declared ourselves pleased to meet one another.

He kept hold of my hand between dances and half way through the evening took me to the café for refreshments. I was so happy that I couldn't help laughing. I laughed so much I had to put down my coca-cola.

'What's the joke, Cora? Tell me!'

I couldn't tell him. How could I say I was laughing because I was a success at last?

'Can I leave you home?'

I nodded and smiled, as if I had done this a thousand times over.

'What about us going early and taking a wee walk?'

I was less keen on that idea – I would have preferred to have enjoyed every moment of my glory within the dancehall itself – but I did not like to refuse. He might think me childish. Unsophisticated. I went to collect my coat. I had never danced the last waltz and was to be done out of it again. My ecstasy dimmed a little.

Rosie came rushing into the cloakroom behind me. 'Well?'

'Well what?'

'Do you like him? Is he nice? What does he do? Do you think there's any future in it? Where are you going?'

We were going on 'somewhere else', I told her; I wasn't sure where. But I was sure it would be somewhere interesting. A *walk*? I was not going to tell Rosie that. She might laugh. Perhaps anyway we could go downtown and drink coke in White's Milk Bar. If he asked what I would like to do I would suggest it.

'Have a good time!' cried Rosie.

So my time for the good time had come.

He was waiting for me in the foyer wearing a thick overcoat and a striped scarf. A man was waiting for me! He took my hand and tucked it into his pocket with his own.

'Shall we go up the hill and take a look at the lights?'

When we took the path and started to climb upward he disentangled our hands and slid his arm round my waist pulling me towards him. It was a very awkward way to walk and we kept kicking one another. After a few yards he stopped to kiss me. His kiss was long and devouring and as his tongue probed my mouth I felt panic rise inside me. I was going to choke. He released me and I gulped open-mouthed swallowing draughts of night air. He laughed, well pleased with me, it seemed. I thought of Rosie and Eithne and Deirdre and Angela under the coloured lights below.

'Look down!' I cried.

He looked. Pinpricks of light glittered round the edges of the Lough, and in the middle of it was a ship, moving slowly, lit from stem to stern, its funnel blaring. I wished I were on that ship heading out to sea.

'Let's go on, eh? Come on, Cora love.' Love? How could I have become that for him so soon?

I did not want to go on (how was it that I did so many things I did not want to do?) but I did, allowing myself to be led upward, away from the lights and the other couples who were wandering around. We turned off on to a smaller path. He took off his thick coat (he was well prepared) and spread it on the ground. But he was not playing at being Sir Walter Raleigh. He laid himself down on the coat and held out his hand. I could just see it, and his face, two odd white shapes glimmering. I wanted to turn and run. But I couldn't spend my life running. I was no longer a child. I was sixteen going on seventeen.

'Cora darling.' His voice was soft, and urgent. 'Come on.'

I took his hand and let him pull me down beside him. He rolled over so that he was half on top of me. I felt his knee pushing my legs apart. I should have run! Oh how I should have run. I thought of Teresa sitting in her warm kitchen reading Jane Austen. I thought of Gerard sitting in the library at Hastings Court reading the Odes of Horace.

I cried out.

'Did I hurt you, darling?' Oh why did he have to keep calling me that? I was not his darling.

My mouth felt bruised. I could not speak, I seemed to have lost the power. He sounded excited. My coat was open – I had not been aware of it happening – and all the buttons of my blouse were undone. His hands were inside my bra. 'What beautiful breasts you have!' An unseen blush was suffusing the top half of my body. I struggled and he gripped me tighter, laughing, as if it were all part of the fun of the fair. I remembered Mrs Robinson and her fancy man laughing. I remembered Mrs Robinson's breasts swinging free. And then I realized that my skirt was around my waist and that his other hand was on my leg moving up and up. I made another attempt to struggle, to push him backwards, but he was so much heavier than I and so swept up in his own desire that it was futile. I was helpless. His finger probed. 'Please!' My voice was feeble. His finger went home and I cried out.

'Feel, Cora, feel! You'll like this better.'

I knew I would not. 'Please don't, I don't want you to,' I said in a pathetic whimper, but I doubted if he heard. He was right up on top of me, inside me, pushing, splitting me in two, heaving and panting and grunting; and then he collapsed, crushing my chest with his weight. I cried. I could not stop. I wanted to die. For now I believed in death.

'Don't cry, love, don't cry.'

'Don't call me love! You don't love me.. Leave me alone!'

My voice returned, and my temper with it. I struck him wildly across the face and he cowered backwards. Why had I not done it earlier? *Why*? 'I hate you! Hate you, hate you, hate you!'

'How was I to know you were a virgin?' Now he was buttoning himself up and his voice was no longer soft. 'What did you come up with me here for if you didn't want it?'

'I didn't want it, I didn't! I didn't know–'

'Tell that to the Marines!' He put on his coat. 'I'll leave you down the road.'

'There's no need.' Nothing else that could happen to me now would matter. To be hit on the head and left for dead would be a fate I would welcome.

'Suit yourself!'

'I will,' I shouted after him. 'That's what I'm going to do – suit myself!'

The night took on a sudden quiet. Something rustled close by. The wind seemed keener. My survival instinct surfaced. I sorted my clothes as best I could and slithered and ran down through the trees on to the road below, where I found that I must have dropped my bag with my money in it up on the hill. I could not go back.

I set off to walk. And now that I had physically survived, I was conscious only of a sense of shame. Putting my hand to my cheek, I felt heat like the heat of a furnace coming off it. Surely the heat that Shadrach, Meshach and Abednego experienced was no greater than this? But God would not bring me out unscorched. Why should he? For I had sinned. There is no sin, disease or death. But I felt the sin inside me, stifling me, devouring me, burning me up. I would never be able to let anyone look at my face again. I would never be able to let Gerard look at me for if I did then he would know. I saw his face with the strange green light falling over it and I burned even more fiercely until I thought I should be consumed in a ball of fire. I wondered that people did not see me lit up like a meteorite moving through the dark night. I wanted to crawl into a manhole, pull the cover over my head and never come up again.

What if I were to have a baby? I *would* have a baby, I was bound to. I would have to go away from home, into the wilderness. But for more than forty days and forty nights. Nine months. *Nine*? It would be an eternity.

A drunk bumped into me. I pushed him aside so hard that he staggered and went down on one knee. I walked on. Rain began to fall but I only noticed it in an extraneous sort of way as if it had nothing to do with me and could not touch me.

I trudged the length of the Antrim Road, skirted the docks and headed east. Now my mind was blank and my legs moved beneath me as if they belonged to someone else.

A man coming towards me was calling, 'Cora, is that you, Cora?' I almost denied it, then I saw that the man was my father. We met under a street light. His hair was plastered to his skull, water dripped from his nose and hung on his eyelashes. He might have been under the sea. I put out my hand to touch him and he caught it and held it against his wet chest.

'Cora, are you all right? Where have you been? We've been so worried.' Yes, even my mother had been worried, although she had been Knowing the Truth, for the last bus was long gone and Rosie had been home for ages. Rosie had been worried too, said my father. He put his arm around me and took me home.

'Did anything happen?'

'No, nothing. I lost my bag, my green shoulder bag, the one you gave me for Christmas.' I started to cry again.

'Don't fret about that, love. We'll get you another. A bag's easily replaced.'

Next day I had a temperature, a headache, a sore throat, a pain in my stomach. I lay in bed with the covers pulled up to my eyebrows. My mother read to me and Mrs Hastings-Smith called. When Rosie came to see me I closed my eyes and simulated death.

After a week I had to get up.

'What happened, Cora?' asked Rosie. 'After you left the Floral Hall? Where did you go?'

'Night club. The Follies Bergère.'

'Don't be silly. There aren't any night clubs in Belfast.'

'That's all you know!'

'What's wrong, Cora?'

'I'm pregnant. I think I'm going to have a baby.'

'Don't be–' She stopped as my tears started rolling. 'Tell me,' she said softly.

I told her everything.

'*Jesus Christ, Jesus Christ!* How could you be so stupid? What a blithering blithering idiot! No girl in her right mind would go up Cave Hill with a strange man at night.'

So I couldn't have been in my right mind then, I was all too ready to believe it. And I was more than ready to agree that I was stupid and ignorant and an idiot. I hadn't known the score: that appeared to be my biggest sin, in Rosie's eyes. But why hadn't she told me the score? She wouldn't have believed I was *that* ignorant. She had never heard of anybody being *that* ignorant. Well, she'd heard of it now. 'Oh heavens, Cora.' She put her arms around me and held me tight. 'Don't cry – you might not be pregnant. It doesn't happen every time, it can't.'

Even I in my despair could see that the world would be overpopulated if it did. We must be hopeful, said Rosie; to be a couple of days late didn't necessarily mean anything. Shock did things to the system, especially a woman's system. I wished I didn't have a woman's system. A man's would be so much simpler. But I wouldn't want to be a man, said Rosie, shocked; men had to work all their lives and keep families and go to war.

She told me to take hot baths and leap about as much as possible. I laid in the bath until I almost passed out and emerged looking like a peeled boiled beetroot. I ran round the railway path and jumped down from the top of the bank, and on one landing staved my ankle. Accident prone! I remembered Gerard's words. I am God's child, I declared to myself as I hopped homeward. I could not even limp, my foot was too painful to put to the ground. For the next few days I laid on the settee contemplating my self-disgust, unable to think of the American war of Independence or the Odes of Horace. Rosie came daily after school. 'Well?' she would demand and I shake my head. '*Courage*!' she said in French, one of the few words she knew in that language. 'You could always have an abortion. There are women who do these things, Deirdre says.'

'You haven't told Deirdre?' A new panic seized me.

'I haven't, cross my heart! You know I wouldn't tell her a thing like that, Cora.' I made her promise that she never would and she did, and am confident that she kept faith with me.

And then one morning I awoke to find the sheets sticky and wet. I promised God that I would never ask him for anything again.

'Thank God,' said Rosie too, as we walked down the hill to school together. 'That was a narrow escape. You must never ever go for a walk with an unknown man again, Cora.'

I reassured her that I never would, nor to the Floral Hall either. For what if I should see him there? I would die of shame.

'It should be him that'd be ashamed,' said Rosie.

'Fat chance,' said I. He would look through me as if he had never set eyes on me: that was how it would be.

Now on Saturday nights which everybody loved I worked at my books and when my eyes were hot and I was tired of my parents telling me that it wasn't good to study all the time, I would slip down the road to the Laverys'. I found Teresa's company comforting. She was reading *Pride and Prejudice*. We talked about Jane and Elizabeth and agreed on the awfulness of Mrs Bennet – 'Imagine,' I almost said, 'having Mrs Bennet for a mother,' and then stopped – and we laughed over Lady Catherine de Burgh.

And on Sundays I stayed away from Hastings Court.

EIGHT

'Is there anything troubling you, dear?' asked Mrs Hastings-Smith. 'You haven't come home with me for weeks.'

I made the excuse that I had for everything now.

'A few hours in country air would refresh the brain.' She looked into my face. '*Let not your heart be troubled, dear, neither let it be afraid.*'

During the week I thought about that and came to a decision: perhaps I could not stop my heart from being troubled but I need not let it be afraid. The following Sunday after church I went back to Hastings Court with her.

It was the kind of glorious spring day compounded of pale gold sunshine, green fields, lambs capering, daffodils waving (ten thousand at least at a glance), small brooks sparkling, that made me feel it would make more sense to want to be a poet than a historian. Bricked up in my narrow street, I had forgotten how beautiful and how open the countryside was. And how green. The rhododendrons were in bud along the driveway at Hastings Court. The grounds looked much less wild and overgrown than they had when I had first come to visit. I remarked on it to Mrs Hastings-Smith.

'Yes, Gerard's doing a good job. I don't know what I shall do without him when he goes to university next year.'

Did she think he would make it?

'If one desires something very much, Cora, and if it is the right thing for one, then one will make it.'

I doubted if she would consider Gerard to be the right

thing for me, in spite of his success at taming her wilderness.

He was standing beside the garage. His face lit up when he saw me, the way a field lightens when the sun touches it, there was no denying or mistaking it, and he seemed not to notice anything different about me. The trouble in my heart eased, just a little.

'Cora!' He opened the passenger door, forgetting Mrs Hastings-Smith. I smiled and said hello and managed to get out of the car without catching my skirt or tripping on the running board.

'How's the Latin doing?' I asked and he made a face. 'I'll come and give you a hand with it after lunch shall I?'

'That'd be great!'

We stood smiling at one another until I realized that Mrs Hastings-Smith was waiting for me to accompany her to the house.

Over lunch she seemed preoccupied. I ate quickly.

'Some more, dear?'

'No thank you.'

She blotted her lips on the frayed serviette and said, 'You're growing up, Cora, aren't you? You might soon even be falling in love for the first time.'

I looked down at my hands which were folded patiently in my lap.

'You must make sure that when you do fall in love it is with the right person.'

My head went up. 'But one can't control that.'

'Oh yes, I believe one can, dear. There is always an element of choice, before one falls. If "falls" is the correct word for it. I have never been convinced that it is. It suggests an accident, and we do not believe in accidents, do we?' She rolled up her serviette and pushed it through its greenish-silver ring. I got up to clear the plates, scraping the bits of lamb fat together.

'I thought I might ask Robert Montgomery to lunch next Sunday,' said Mrs Hastings-Smith.

'Robert?'

'Such a nice boy, don't you think?'

'Oh yes, very nice.' I loaded the tray and carried it into

the kitchen. Marcellina had gone out with her not-so-young man.

Robert Montgomery had been in my Sunday school class, had always had the best experiences to tell; he had recovered from wasp stings, sprained ankles, sore throats, almost before he could open the first page of *Science and Health*. He was earnest, he was without humour, and his faith seemed total. (He was to go berserk before he was twenty-one.) He had no doubts, he told us. Unlike me. Each morning when I wakened mine seemed to have grown like fungus on a damp wall.

I boiled water in a kettle – the range had gone out – and as I washed the dishes I thought about my doubts. I had been unable to talk to anyone about them. My mother would not leave me alone if I were to talk to her and my father would be unhappy, and when I had tried to raise the subject with Mrs Hastings-Smith she had bid me not to let Error in. *Get thee behind me, Satan*!

Washing the dishes, I sang a song low and soft. *If you were the only boy in the world and I was the only girl . . .*

Gerard was waiting in the library. 'You're not going to be very pleased with me.'

'I'm sure you've been doing fine on your own.' But I could see that he had not. He needed me!

We worked all afternoon and at the end of it yawned and stretched well pleased with what we had done.

'Let's go for a walk,' he said 'and clear our heads. I want to show you the bluebells in the orchard.'

There would be no harm in going for a walk with a man I knew. Even I knew the score about that. And I did not think that Rosie could disapprove, except on the grounds that he was a Roman Catholic. But I was not thinking about that this spring afternoon.

We passed the conservatory, waved at Mrs Hastings-Smith all in mauve amidst the green jungle of plants. We crossed the lawn and were out of sight of the house.

Sweet lovers love the spring . . .

Had I been humming the tune aloud? I felt myself blush but Gerard showed no signs of having heard; he was talking about the rhododendrons, and what a fine showing he thought they would make this year, and about the vegetables he had planted in the kitchen garden, and how quickly they seemed to be growing, amazing really, for he had never watched plants actually grow until he came to Hastings Court, had never thought he would be interested to watch them. We came to the orchard.

The bluebells made rivers of blue between the trees. There never could have been a more beautiful spring.

He took me then to see a patch of late crocuses. Standing proud and spearlike, purple, yellow and white, they looked so fresh and pure. Yes, that was what I liked about them: their purity. Could I tell Gerard that? I did.

He nodded. 'I know what you mean.'

I felt at peace.

We walked on through the late afternoon sunshine. He did not take my hand or try to kiss me and I was grateful that he did not for I was not yet ready to move into that stage. Nor did he suggest that we lie upon the ground and I was sure that he never would. If a man loved a girl and respected her – that was important, said Rosie, to be respected – then he would not try to get her to do things that were wrong. Once they were married it would be different. But even then they would not lie on the cold ground on an overcoat.

Don't think of that now! Don't let the memory intrude and spoil this perfect spring day, but already, because I had recalled it, the day was slightly less than perfect.

Think of the crocuses, concentrate on them! See how delicate the filaments are. I remembered the man's heavy dark bulk crushing me, smothering me; I remembered the way his knee moved up between my legs. No, don't remember! Think of Gerard Lavery who is here beside you, squatting on his haunches, one thin brown hand held out to cup a bright yellow flower. Think of Gerard Lavery who loves you. For he does love me, I know he does.

I desired him and he was right for me. Only I could judge who was right.

The following Sunday Robert Montgomery came to lunch. He was not interested in Latin. Gerard and I spent the afternoon in the library and Robert spent the afternoon in the conservatory talking about his experiences to Mrs Hastings-Smith. The sun shone and steam rose from the spotted leaves. Mrs Hastings-Smith dropped off to sleep before tea-time. She did not ask him to lunch again.

The days became warmer and longer; we withdrew to our rooms and bent our backs. Why did they have exams in summertime, demanded Rosie, when there were horrid winter days that were more suitable? In the street the Lavery children played. Skipping was the current craze. The ropes birled, the feet flew. Teresa sat on her front doorstep, knees hunched up, a book spread across them. She was reading *Emma*. Lucky Teresa! No, of course I didn't mean that. I only meant lucky Teresa at that moment on a summer's evening to be reading about Emma Woodhouse and Mr Knightly – for pleasure! – rather than numbing her brain with facts. I threw down my pen and went out into the street to breathe the air.

She made room for me on the step.

'I wonder how Gerard's getting on.' I introduced his name into every conversation I had with her nowadays, and was well aware that I did, but could not seem to stop myself. We discussed his chances of getting into university. I was confident that he would do well enough in Matric and next year have a good chance of winning a scholarship. Teresa was less sure about it all. Would he get enough to keep himself? And was university for the likes of him? And then there was her father who relied on Gerard to help bring money into the house.

'Brian's working now though isn't he? And after the "Twelfth" Bridie'll be starting in the Rope Works. Anyway, I'm sure Mrs Hastings-Smith will do what she can.'

'She's a good woman that.'

I nodded.

The children called to us to come give the rope a birl. Teresa put down her book and we each took an end of the heavy rope and turned it, swinging it low under the children's feet, high over their heads, and as I felt the familiar touch of the hemp in the palm of my hands I remembered the days of swinging round the old lamp-posts. Now we had new tall lamp standards with fluorescent lights that made faces look unnatural.

'Faster, faster!' we spurred the children on. The ones on the side lines clapped and called.

She is handsome, she is pretty,
She is the girl from Belfast city.
She's a courting one, two, three . . .

'Excuse me!' Uncle Billy's voice stopped us in mid-swing. He wanted past and we were blocking the pavement.

'There's plenty road to walk in, mister,' said Mary Lavery.

Uncle Billy was not amused.

Teresa cuffed her sister's ear and told her not to be so cheeky and to the rest she said, 'Let Mr McGill go by now.'

He went.

'I'm surprised at you, Cora,' he said to me later, 'encouraging those Papes in their wild behaviour.'

'They were only skipping.'

And obstructing the public highway. *And* making so much noise that Granny McGill had had to take an aspirin for her headache. *And* leaving litter lying around in the street afterwards. If it weren't for the Laverys this would be a well-kept, quiet street.

'I wish them no ill, Cora,' said Mrs Meneely, 'but I can't help wishing they'd go back to the Falls where they'd be more at home.'

'Well, they obviously aren't going to, are they?' said Rosie. 'They've been here for seven years after all.'

Rosie and I went for a walk and she said, 'God, they get on my nerves! Do you think they could give over once in a while?' She was changing her tune, no longer wanted to sing the songs her grandfather had sung, and said she had no intention of going anywhere near the 'Twelfth' parade this year. Anyway, Deirdre Fish had asked her to go with them to Portstewart for the first two weeks of July.

'So I'll be well out of the place.' She took my arm. 'I wish you could come too, Cora. If I were to ask Deirdre–'

'No!'

My mother was talking about renting a house in Portrush for a week and we had been going to ask Rosie to join us. 'We're taking a week in Portrush in August,' I said. 'And we're going to see if Teresa could come.'

Tit for tat! We still played at it at sixteen going on seventeen, regressing at times to behaving as if we were six going on seven.

Neither of us ever quarrelled with Teresa: she had a passivity that made us retreat from dispute.

'You are so angelic, so truly angelic, Teresa!' said Rosie, making Teresa laugh. We were having tea in our back living room. As I lifted my head I became aware of a wide shadow crossing the yard.

'Here's your mother coming, Rosie!'

'Well, what of it?' She kept her head up, her elbows on the table, her cup supported between her hands. 'No, stay where you are, Cora.'

Mrs Meneely knocked and came straight in and when she saw the three of us she stopped dead, which she was able to do in a second since her walk never amounted to more than a shuffle. Her lazy eyes flickered over us one after the other then moved down to the table and the half-empty plates and came back up to rest on her daughter again. With a soft grunt, she turned around and padded out. Sighing, Rosie got up and followed her.

Two hours later she was back. 'I'm raging!' she said, though that we could see.

'Sit down,' said my mother.

Rosie would not. She needed to be on her feet. 'To think they're trying to tell me who not to be friends with at my age! They said if Teresa Lavery was more important to me than they were I could leave the house so I left it!'

My mother was uneasy. 'You mustn't fall out with your family, Rosie.'

'You should have thought of that before shouldn't you, Eileen?' said my father.
'What do you mean, Desmond?'
'You know quite well what I mean.'
Were they on the verge of quarrelling for the first time? My mother picked up Mary Baker Eddy but, before she had time to consult her, there came a heavy knocking at the door.
'That'll be them,' said Rosie, taking up a position in front of the empty fireplace with one elbow propped against the mantelpiece. My father went to let them in.
Mrs Meneely had removed her slippers and managed to squash her feet into a pair of old court shoes and Uncle Billy had on his Lodge-going no-longer-dancehall-going suit.
'Now we've nothing against Catholics,' began Mrs Meneely.
'Except that their religion is a curse upon this land,' said Uncle Billy.
'I intend to remain friends with Teresa Lavery and that is that,' said Rosie. 'Good friends.'
Uncle Billy looked at my mother. 'You have allowed this to happen under your roof, Eileen. You have set a daughter against her mother.'
'The Bible tells us to love thy neighbour.'
'That's as may be but it doesn't say you have to consort with them. And not every word of the Bible has to be taken literal like.'
'You take the words *you* want,' said Rosie.
'The devil has entered into thy soul, Margaret Rose.'
'I don't mind you *speaking* to the Lavery girl, Rosie,' said Mrs Meneely. 'Now and again like. It's just that I don't want you to get too thick with her.'
'We shall be as thick as thieves if we wish. This is 1950 not 1690 and I don't have to cry No Surrender!'
That was a mistake! Uncle Billy stepped into the middle of the room and gave forth. 'Our forebears died for our faith, let us not forget that. If it had not been for their courage and their strength we might ourselves now be under the rule of Rome!' His voice bounced off the narrow

walls of our living room. He might have been speaking in the Ulster Hall.

No solution was found that day. Uncle Billy took his sister home – 'The ingratitude of you, Margaret Rose, after all we've done for you!' – and Rosie spent the night with us. She sighed in her sleep and ground her teeth.

In the morning, with mauve pouches under her eyes and her hair looking like a bird's nest, came Mrs Meneely to say that they'd allow Margaret Rose to be friendly with Teresa Lavery when she met her in the street like she would with any other neighbour but she must promise that she wouldn't spend time with her in our house or anyone else's, and certainly not the Laverys'.

'A street friendship, Ma? That'd be more public. What would the neighbours say?'

'Just promise, Margaret Rose, so that we can get some peace! I've been sick to my stomach with nerves all night.'

Rosie would not promise.

'Honour thy father and thy mother,' intoned Uncle Billy on his return. 'Haven't I always been as a father to you, Margaret Rose? And look at your poor mother – near worn to a shadow. But I don't suppose that troubles you. As long as you can get doing what you want.'

Uncle Sam was miserable. Rosie and I went to see him in the shop. 'We miss you, Princess.' He held her hand. 'Does that Lavery girl matter so much to you? Sure you hardly know her.'

'Yes, she does matter, Uncle Sam. And it's also a question of principle.'

Ah that!

'Principles can be a pain in the neck at times,' said my father. He was sawing up a plank of wood in the shed and I was holding the end. The shed was just a shed now, where my father kept tools and fiddled about – no more did Moses call in the animals two by two or the Red Queen talk to Alice. The looking glass had long since been shattered.

'But you think Rosie's right?'

'Of course I do. Though this business of right and

wrong is difficult isn't it? Nothing ever seems black and white to me. Hold tight now, Cora, it's nearly through.'

The smell of the fresh sawdust filled my nostrils. I watched the blade come closer and closer to my fingers but I held tight, did not waver, for I must show trust in my father, even though his hand was none too steady these days and his eye less than straight. My arm juddered, the blade broke through and the wood was halved. 'Bravo!' I held my piece aloft.

He began to cough. It had a bad sound to it, that cough. I rubbed his back. 'Are you all right?' It was just the sawdust catching his throat, he said.

I told him that I knew what he meant about things not being black and white, of course I did, I wasn't a child any longer, but where the friendship of Rosie and Teresa was concerned, could one not say that was right? 'I mean it's based on love and the McGill's objection is based on hate.' Love and hate. Was love always white and hate black? No, the shades merged there too. But, still, love *was* commendable, wasn't it, and hate damnable? My father laughed.

'OK.' I said, 'it was all right to hate Hitler because he was evil but it's not all right for the McGills to hate Teresa because she's a Catholic.'

'It's not so much hate as fear, Cora. You can smell it on them. There's nothing rational about it. And it won't go away either by reading to them from the Bible about loving your neighbour.' We glanced guiltily at the open door as we heard my mother's voice calling. I went outside.

On the pavement Rosie stood chatting with Teresa who had been told nothing about the dispute but sensed that something was going on.

'Tea-time, girls.' My mother appeared on the front step.

'I'll away in and get myself washed,' said Rosie.

Teresa watched her go into the house. 'Why is she staying with you, Cora?'

So that we could revise for our exams together, I told her, but she was not convinced.

Rosie and I pressed on with our revision, sitting

together at the living room table, but she found it difficult to work and her results, when they came, reflected her lack of concentration. Rosie's stand over Teresa cost her her place at college.

'Now see here, Margaret Rose,' said her grandmother, 'you've got a good home up the street and that is where you belong. You can't stay here for ever!'

'I'm ready to come home when you're all ready to have me. You know my terms.'

'Terms! The impudence of it!' Granny McGill stumped off, always having known that no good would come from RCs moving into the street.

'You *should* honour your mother, Rosie,' said my mother sadly.

The day before we sat our first exam a compromise was reached. Uncle Sam came with the new proposal. Rosie could be friendly with Teresa on just one condition: that she would not enter the Laverys' house. 'That's not much of hardship is it now, Princess?' Rosie said she would think about it. She thought. She knew that her family would never back down on this condition and she also knew that she could not stay with us, never mind for ever, even indefinitely.

'Perhaps the answer's to get married,' she said.

She went home in the meantime.

Her birthday fell in June, at the end of our examinations. 'We'll have a double celebration!' Deirdre Fish offered her house. It was much more suitable, said Rosie to her mother, being three times the size of their house, and they were going to light a fire in the back garden and cook potatoes and sausages. Teresa was not invited of course nor would she have wished to have been since she would have been out of place.

I felt misplaced myself. The party started in the late afternoon and would go on until midnight or later. Rosie and I were to stay the night. The afternoon was not so bad, spent out of doors gathering wood, burying potatoes in the embers, frying sausages, drinking cider. We mingled freely, absorbed by the fire and the food, and as

I sat bemused by the heat and the flicker of the flames I thought that perhaps parties were bearable after all. But after we had cleared up and gone indoors, the mood changed. The kissing games began.

They mocked themselves for wanting to play, saying you'd think we were fourteen again but oh well why not anything for a bit of fun and a laugh. They made it quite clear that they could all kiss when and where they wanted. I wished there were ladies' cloakrooms in private houses where one could linger adjusting one's petticoat; but if one stayed in the bathroom too long somebody came rattling the door knob asking if there was anyone in.

'Postman's knock!' cried Deirdre.

We were given numbers on pieces of paper – I got three – and we sat around the room trying to look nonchalant. Or perhaps the others really were and it was only I who was putting up the pretence. I took the seat nearest the French window where I could smell the bonfire smoke and look at the gean tree.

Hugo Fish was the first to go out. Wet Fish, Eithne and I called him; we had heard he slobbered when he kissed. My lips puckered at the thought.

We were silent, at Deirdre's command. The knocking came. One, two, three.

'Three!' cried Rosie. 'Who's number three?' Her eyes swept the room and stopped at me. She always read me well. 'Cora! Come on now, Cora!' I got up and trudged to the door keeping my head down and face averted.

'He isn't going to eat you alive,' said Quentin.

'England expects,' cried Randolph.

I closed the door on their laughter.

Hugo Fish was waiting expectantly in the hall jiggling about on the balls of his feet the way a boxer does before coming out from his corner. He came down flat on his heels when he saw me. 'Cora – oh–' He had probably hoped for Rosie – he was always trying to get her back – or Susan Orr with her sleek black hair and scarlet lips. Or any other girl in the room except me. But he must do his duty, to God and the King. He came a step closer. I closed my eyes. I felt his damp lips brush my cheek. He had funked it.

When I opened my eyes I saw only the back of his head as he turned to open the door. He went into the room to the noise of catcalls. I scrubbed my cheek with my handkerchief.

I contemplated the closed door on which I was expected to knock. I funked it.

Running, I went along the hall, slipping a little on the polished wood, and up the stairs, taking two, three, four at a time, and into the bedroom where I yanked my jacket out from under the pile and was back down again before the drawing room door opened.

I rode out to Hastings Court on the front seat of the bus enjoying a good view of the burgeoning countryside. On the narrow country lanes branches scraped the bus windows.

Mrs Hastings-Smith had gone to Rostrevor and would not be back until next day. 'One of her missions,' said Marcellina. 'But sure stay the evening and I'll cook us a good dinner and stay the night too if you want. Your old bed's up the stair doing nothing.'

I rang the Fishes and asked for Rosie.

'Honestly, Cora, you are hopeless! Fancy disappearing into thin air like that! We turned the place upside down looking for you. What on earth am I to do with you?'

We ate in the kitchen, the three of us, Marcellina, Gerard and I – how much more easily I fitted here – and afterwards Marcellina's not-so-young man came and they went walking.

And my young man and I went walking too, down through the flower gardens into the orchard. The night air was sweet with the scent of grass and roses. The blossom was over, all but for a few last flowers which were holding on. We compared notes on our exams, not bothered to be talking about that on a summer's night, for why should one not talk about what one wanted to talk about? We both thought we had done well enough, which indeed we had.

We stayed outside as the long evening dwindled and a

small crescent moon appeared. Coming back up to the house, Gerard took my hand.

'I don't know what I'd have done without you, Cora. I'm really grateful.'

For most of that summer night I lay awake with the window up so that I could smell the air and with the curtains drawn back so that I could see the thin slice of moon. Dawn came early, pale pink and green and quiet. I wanted to stay at Hastings Court for ever. I felt myself to be in a state of bliss. The first cock crowed and then I slid down into a sleep which brought with it only happy dreams.

Waking, I heard voices, and slipping out of bed to go to the window, saw Gerard and Marcellina coming up the path in their Mass clothes. I remembered the day I had run from the Catholic church. But I had been young then and full of silly prejudices about priests and nuns. And I was no longer a totally convinced Christian Scientist. *There is no sensation in matter. There is no sin, disease or death*. I could recite the words – oh so easily! – but could not believe them. I wished that I could so that I could remain in the fold, for it was comfortable there, and if I left it I would distress many people. People whom I loved. Was I thinking then that I might turn? Go over to the Church of Rome? Gerard and Marcellina were gone now, round the corner of the house. I shivered, pushed up the window and returned to the bed where I sat examining my thoughts.

NINE

'Why are you asking me all these things?'

'I'm interested, that's all.'

'In a – well, intellectual sort of way?' Gerard used the word uneasily, had probably never spoken it aloud before.

I said yes, which appeared to relieve him.

'It's just – I wouldn't want anyone to think I was trying to convert you.' He gave me a half-smile.

'Oh, I wouldn't worry about that!'

He was willing now to talk, to answer my questions on the virgin birth, transubstantiation, sin. We skated lightly on the surface of such large topics and I did not probe too deeply, not wanting to start cracks under our feet. I was particularly interested in sin. Mortal sin and venial sin. Sins of omission and commission. The seven deadly. Original sin. So many different kinds and I had been brought up to believe that there was no sin.

We talked religion only out of doors, by mutual, unspoken agreement; inside the house we continued our exloration of the history of Ireland. I brought books from the central library in Belfast, we found others in the bookshelves at Hastings Court.

'What do you want to keep on raking up the past for?' said Mrs Hastings-Smith, coming into the library when we were discussing the signing of the Anglo-Irish treaty in 1921 and the rioting that followed. She cast an eye at the book. 'All this old fighting, it's not the thing for healthy young people to be dwelling on. It's all behind us anyway, Ireland is at peace now. Cora, I'm going to visit old Mrs Dowson in Ballyholme, I think you should come with me. She loves young people.' It was not an offer open to refusal.

Driving through the Hollywood Hills in the Lagonda, she talked about influences. Sometimes bad influences came through good people; one had constantly to watch and pray. I did not pray at all now, had found that I could not, got stuck at the end of *Our Father*.

As we parked the car along the sea front at Ballyholme, a woman came forward to hand us a leaflet and ask if we'd seen the light.

'We have our own light,' said Mrs Hastings-Smith giving the woman a smile and returning the leaflet. 'Thank you so much.'

On the sands were etched the words JESUS SAVES. Gospellers were gathering. *Stand up, stand up for Jesus . . .*

'They are so joyless,' said Mrs Hastings-Smith, ' in spite of all that singing. Such a pity they cannot know *Science*.'

We drank tea with Mrs Dowson, a sweet, russet-cheeked old lady who had gone to Boston before the First World War and met Mary Baker Eddy, and across the road beside the sea the gospellers sang, drowning out the sound of the waves. I hummed a different song inside my head. *Oh I do like to be beside the seaside . . .* Mrs Hastings-Smith gave me an odd look and drew me into the conversation.

'It is a marvellous experience, Cora, to go to Boston and see the First Church. You must do it one day.'

The tide was coming in when we returned to the car. The gospellers had gone, the waves were eating at the edges of their message.

Mrs Hastings-Smith drove me home along the coast road thus avoiding Hastings Court.

'You go to Portrush on holiday next week don't you, dear? That will be nice for you.'

'We're taking Teresa.'

'Teresa! I thought she was so much needed at home?'

'Bridie is to take over for the week.'

'How nice,' said Mrs Hastings-Smith with uncharacteristic insincerity.

On Sunday morning in Portrush Teresa rose early. I would have walked with her to the church, going only as far as the door, but I knew that it might disturb my parents.

'You don't talk about religion with Teresa do you?' asked my mother.

'No, hardly ever. Why?'

'I just wondered. But I thought not. You know of course, Cora, that religion is not really a topic for discussion.' She broke off as my father's coughing deepened in the next room. 'One does not *discuss* the truth.'

'Mother, listen to that cough!'

'A week's sea air will do him the world of good, dear.' She got up and went to him.

I went out to meet Teresa. She came from church smiling, a scarf tied about her head, but she smiled not because she came from church but because she was beside the seaside. How she liked it! She was in seventh heaven, as she put it. 'I can't believe it, Cora – seven whole days!' She sniffed the sea air. She laughed. She tucked her hand into the crook of my arm and let the scarf slide backwards and the wind take her hair. We walked down to the shore. We skipped barefooted along the sand and, turning towards the sea, ran in to the Atlantic breakers which crashed and surged around our legs soaking our skirts and making us dance and squeal with laughter.

'So this is heaven is it, Teresa?' This kind of heaven would be all right for me. Angels and harps had no appeal. Too sickly and too sweet. Better than Purgatory though, said Teresa, or hell. She believed in a place where damned souls wandered and fires crackled. I considered hell to be a state of mind. That, too, she agreed.

My seventeenth birthday fell that week. Rosie came up on the train for it. I had not seen much of her since the end of term – she'd been to Portstewart with the Fishes and then had stayed with Deirdre to keep her company while her parents went off to Venice – and for a moment, when she came out of the station, I almost did not know her. Men turned to look at her and whistle, though of course they always had. She sauntered on white high-heeled sandals, white earrings swinging, grazing her apricot-coloured cheek.

'Cora!' She kissed me and I smelt her perfume. 'You've been in the sun.' I wrinkled my freckled nose at her. 'And you too, Teresa – goodness, you're brown! Come on, let's go for a cup of coffee, I'm dying for a fag and I know I can't smoke under your mother's roof.' Nor her own either. I had known that she smoked from time to time but not that she had reached the stage when she might die for want of it.

We sat at the back of a café where the light was poor and Rosie smoked flat Turkish cigarettes with a powerful aroma. She lounged against the back of the chair, not huddling over the table as Teresa and I did. She crossed her legs at the knee revealing apricot-coloured thighs. She looked around the café. She offered us cigarettes which she knew we would not accept. We must be dull for her, I thought, after Deirdre Fish; two awkward, clumsy girls who preferred walking barefoot on the sand to more sophisticated pleasures. I wished she had not bothered to come.

'Rosie!' A young man in flannels and blue blazer had sighted her. 'What are *you* doing here?' It seemed that Teresa and I were invisible. I pinched my arm and feeling pain supposed that I existed. 'I've got the car, why don't we go for a spin . . . ?'

Like a record on a turntable.

'We'll see you later,' said I, getting up and pushing back my chair. Teresa followed. We walked glumly down the street. 'She's not the same any more, Teresa, we've got to face it.'

'Cora! Teresa! Hey, Apple Core!' Rosie was shouting.

I was tempted to walk on, to punish her, but we turned and waited. She came flying towards us, blonde hair streaming behind her. She almost went over on one ankle. 'Drat these stupid shoes!' She took them off. 'Why didn't you wait for me? You didn't think I'd spend the day with a creep like that did you? On your birthday?' She came into the middle, linked arms with us both.

We spent the day on the beach. It was the best day we had ever spent together, we were agreed upon that, and it was to be the best we ever would spend. It was one of those seaside days that seemed to hold a promise of eternity like the sea itself. We swam, sunbathed, swam again, and so the cycle was repeated. We built a sandcastle. The biggest sandcastle in the world, said Rosie, big enough for all three of us to live in. It'd be great to live in a castle, said Teresa, digging deep to make the moat. We would pull up the drawbridge, said Rosie, and let no one else in. No one? I thought of Gerard. Well, maybe once in a while, Rosie conceded, we might be able to see our way to letting a few other, carefully selected people in. She could not be in love then.

That night in bed we asked her if she were. She considered. 'I suppose not. I quite like Harry Dunbar at the moment but I guess that's not the same thing?'

'Indeed it's not,' said Teresa sharply and made us laugh.

'I shall have to wait for Mr Right then. What about yourself, dark, secretive Teresa?'

I suspected Teresa blushed unseen in the darkness. She fancied a boy who went to her church, she had confided to me, a handsome lad by the name of Dominic Quin. 'How would I've time to fall in love?' she demanded.

'It needn't take much time. What about love at first sight? That'd only take a minute. And what about you, old Apple Core? You're lying there awful quiet, I'm thinking, keeping your secrets to yourself.'

I protested – what secrets could I have? Rosie was open with us, but we were not with her. She entertained us until the small hours with tales of assignations and falling in and out of love. She seemed to know half the men in Belfast. The Protestant half.

We were quiet after she left in the morning.

'She's a bright spark is Rosie,' said my father.

The spark seemed to be going out of him. I tried not to think about it, to tell myself that he would be all right, that lots of people had coughs.

Rosie started work in the Head Office of the Ulster Bank. She liked it, well enough at any rate. 'As much as I'd ever like any job. It'll do in the meantime.' To begin with she was given the job of sorting out banknotes and then twice a day was released into the streets of Belfast to deliver statements. It was that which suited her. The freedom of the streets. For that was how it felt to her. 'It's almost like being a child again, roaming about.' I, closeted in my school classroom, envied her that. The streets had always drawn us, the life of the out-of-doors. She strolled up Royal Avenue and Donegall Place, encircled the City Hall, met people and had a crack, stopped off at milk bars and drank coffee and coke. And she delivered the statements, going up narrow dark staircases into the offices of solicitors, getting to know the solicitors and their clerks of course. Her daytime wanderings reaped many evening dates. How many more times was I to watch her getting ready and tell her to have a good time?

'She's a popular girl is our Margaret Rose,' said Mrs Meneely.

'She's quite right not to get tied down too soon,' said Mrs McGill. 'She'll can take her pick when she wants.'

There was one young solicitor, Tom Thorburn, whose cause they came gradually to espouse above the others. He brought flowers for the women, freesias, anemones, violets, when he called, and to Margaret Rose he gave boxes of chocolates to eat in the pictures or at the theatre. He quickly learned that Milk Tray was Mrs Meneely's favourite. A right nice class of person, said Mrs McGill. Couldn't get better, said Mrs Meneely. (She liked the soft centres best.) Even Uncles Billy and Sam could find nothing wrong with him. He was from a very good family, comfortably off, Unionist, connections at Stormont. Father was a solicitor too, Tom was in the family firm. He'd been to Campbell College and only the best went there. He was obviously not short of a bob or two, said Mrs Meneely, chewing on the remains of chocolate fudge brought back from *The Pirates of Penzance*. Margaret Rose could do a lot worse when all was said and done, said Granny McGill.

But all was not said and done, for the Thorburns had a few things to say too and they thought that their son could do a lot better for himself. I heard from Eithne Potter, who lived next door to them, that Mrs Thorburn had told her mother that they liked Rosie and they thought she was a lovely girl but – Well, her family was not quite what they were used to. Look at the mother, nothing but a moving tub of lard! And those uncles! They were just the kind of bigots to give Ulster a bad name. 'My father says the Unionist party would get on a damned sight better without the likes of them,' said Eithne.

It seemed to me that it did well enough as it was: in the Westminster election in the previous October out of twelve MPs returned nine were Unionist. At the end of one candidate's election speech a Stormont MP (Unionist of course) who'd been present had shouted out, 'And to hell with the Pope!' in response to the declaration, 'God Save the King!'

'What about that?' I asked Eithne. 'Would he not give Ulster Protestants a bad name?'

She shrugged. 'Well, I suppose that was going a bit far.'

How far can you go? Until someone objects strongly enough? With a loaded gun or a stick of gelignite. Mr Potter said Northern Ireland was the safest part of the United Kingdom to live in. The crime rate was low. Why then did the police need to carry guns? 'Just in case,' said Eithne.

She and I were the only two of our group left at school; the others had dispersed into the Civil Service, banks, secretarial colleges. Deirdre Fish was abroad. She had been sent to Switzerland to be finished off: that was how I put it to Teresa. In my nastier moods I wished that she would be, literally. But it was to be the end of Deirdre and Rosie's friendship, more or less, for when Deirdre returned we saw that she had shifted her sights; she talked of Persian girls whose fathers were millionaires and of young women whose ancestors had sat on the thrones of Europe. 'God, Maria Teresa and her merry band!' said Rosie. 'They always did make me sick.'

'Cora dear,' said Mrs Hastings-Smith, 'what about you and I having a little talk? We don't seem to have talked much recently, not really talked. Let us go into the conservatory. So much nicer to be amongst plants in wintertime I always think.'

The plants grew higher and wilder every year, interlacing one with the other as they climbed and spread, making the light within patterned and green. I watched a shaft of sunshine play across Mrs Hastings-Smith's smooth serene face. I waited.

'You are a woman now, Cora, in your eighteenth year. And growing bonnier all the time.' Ah, she warmed my heart there! And softened me. I wished that I would be able to please her in return, but knew I could not. 'Oh yes, indeed you are. And I'm sure young men must see it too. I must speak plainly to you, Cora – I consider that you are spending too much time in the company of Gerard Lavery. Now I'm very fond of Gerard and I believe him to be an excellent person, hardworking, reliable, trustworthy–' My heart sang. I believed him to be excellent too. 'But he is not suitable for you, Cora, you know that he is not.'

I denied all feeling for him, in the way that she implied. We were just good friends! We enjoyed working together, he had a good mind, but that was all, well of course that was all, for I would never let myself become *involved* with a Roman Catholic. I spoke ardently, and was convinced that I convinced her. It was necessary to allay her fears, lest she try to keep me from the house. Her goodness made her ready to believe. She said, 'You are a good child.'

That stung. I knew that I was not good.

In my bag I had a book about saints. Going home on the bus I looked at it. I found the idea of saints difficult, disliked especially the idea of praying to their graven images. There was still much in the Roman religion that I found unacceptable.

As I came into the house, I heard my father coughing. And my mother reading from the book. I pushed open the living room door.

My father's face was greyish-yellow, his cheeks sunken. How had I not seen his colour before? I had been too preoccupied with my own selfish concerns! I knelt down beside him and laid my hand on his arm. His chest was heaving, he gasped for breath.

'Go and ring Mrs Hastings-Smith, dear,' said my mother. 'Ask her to work for us. I'm sure you could use the McGills' phone.'

'Put all fear out of your heart, Cora,' said Mrs Hastings-Smith.

The McGills were having supper. I accepted a cup of tea and sat down at the table beside them.

'Is he bad?' asked Rosie.

'Not good.'

'Your mother should give in and send for the doctor now,' said Granny McGill. 'You can't fool around with a man's life.'

'Do you mind that time I got one and saved your life?' said Uncle Billy.

I wished that he would get one now and save my father's life. If only it were that simple! But something had to be done and there was only one person who could take the responsibility. I asked if I could use the phone again and did they have their doctor's number?

'Just you go ahead, Cora,' said Granny McGill. 'At least you've got some sense. If your mother won't do it then you've got to.'

She might never forgive me, but it was a chance I had to take.

My hand shook as I dialled. The doctor said he would come at once.

Oh ye of little faith. . . .

My mother did not reproach me when I brought in the strange man with the black bag, but her eyes filled with sorrow. I saw them fill before she turned her head. She made no objection to the doctor examining my father nor to the suggestion that an ambulance should be called and my father taken to hospital. She was not against doctors, she said later, not in the way that Plymouth Brethren were, going so far as to refuse blood transfusions for their children; at times doctors fulfilled a function. At times Christian Science and orthodox medicine could work together. My father did not protest either, would have been too weak to do so had he wished. I organized his departure, laying out pyjamas and toothbrush. My parents had become passive; they stayed quietly together, waiting for the ambulance.

The house in a moment became full of people: ambulance men, Rosie, Mrs Meneely, Granny McGill, Uncle Sam and Uncle Billy. My father panted for breath again. I kissed his forehead and stepped back to let them put him on the stretcher. My mother, book in hand, went with him into the ambulance. The doors closed. Rosie took my hand and squeezed it tight.

'He had to go.'

'You've done the right thing, Cora,' said Mrs Meneely.

'May the Lord have mercy on him and watch over him,' said Uncle Billy.

'Amen,' said Uncle Sam.

Teresa lit a candle to the Virgin and asked her to intercede for my father. I prayed too. Please God, I gabbled in my head, make him better and I will never ever doubt you again, *please God*. Promises, promises . . . I knew it was not the efficacious way to pray. Who would listen to such a prayer, anyway? Who would be fooled? I would have sold my soul to the devil if it would have helped.

In the hospital they x-rayed and tested and found my father to be suffering from carcinoma of the lung well advanced. There was no question of surgery. My mother brought him home. The doctor called every evening to inject him with morphine and then he slept whilst she watched over him. Teresa and Rosie sat with me during the long black hours. My mother and father grew closer as his life ebbed away; there seemed no place for me to get in. I went to his room, put my hand over his, said his name. 'Cora.' He said mine and smiled faintly, but nothing else. I wanted him to justify my action and exonerate me from all blame.

'You've nothing to blame yourself for,' said Rosie.

'But what good did it do – sending him to hospital to find that out? They would have preferred not to know.'

'But it mightn't have been too late,' said Teresa. 'You had to give him the chance.'

It was all right for Teresa: she could get rid of her guilt by speaking through a grill to a faceless man. She could emerge spotless, her sins forgiven. She must feel light as air. I felt as heavy as a stone-filled sack at the bottom of the Dead Sea.

My father went peacefully. My mother was calm. 'He has passed on to a better and higher state, dear.' I wept against her shoulder and she comforted me, but did not cry herself. I sought relief in the noise of the McGills' and the Laverys' houses.

Another funeral in the street. No men of the Lodge this time, or black bows on the knocker, no minister either, only Mrs Hastings-Smith reading from the Bible and *Science and Health with Key to the Scriptures* by Mary Baker Eddy. A quiet, dignified affair.

Aunt Belle came from London where she had a good job and Aunt Kathleen, my father's sister, from Armagh where she lived a pious life (Presbyterian) behind lace curtains and half-pulled blinds. She had an aversion to sunlight. We had no men of our own to go with the cortège. My mother asked Uncle Billy and Uncle Sam to lead the mourners, a handful of neighbours.

'Not like a proper funeral is it?' said Granny McGill. 'Now, Cora, I'm not meaning nothing . . .'

They were good to me, the McGills: they made a place for me at the fire, gave me tea and warm bread, they told me that time was a great healer and that my father had been fond of me, and that I had been a good daughter to him. They said all the things that I needed to hear. They said too they could understand why I had given up that odd religion. For since I'd called the doctor I had been unable to go back to church.

I need not reproach myself for that, said Mrs Hastings-Smith, nor would God for he did not make judgments. She was for the God of the New Testament, not of the Old. 'You will come back to the church one day, Cora, I am confident that you will, for that is where you belong.'

Suddenly I seemed not to belong anywhere, except perhaps in her library, amongst the books, with the green lamp lit, and Gerard seated at the table beside me, his head resting on his hand. He would look sideways at me and smile and I would think, yes, perhaps some day it might be possible to be happy again.

TEN

'Isn't it about time you took me to Hastings Court?' said Rosie. 'You've always been going to and never have.'

I said that she had always been too busy.

'Well, I'm not busy now.'

And so we went.

'What a place!' said Rosie as we came up the drive between the rhododendrons and saw the house ahead. 'You could stash a couple of hundred people in there and never notice. Do you mean to say Mrs Hastings-Smith lives in it alone?'

'With Marcellina. And Gerard Lavery,' I added as casually as I could.

'Doesn't he live over the stable or something?'

He appeared at that moment from between the rhododendrons. He looked startled; we had taken him by surprise.

'Gerard, you remember Rosie don't you? Rosie Meneely?'

Rosie laughed. 'Have I changed that much?'

They were staring at one another. I felt a chill rise up from the cold ground into my body. It need only take a minute, I remembered Rosie saying. I don't know what else they said whilst we stood there, probably nothing very much, just a few civilities about it having been a long time.

One couldn't call it love at first sight exactly since they'd seen one another off and on since they were children but, undoubtedly, love blossomed at that moment. Or was it just a very powerful sexual attraction, at least initially? Or is romantic love always sexual in its beginning? I was ill-equipped to judge, but whatever it was, I was conscious of something like an electric tingling in the damp air. Had I put out my hand I might have received a shock. And in the kitchen later, drinking tea, I was conscious again of the heat that glowed between them. Rosie's cheeks were pink; she laughed excitedly. Gerard scarcely took his eyes off her. She was beautiful, of course, quite beautiful. I understood a man desiring her.

On the way home on the bus she chattered, she could not help it. 'Oh Cora, isn't he fabulous? Why didn't you tell me? He's got such beautiful eyes, when he looked at me I felt I was drowning.' She used the universal language of love, or infatuation. 'But he's a Taig by God!' Her laugh was edged with nervousness. 'Don't tell my family – they'd kill me! Do you think I'm mad, Cora? I feel slightly mad. I'm hot – feel!' She took my hand and pressed it against her forehead. The soft curls fringing it were damp. 'Say something, Cora, for God's sake, don't just sit there!' But I could not speak. 'And don't tell Teresa either will you? Promise! She'd be worried, I know she would.'

What was there to tell? Nothing much yet. But soon there would be. She told everything to me, her best friend.

When she finished work she would take the bus out to Hastings Court. It was a many-roomed mansion, ideal for lovers. Rooms, relics of an era when week-end guests arrived with trunks and maids, had not been opened for years. The wardrobes were full of silks and satins and taffetas; fine wool shawls and moth-eaten fur stoles rotted in the chests of drawers. Mrs Hastings-Smith was uninterested in all that old stuff, though from time to time supposed she ought to do something about it but couldn't think what. 'Not even the Army (Salvation) would want it. It's not quite their style.' It was Rosie's style: the lace ball dresses, the gaudy kimonos, the whaleboned corsets, the delicate silk underwear. They made her feel wild, and romantic.

In a room lined with silk paper the colour of peacocks' tails there was an antique gramophone which, if wound long enough, could be persuaded to wheeze into a lop-sided spin. The records were cracked but the tunes unmistakable. *If you were the only girl in the world and I was the only boy . . . Daisy, daisy, give me your answer do, I'm half crazy . . .* The tunes went round and round inside my skull as if my head itself were a turntable.

In the peacock room waltzed Rosie and Gerard, far far away from the jungle in which Mrs Hastings-Smith sat peacefully reading and from the red-brick house in which the McGills sat gathered round their well-banked fire lamenting the absence of Margaret Rose.

'The house is dead quiet so it is,' said Uncle Sam.

'Where is she anyway?' said Uncle Billy. 'Who are all those girls she goes home to tea with?'

'They're nice girls,' said Mrs Meneely. 'They work in the bank alongside of her.'

'I don't know what she had to break off with that nice Tom Thorburn for,' said Granny McGill.

'Why can't she come home to her own house once in a while?' said Uncle Billy.

'She's getting on for eighteen, Billy,' said Mrs Meneely. 'You can't expect her to sit in the house can you, Cora, when she could be out enjoying herself?'

'Cora sits in the house don't you, Cora?' said Uncle Billy.

My own, or Teresa's, and sometimes here, in the McGills', which I seemed to be unable to stay away from, even when Rosie was not there. I no longer sat in Mrs Hastings-Smith's. The centre of my life had shifted. I felt off-centre, and when I walked down the road to school I wondered that I did not list, like a ship tilted over.

'Of course Cora's working for her scholarship,' said Granny McGill. 'You're quite right to stick in, dear.'

Stick in and you'll get on. But where would it get you? Now if I were to leave school and take a job in the bank, we'd have more money coming in. My father had left us badly provided for and my mother was not qualified to earn her living, had never done so, having helped at home until she married my father. She thought of trying to get a job as a shop assistant but I was horrified and would not let her consider it. 'We could take a lodger,' I suggested. We put an advertisement in the *Belfast Telegraph* and two young men, brash and pimpled, came and one young woman whom we recognized as a Salvationist the moment she put a foot over the threshold. She had pamphlets with her and if she was not going to rent our room she was at least going to try to convert us.

We decided that we could not accept strangers in our house: it was not large enough for that. The other alternative, said my mother, was to sell up and move into something even smaller. Leave the street? That was also unacceptable to me. I would have preferred to leave school first. I was bored with it anyway, was much too restless to sit in its chalk-laden rooms listening to virginal women reading from notes written in the dark ages – the dark ages of their minds, an everlasting state for some, I had long since decided – and I was bored too with Eithne Potter who now regarded me as her best friend and was reluctant to let me out of her sight, accompanying me even to the toilet where she would stand outside talking about how we must stick together. Stick in and stick together. Her hands were gluey and her breath smelt. I shrank away from her and couldn't bear to think that once we'd been 'married' and lain on the ground and kissed mouth to mouth.

There was a shortage of teachers in the country and in primary schools they were taking on people untrained. I talked my mother round and applied.

A telegram came summoning me to a school. I pulled off my green uniform and put on my best dress and, in that short passage of time, switched roles.

The school looked so much like a decaying warehouse that I almost passed it by. The building had been condemned pre-war, I was to learn, but whether it was first or second I forgot to ask. I entered into that gaunt gloomy place where children marched up and down stone stairs in time to the clunk, clunk, clunk of the headmistress's bell, where they sat in rows with their hands clasped tightly behind their backs, where they chanted and recited until they put themselves into a state of semi-hypnosis. The headmistress, gaunt and gloomy also, reigned by overt terror, no attempt to conceal iron hands in velvet gloves or any of that nonsense. Her chief implements were the bell, the cane, and a cold voice.

'The main thing is not to let them take advantage, Miss Caldwell. Once you do that you are lost.'

I was lost already, had little hope of being found, and so I ignored her warning.

'Keep your head up, Miss Caldwell, well away from theirs. Many of the children are dirty, unfortunately, though we do what we can.'

She led the singing at morning assembly. *Jesus loves me this I know . . .* The staff, a motley bunch made up of ex-Servicemen who'd done the six month training and other totally untrained girls like me (all they could get for a condemned school), stood on the sidelines glaring, looking like wanted men and women in police posters, their facial twitches intended to deter defaulters, whilst the camp commandant walked between the rows swishing her cane, catching a shin here, a fidgeting hand there, urging on the apathetic, the lazy, and the poseurs. 'Sing up, I can't hear you!' She bent an ear, though not too closely, to an opening and shutting mouth. 'Louder, louder!' A tap on the buttocks worked wonders, brought a singing voice out in full throttle; or better still, a whack across the back of the knees, since they were unprotected. Up and down the lines children winced, buckled, and straightened up again. *Little ones to Him belong . . .*

'That's better!'

You in your small corner and I in mine . . .

'Now stand no nonsense, Miss Caldwell, right from the beginning. It is important to begin as you mean to go on.'

She handed me the register for Second Infants. The names ran on and on. How many were there? Fifty-eight, said the commandant. 'Two left last week, two of the worst, so you're lucky.' Fifty-eight? My voice faltered. There were seventy in First Infants, she informed me. I apologized and went to face my class.

On the threshold I paused to try to accustom myself to the smell and noise. Their curiosity quietened them: I was their third teacher in three months. Good morning, children. Good morning, miss. A sea of clicking fingers waved in the air. *Please miss please miss . . . What's your name I like your dress where do you live . . .*

Please sit please sit, I begged, most humbly.

The door opened, the hubbub died like a turned-off tap.

'I told you, Miss Caldwell, to stand no nonsense from the start. Hands behind your backs, heads up!' They performed like seals. She left me with them, transformed into statues. I made an appeal. Listen, I said, let us be as quiet as mice together and then she'll not come in and if she doesn't come in we can have a good time together, I can tell you stories and we'll do all sorts of marvellous things. Well, I was young. And so were they. You're on, they said.

I told them my first story. 'Once upon a time there was a man called Bluebeard . . .' Mouths opened, eyes became round, hands slid round from behind their backs but did not fidget. I held them in thrall. My heart glowed.

She came back.

'What *are* you doing, Miss Caldwell? You're supposed to be teaching RI at this time. We always do RI first thing. Haven't you even looked at your timetable?'

She stayed to hear me tell the story of Jesus and the man sick of the palsy. I did not think she liked my style. Once upon a time there was this man . . .

'Keep to the words of the Bible, Miss Caldwell, whenever possible.'

I liked the words of the Bible myself, they flowed so beautifully, but the children were small and illiterate. They came, however, to see that I had not talked loosely: whenever possible we did do marvellous things together. I told stories that changed in mid-sentence at the opening of the door, I let them paint or draw when I knew she was otherwise engaged, teaching a class for a sick teacher, or better still, gone to the education offices on business. Those were the good times, when she left the building; the staff knocked on one another's doors and had a crack or sat in the toilet smoking fags.

I went home with fleas on my body and nits in my hair. My mother cut my hair and sluiced it with paraffin. 'I wonder if what you are doing is wise, dear . . .'

I met Miss Lightbody walking her dog. She seemed like a shaft of light after our commandant. 'It seems such a waste, Cora, for you not to go on with your education. Wouldn't you like to reconsider?'

But I could not go back to my past life. All my habits had changed.

Sundays were my bad days, my dead days, whose hours I counted in their long slow passing. I had ceased to go to the white church where I had known peace and I had ceased to go to Hastings Court where I had known happiness. I spent the day alone. Teresa was relative-bound; Rosie was with her true love, her Mr Right, the one she had been waiting for; other school friends I had drifted from. I could not stay in the house. I roamed the Sunday, God-gripped streets of Belfast, my ears assailed by the sound of church bells tolling, my eyes transfixed by the sight of congregations, hatted and gloved, carrying hymn-books, piously smiling, emerging from solid high-soaring edifices bringing with them the smell of sanctity. Church of Ireland, Presbyterian, Methodist, Roman Catholic, Baptist, Congregational, Church of God, Salvationists, Mooneyites . . . Sects without end. Adherents without end. Clotting the streets.

They had seen the light. They would be saved.

I had no hope of salvation, nor interest either. I looked into a long dark tunnel at the end of which there was not even a blink of light.

My only salvation (in a manner of speaking) lay in my pupils. I welcomed Monday mornings, lingered on Friday afternoons sorting chalk, cleaning blackboards, talking to children with no home to go until mother would come back from the mill. On Saturdays I took them out. They huddled close to me, three, four, clinging to either arm. We went to the zoo, the museum, to Bangor on the bus. People looked at me as I passed. A female Pied Piper with her ragged band.

The commandant found out. Commandants always do

– they have ways. 'You do not have my permission to conduct school outings on Saturday afternoons, Miss Caldwell.' Nor on any other day. She did not believe in outings, any more than I believed in God. Run about zoological gardens looking at monkeys and baboons or idle around beaches picking up shells? You would have to be joking, Miss Caldwell! There was to be no more of *that*. Or else. She did not need to remind me that I was only temporary staff. Here today and gone tomorrow. That was what had happened to my predecessor who had been caught smoking in a classroom at lunchtime. The only place to smoke, apart from the toilet, there being no staffroom; if one smoked at all, that was. One needed to do something to stop one's lid flying off. An ex-RAF flyer tippled behind the door from a bottle marked Cough Linctus.

I brought in bags of dolly mixtures and jelly babies to give out as rewards. (Rewards were permitted, within reason, in order to single out the sheep from the goats.) Ten out of ten for spelling. Ten out of ten for mental arithmetic. Perfection was deemed worthy of rewarding. But there was nothing wrong with nine out of ten, as far as I could see, or eight, or seven. And six or five was at least a pass, and for some four was a good effort. And those who could reach no higher needed consolation. I understood the need for consolation. We chewed, all fifty-nine of us, eyes on the door, ready to swallow fast. For her step was swift and stealthy, and her wrath terrible to behold.

'Two out of ten, boy! Did you learn your spelling last night? Do you expect me to believe that? What do you think, children? This lad's a joker if you ask me. How could anybody who *learnt* spelling get *two* out of *ten*?' She expected laughter. Some, trying to be obliging, tittered. 'Hold out your hand, boy!'

I was a coward, had to look away. I heard the swish of the bamboo and the child's yelp of pain and I shook. Her violence unnerved me. I feared that one day I might seize the cane from her hand and break it over her back.

'They don't bother about it as much as you do,' said

the ex-flyer. 'They're used to it, brought up to it, it's a way of life. You have to beat them or they'll think you're soft.'

They did not think of me as soft; they loved me, I knew they did. They waited for me at the bus stop in the mornings, round the corner of the school wall in the afternoon. They craved affection. Any fool could see that.

It was outrageous, said the commandant, for a teacher to walk along the road holding hands with pupils. 'It's got to stop, Miss Caldwell. The class is getting quite out of control.'

When I pinned up pictures on the walls they clustered round. 'This is the grand canyon, children, and this the mighty river Amazon in Brazil. One of these days I'll take you up the Amazon–'

'And just what is going on here?' We had neglected to keep watch. 'To your seats at once!' The children scattered. 'Ah, Miss Caldwell! I hadn't realized you were in the room.'

'I am not small,' I said, holding my head high.

'I would like a word afterwards, if you don't mind.'

Of course I minded but what was I to do? In the cupboard which she used as an office she told me she would have to ask the education authority to terminate my employment. One more chance, I pleaded, prepared to go down on to my knees. Please! I would promise anything, that I would be cool to the children, stand no nonsense, not let them take advantage or be my friend. One more chance, she said; the last one. But I had let the children too far and could not call them back. They went even further out of control like a car skidding on black ice and I, the driver, could not even keep hold of the wheel. A crash was inevitable. They ceased to listen when I talked and one day, provoked by one small demon, I lost my temper and slapped him hard across the face. There was total silence in the room. I burst into tears.

'Don't worry,' said my mother. 'I'm sure there must be something that would suit you better. What about the bank? Rosie seems to be doing well there.'

But I would not follow in Rosie's footsteps. I took to staying in bed late in the mornings, rising around noon; I bought doughnuts in the bakery where Magenta Lily no longer worked and ate them by the half-dozen.

'You'll get fat,' said my mother. 'Like Mrs Meneely.' That was meant to make me smile.

She 'worked' long hours for me, her lips moving as she read. Perhaps we needed a change? She had been wondering whether we should pack up and go and make our home with Aunt Belle in London. I went out and got a job in a solicitor's office.

The place was poky and dark, up a rickety stair. There was an elderly woman and the solicitor who was an elderly man and myself. We spoke no more than was necessary.

Rosie came tripping up the stairs bringing our bank statement. Her laugh broke up the gloom. The elderly man and elderly woman smiled. 'Meet me for lunch,' said Rosie. 'I hardly see you these days.' It was not my fault, I muttered, but she was gone, singing, back down the stairs and out into the street.

'What a nice girl,' said the elderly woman.

'A lovely girl,' said the solicitor. 'A ray of sunshine.' And then, astonished at having said so much, he picked up his pen and bent his head.

In the cracked mirror in the toilet, I saw that my face looked like the dark side of the moon.

Over lunch Rosie said, 'I'm so happy, Cora, you've no idea! I still can't believe it. That I should fall in love with Gerard Lavery! Can you believe it?'

Yes, I said, I could.

The days were drawing out, the daffodils and crocuses would be blooming at Hastings Court, soon the bluebells would come and make rivers of blue between the apple trees. Sweet lovers love the spring . . .

At four o'clock we had a cup of tea, the elderly woman and I, and she brought out the Coronation tin in which she kept the digestive biscuits. She raised the lid taking care not to put her fingers over the faces of the King and Queen. I saw myself forty years on, drinking tea, eating biscuits, with a young girl with her life ahead of her. No,

I lie, I did not see myself looking like that elderly woman, ever. I was only seventeen going on eighteen.

A man was waiting for me in a pool of darkness at the bottom of the stairs as I went down. For a moment my heart leapt and then I saw it was Tom Thorburn. Would I come and have a cup of tea with him? We went to Campbell's tea shop and he bought me tea and hot pancakes dripping with sugar and lemon. He ate nothing himself, smoked one cigarette and then another.

'How is Rosie? Do you know why she doesn't want to see me any more? Is there somebody else?'

He was dejected, miserable. I understood his state of mind, but could be of little help to him. I ate three pancakes and refused another not wishing him to think me greedy.

'She must be doing something. She's never at home when I call. They say she's having tea with friends . . .' He lapsed into silence. He left me to the bus stop. 'Tell her if ever – Well, just tell her–'

The trolley bus came.

I was to baby-sit that evening for Teresa who had been invited out by Dominic Quin. Bridie also had a date and Brian said he had other things to do than mind children. That was women's work.

'Are you sure now you don't mind, Cora? Do I look all right?' Teresa spun around in Rosie's red dirndl skirt and my white blouse.

'Have a good time,' I called after her. *Good time, good time* . . . The words echoed in my head.

I tidied up the living room. The older children were still playing outside, Paul and Anthony were supposed to be in bed. Paul slept, Anthony did not. He was a hyperactive child, then in his fourth year; he would not rest until he fell down exhausted. He ran up and down the stairs, he stamped his feet, he jumped and yelled and screamed until my head pounded. 'He'll try it on,' Teresa had said. 'Just smack his bottom and put him back into bed.' I was not successful in my attempt to follow her instructions; he suspected no doubt that my heart was not in my smack and lunged back at me catching me in the solar plexus and winding me. He was greatly amused. I straightened up. I hit him. He fell over catching the side of his head against the iron bedstead.

I sent Peter for the doctor who put three stitches in Anthony's temple. My mother, seeing the doctor's car, came hurrying.

'What happened, Cora?'

'She hit me,' said Anthony. 'Right there. Wham! She wanted to kill me so she did.'

'Don't upset yourself so,' said Teresa when she came home. (They'd been to a youth club dance and had a great time.) 'Sure you know Anthony is a right devil. I don't blame you for one minute and our father won't either. We've all wanted to kill Anthony before now.'

ELEVEN

A hired car had drawn up outside the portico of Hastings Court. Out had come a collection of trunks and boxes followed by a middle-aged man whose skin was yellowed from years spent in a hot climate. He had not been recognized by Gerard nor Marcellina, nor initially by Mrs Hastings-Smith. He had shaved off his moustaches since she had last seen him.

'Bertrand! Good gracious me, how the time has passed! Do come inside, boy, and Marcellina will make up your bed and bring us tea in the conservatory. And Gerard here – our estate manager – will take up your boxes. We manage on very few staff nowadays, I'm afraid. You will find that times have changed, Bertrand dear.'

Bertrand, having found post-Independence India not to his liking, had decided to come home.

'It is delightful to see him again of course,' said his mother, taking tea with my mother in our house. 'Though I must say I do find my days much more broken up. He is so restless, he cannot seem to leave well alone. It is those years in a hot climate, I daresay.'

Bertrand walked the length and breadth of his demesne carrying a tape measure and a notebook. Inside the house he went from room to room opening drawers, wardrobes, chests, windows.

'The place is freezing since Bertrand came,' said his mother. 'Draughts whistling up the corridors, doors banging in the wind. He does not seem to realize that this is not India.'

He questioned Marcellina about her spending and his mother about accounts.

'Accounts? Well, you know, Eileen, that I am not

money-minded. I have never cared for material things. I keep a few odd bills in the bureau drawer and I never neglect to pay any – I have never been in debt in my life – but as to keeping records . . .'

Bertrand was not satisfied by a few odd bills in the bureau drawer. Nor was he satisfied by Marcellina telling him she got money from the lady when she needed it.

'He asked me, Eileen, if I had any idea where the money went. What she did with it. She spends it on food, Bertrand, I told him, and coal for the fires. I also told him that I trust Marcellina totally; she has been with me for years. Of course I realize that it has been different for him in India with the coolies or whatever it is they have there. Very nice people they are I'm sure but just different standards. They do not keep the ten commandments for one thing.'

'They get their hands chopped off if they steal,' I said. 'That's if they're Muslims.'

'I am sure Bertrand would never chop off anybody's hand, dear,' said his mother. 'He was always a kind, gentle boy, even though he was not fortunate enough to be brought up in *Science*. I often wish I had come to it earlier myself so that he might have known it.'

'It is not always a guarantee though,' said my mother.

'Perhaps not, Eileen, but one must have faith that the seed sown early will not wither entirely, that it may lie dormant to blossom again.'

'More tea?' said I.

'Thank you, dear.' Mrs Hastings-Smith sighed. 'Poor Bertrand. The trouble is he cannot bring himself to face up to post-war Britain. He has to learn to adjust as we all have done. He keeps going on about dust and cobwebs and damp patches. He doesn't give poor Marcellina a minute's peace.'

Marcellina dusted and scrubbed, climbed ladders to disperse spiders' webs, washed windows that had never been cleaned in living memory, removed from drawers newspapers dated 1914. Gerard – there was to be no peace for him either – cleared his books from the library, trimmed the borders, weeded the drive and tilled the soil from dawn till dark.

'He wants his pound of flesh that one,' said Marcellina. 'Who does he think he is?'

Bertrand brought in men who crawled over the roof and tapped and banged on the walls. The tapping went on all day. Like a ghost house it was, said Marcellina, crossing herself.

One evening at dusk, Bertrand came to the conservatory.

'Mother, I must talk to you.'

'Of course, dear, any time. You know I am always delighted to listen.'

'Not this time though, I suspect.' He lifted a geranium and sat himself down on the bench. She only could see his face glimmering, and his hands. He lit a cheroot. He began to talk. The tip of the cheroot glowed, drew circles in the air. There was dry rot in the east wing, wet rot in the west, rising damp in the pantries, mildew in the scullery, woodworm in the rafters, a million holes in the roof, and trouble with the gutters. To say nothing of minor blemishes. Such a catalogue of woes. Such a pity Bertrand could not have known Christian Science for then he might have been prepared to look on the bright side and list the good things.

'After all, dear, the ground floor is perfectly dry, except when the rain is very heavy, and this conservatory is extremely warm. It catches the sun all day long. Look now, look at the sunset!'

But Bertrand would not look at the sunset. He said, 'The place is crumbling about our ears, Mother. We must get out.'

'He is thinking of selling, Eileen,' said his mother to my mother, complacently. 'But who would buy if there are as many faults as he says? People tend to get very excited about rot and things.'

The house went on the market. The picture looked imposing in the *Belfast Telegraph*, the *Irish Times* and *Country Life*. Prospective buyers came, and went. Marcellina was not tactful about the dry rot or the rising damp, though she did assure the viewers, whilst pointing out the affected areas, that one got used to such afflictions in time and the smells were bad only when it was damp or hot or the wind was from the west.

And then an American came. He had a soul, which put him above concern for rot, wet or dry; he had a feeling for the past; he had money.

'You'll need to watch that one,' said Marcellina to Mrs Hastings-Smith.

The American bought, lock, stock and barrel, not excluding the mouldering silks and satins, the leather tomes in the library, the chipped china, the antique gramophone, and the cracked records. He wanted to buy himself a complete past.

'I can't believe it, Eileen. It's Bertrand's birthright,' said his mother. 'What use is birthright, he said to me, if it's full of holes?'

Bertrand was kind though, would not put his mother in the street; he bought her a bungalow at Cherryvalley. He repacked his trunks and boxes and went off to make a new life in Rhodesia. The American offered Marcellina a job but she refused. She was not going to work for a Yank no matter how much dough he had. She married her not-so-young man who was not so not-so-young any more and enjoyed reminiscing about the good old days at Hastings Court.

And Gerard Lavery came back to live in the street.

You must help us, Cora, they said, you are our friend, our best friend. With the coming of Bertrand Hastings-Smith from India, the idyll of Rosie and Gerard was over. No more walking hand in hand through the orchard, no more dancing in the peacock room. We are in love, Cora, they said, we want to be together, what are we to do?

They spoke to me separately, each using different phrases; Rosie was more specific, more impassioned, whilst Gerard, quieter, used fewer words, but one could see that he meant what he said.

'What are we to do, Cora?' He looked tired, had quickly lost his out-of-doors look. He was baby-sitting. Teresa and Bridie had gone out on dates. I sat drinking tea with him at the kitchen table. He had other problems beside Rosie. The younger boys were wild and troublesome; he needed work, money, space to live in. Washing hung from a pulley over his camp bed at night and he had had to abandon his studies, at least in the meantime. Why not try for a job as a solicitor's clerk? I suggested.

He got one, in an office only a hundred yards from where I worked. My solicitor knew his, vaguely. 'Oh yes, Brady.' Brady was of course Catholic. We met in the street near our offices and exchanged notes. Our lives in office hours sounded identical. We talked too of Rosie, which was only to be expected. I carried messages from one to the other. I became the go-between.

After work they took buses to parts of the city where they knew no one, as far as they knew. They went to picture houses and saw the same film round twice; they drank vile coffee in sleazy cafés but did not care about the vileness; they ate fish and chips in horse-box chip shops. They moved around.

'It's quite exciting in a way,' said Rosie. 'But frustrating, too. We never seem to be properly alone.'

What about Cave Hill? I did not make the suggestion. When I stood at the edge of the Lough and looked across at the hill, I still felt revulsion, fear, disgust, sweep through me. I didn't really care about the loss of virginity itself, but it was the way in which it had gone that haunted me. It had been so ugly. But what disgusted me most of all was the thought of my stupidity. I did not often look at the hill.

'We can't go on like this much longer,' said Rosie. 'I wish I could get a room somewhere, on the other side of town.'

'Leave home?'

But in those days we did not think about leaving home, except to get married.

Rosie's eighteenth birthday passed off quietly. She stayed at home to placate her family and I went for tea.

'Just like the old days eh?' said Granny McGill. 'You and Rosie sitting side by side at the table.'

'It's a wonder they've no young men sitting with them though,' said Mrs Meneely, who still regretted the rebuff of Tom Thorburn. Rosie might not get a chance of someone in such a good position again. Cousin Deanna had got engaged and was saving to be married so if Rosie didn't hurry up she would find that *she* had to be Deanna's bridesmaid.

'They've plenty time,' said Uncle Sam, giving us a wink. He leant over the table to light the candles on the cake.

Rosie closed her eyes and made a wish, a long one, then, taking her time but not releasing her breath, she blew out every one of her eighteen candles. She should have been lucky!

'Bravo!' cried Uncle Sam. 'You've good puff in you, Margaret Rose.'

She wore a pink dress with a faint white stripe in it for her birthday. The sun gleamed in her hair. We each ate a slice of cake and then Mrs Meneely had another. She had to keep her strength up and it wasn't every day that her daughter was eighteen.

'Let's go for a walk, Cora!' said Rosie.

'You're a restless one right enough,' said Granny McGill. 'Can't sit still for two minutes.'

Rosie linked arms with me. We passed the Laverys' house and heard the sound of children – 'My poor Gerard, all those kids!' – and continued down the street towards the railway track. We saw no one on the path. The bank grew high with grasses and wild flowers. 'It's peaceful here,' said Rosie. 'Quiet. Not many people seem to come this way in the evening.' We came out at the local station and sat for a while on the seat among the sweet-smelling wallflowers.

A train puffed in and Deirdre Fish, with a young man holding her elbow, stepped out. 'Rosie, long time no see!' They greeted one another like long-lost friends encountered in the desert. I remained on the seat. 'This is Reginald, Rosie.' Deirdre laughed and squeezed his hand. He laughed and gave his other hand to Rosie. From the cut of his suit and the crispness of the cuffs showing at the jacket sleeves, one could tell that Reginald had a good position and did not sleep on a camp bed in the kitchen. 'We must see one another sometime, Rosie. What about making up a foursome? Why not come with us to the dinner dance at the Country Club on Saturday night?' 'Do come,' said Reginald, very smooth, very polite, his teeth glittering, 'it would be great fun.' 'I'll ring you,' said Rosie.

'It *could* be great fun,' said I, when Deirdre and Reginald had made their way laughing along the platform.

Rosie kicked me in the shin.

Why could she not have gone to the Country Club with Country Club men – she could have taken her pick – and left Gerard for me? Why, why, why? At night the question hammered in my brain. It tormented me to watch her happiness yet I could not stay away from her, for although I hated her, I still loved her.

She and Gerard, tired of trailing around the city, and becoming more complacent, began to take a few risks nearer home. They went to the Astoria Picture House and met up in the back row; they kissed, held hands and when the lights went up for the sale of ice cream they shifted over in their seats and looked the other way. They walked along the railway path when the light was leaving the sky.

At the end of June my mother went to stay with her sister Belle in London and, reluctant to have me sleep alone, asked Rosie to come and stay.

'Can I sleep in your little room? It might be better for you, Cora. I'm restless at nights and wouldn't want to keep you awake.'

After dark Gerard came to the back door. 'Is it all right? Rosie said to come.'

'Of course it's all right,' said Rosie behind me. 'Cora doesn't mind do you, Cora? Come in, love, come in before you're seen for goodness sake!'

He stayed with her until two. The sound of their love-making came through the thin wall. I buried my head under the pillow. When two had struck on the clock in the hall I heard the stairs creak. 'I love you.' Rosie's whisper, loud in the silent night, went after him. 'Come back tomorrow!'

'I don't know where our Gerard goes to at nights,' said Teresa. 'He comes back at two, three, four, last night it was five.'

'He must have a girl.'

'What kind of a girl would let him stay with her till that hour?'

Rosie said, 'I'm fond of your mother, Cora, but I wish she'd stay away for a month. It's going to be difficult to go back to the railway path.'

But my mother returned when expected. I went down to the docks to meet her off the Liverpool boat. Belle wanted us to come and live with her, she said; she had a nice terraced house in Islington which she'd picked up for little money. There was plenty of space and a Christian Science church not far away. Let's wait, I said, let's wait a bit and see . . .

The Lambeg drums were throbbing in the night, the 'Twelfth' was on its way.

'*It's ould but it's beautiful,*' sang Uncle Sam, '*its colours they are fine.*'

'Are you coming on the walk this year, Margaret Rose?' asked Uncle Billy.

'Not this year, no.'

'But you didn't come last year either.'

'Neither I did.'

'When will you come again?'

This year, next year, sometime, never . . .

Rosie shrugged.

Uncle Billy unfurled the Union Jack and hung it above the front door; Granny McGill put a vase of Sweet William and orange lilies in the front room window. Rosie came along to my house.

She said, 'What is going to become of us, Cora – Gerard and I? What are we to do?'

I supposed they could run away, to London or somewhere of the sort, though I wondered why *I* should tell them what to do.

Rosie said she was ready to go but Gerard was reluctant to leave his family. 'He says it wouldn't be fair on Tersea. I know it wouldn't but this isn't fair on me either.'

On the eleventh of July the bonfires were lit. The smell of smoke was in the air. The drums beat louder.

On the twelfth of July Uncle Sam, brushing off his bowler hat, said, 'You used to enjoy the Walk, Margaret Rose.'

Granny McGill, packing the picnic, said, 'What's got into you?'

Mrs Meneely, slicing, buttering, eating, said, 'And what are the two of youse going to do with youselves the day?'

'We might go for a picnic,' said Rosie. 'What about it, Cora? Yes, let's – I know where we'll go.'

We took the bus out into the country. We passed Orangemen going the other way with flag, pipe and drum. As the bus sped on the noise of the music receded. 'Thank God,' said Rosie.

Scaffolding covered the walls of Hastings Court, ladders stood about, tools lay abandoned. The workmen were off for the 'Twelfth', the American was in America. We went down into the orchard and spread our rug under the branches of an apple tree. Bees buzzed overhead, butterflies flitted, white, orange and yellow. 'It's so peaceful here,' murmured Rosie. 'I love this place.' She closed her eyes against the sun and slept, smiling as she dreamt, trembling a little. I, too, allowed sleep to tug me downward and I dreamt and when we simultaneously awoke we looked at one another wonderingly but stayed for a moment caught up in our separate dreams. Separate, conflicting dreams. But only I knew that.

Rosie sighed and opened the picnic basket.

In the early evening we returned to the city. Before we parted she asked if I would give Gerard a message.

I went into the Laverys' house. Teresa's eyes were red. 'What's up?' Nothing much, she said, and then told me that Dominic Quin had broken with her. She blew her nose. 'Ach well, I knew it couldn't last. I mean who would want to take me on with all this lot hanging about my neck?'

'Plenty men should,' I said so fiercely I made her smile.

Gerard came in but I had to wait until Teresa went into the back yard to see if the washing was dry before I could pass on Rosie's message.

'She said nine o'clock. And you'd know where.'

He nodded.

I had to go, I couldn't bear to look at the expression in his eyes, at the line of his mouth, at the way his hair curled on his head. I wanted to run my fingers through those curls and down his bare brown arms. I wanted to sit close to him at a table and talk, about religion, Ireland, anything. I wanted him!

The street was quiet; the Lavery children were playing elsewhere, the Orangemen had not yet returned. Mrs Hastings-Smith had come from Cherryvalley to visit my mother.

'It's not a day I'm fond of, Eileen, I have to confess. All that marching and drum banging. Cemented with love, their banners say. It is a great pity they are not more concerned with Divine Love.'

I sat by the window watching the street. Magenta Lily passed pushing a pram, then came Rebecca Cohen, gowned in yellow, flanked by a swain, holding his head high. The shadows lengthened.

At ten minutes to nine Gerard went by. He waved to me. 'Who's that you're waving to, Cora?' asked my mother. 'Nobody.' 'You can't wave to nobody.' 'Why not?' She and Mrs Hastings-Smith exchanged glances – I knew that they did, even though I did not turn my head – and then smiled reassuringly at one another. 'Would you like to come to tea with me at Cherryvalley one day, Cora?' 'Thank you,' I said and craned my neck to watch Rosie go. She wore a pale green dress and a ribbon in her hair. She seemed to float like a pale green feather.

'Have you heard from Bertrand?' asked my mother.

'Just a picture postcard. Looks very dusty there if you ask me. He said there was no dry rot and much less rain than in County Down.'

'Sounds as if he's liking it then.'

The street came suddenly to life: the Lavery children were back, running, skipping, yelling. Peter and Paul were fighting over a rubber tyre. The tyre swayed to and fro, the boys held on grimly as in a tug-of-war. Anthony ran up our path and squashed his nose against the glass close to my face. He left behind a trail of snot. He laughed triumphantly.

'Little imp,' said my mother.

A car turned the corner and stopped at the McGills' door. Out got the family, their Sunday best looking a little crushed after the long day at the 'Field'.

'I think I'll go out,' I said vaguely.

'Don't be long then,' said my mother. 'It'll be getting dark soon.'

Uncle Sam was standing at his gate, the others had gone in. 'Do you know where our Margaret Rose is?'

I shook my head. 'Did you have a good time?'

'It was great altogether. You missed yourselves, you and Rosie.'

As I approached the gate leading to the railway path, I saw Deanna come out with her intended. She was talking intently and wagging her head about, he was listening. They did not notice me. Sweet lovers love the railway path . . .

It was darker in there, with the bank closing off one side. Bushes cast green-black shadows. Something moved. Only a night animal. The scents were the scents of night, sharp and pungent. Now a man in a flat cap was coming towards me. I felt my heart-beat quicken, the palms of my hands begin to sweat. As we drew level each drawing slightly to the side, he looked me up and down and for a moment I thought he would accost me, then he seemed to think better of it and his stride picked up again. If he had stopped what would I have done? If I had screamed would Rosie and Gerard have come running to save me? Or would they be too absorbed in one another to hear? Where were they anyway? I walked the entire length of the path to the station and half-way back again. And then I caught a sound.

I crept up the bank, grasping clumps of grass to steady myself, and looked down the other side. There they lay sprawled, locked together. Her head was flung back, its green ribbon trailing, just discernible in the fading light; her pale arms were around him, her pale legs also. They were moving; the bank was moving; the earth was moving.

I lost my grip. As I slipped I tried to regain it but could not. I felt the coarse grass lacerating my hands.

I landed on the path with a judder which went right up into my skull. I heard Rosie give a little scream – not of terror – but of pleasure. Then she laughed. 'Gerard!' She said his name. 'Sh!' he said and she laughed again as if she could not stop.

TWELVE

I lay in bed with the sheet pulled over my head. I thought I could hear Rosie crying.

'Cora!' My mother was calling. 'Come down please, Cora.'

I got up. I looked at my hands. The palms were streaked with fine red lines. I put them under my armpits and went downstairs.

My mother was in the back living room with Rosie telling her she would be all right, and that the peace of God was with her. Rosie's pale green dress was torn, her nose was bleeding, her hair had lost its ribbon. Her chest rose and fell; only the sound of her breath came from between her half-open lips. My mother asked me to make tea while she washed Rosie's face and brushed her hair. Her hands were soft and gentle. Mine burned with pain.

Rosie drank the tea, subsided, but the terror stayed in her eyes. Suddenly she spoke.

'They'll kill him!'

I thought my heart would stop.

'Who will, dear?' asked my mother.

'Uncle Billy and Uncle Sam.'

In their church-going Lodge-going no-longer-dance-hall-going suits, their hair slicked down with Brilliantine.

'I'm sure they wouldn't dream of killing anybody,' said my mother soothingly.

'They've gone after him!'

With their wide shoulders and big hands, and firm flat-footed steps.

'After who, dear?'

'Gerard. Oh God, *Gerard*.'

'Lavery,' said I, speaking for the first time.

My mother was silenced.
'They'll kill him, I know they will!'
They did not kill him though they left him for dead, concussed, bleeding from ears, nose, mouth, with an arm and three ribs broken, and the hearing in his right ear impaired for life. He was found by a man walking his whippet on the railway path.
Rosie was claimed by her two closest female relatives. They came for her, her mother and her grandmother, to our front door. They would not come into the living room, remained in the hall with the door left open at their backs letting in a cool night breeze which made me shiver.
'Margaret Rose, you are to come home at once!'
'I don't want to come.'
'We are telling you to!'
'Look at you! Look at your dress!'
'Uncle Billy tore my dress–'
'Don't tell lies now, Margaret Rose!'
'You're no better than a hoor.'
'It would have been bad enough if it had been with one of our own but a Taig–'
'I love him!'
'You're out of your mind.'
'You've brought shame on our house.'
The house of a Worshipful Grand Master of the Loyal Orange Lodge.
It's ould but it's beautiful . . .
'Come home when you're told!'
'I want to go to Gerard.' But her voice was weak. She knew that what she wanted she could not have. 'What have they done to him?'
'Nothing at all,' said Mrs McGill, eyeing my mother. 'They've just had a word with him for his own good.'
'They'll kill me too.'
'Don't talk nonsense, Margaret Rose. Sure you know they'd never lay a finger on you, they never have. That dress getting tore was just an accident. They love you as if you were their own. And *this* is how you betray them.'
Rosie cried then went home. We urged her to stay with us, my mother and I, but she had lost her fire and

resistance. She allowed the women to take her by the arms. She looked like a rag doll between them.

'I'll see you in the morning, Rosie,' I said. I was not to see her for several years.

At first light Rosie and her mother left the street for a destination not to be revealed to anyone outside the family. 'She's gone to relatives to take a wee rest,' said Granny McGill. 'She was overwrought so she was. Sure you could see that for yourself. She's a high strung girl is our Margaret Rose. And Cora, we'll ask you to say nothing to nobody about all this. For Margaret Rose's sake. We know you won't.' I gave her my promise. And I intended to keep it since it was in my own interest to do so, but with Teresa I failed.

'Holy Mother of God save us!' cried Teresa when the police arrived to tell them about Gerard. They came in the morning, after he had regained consciousness, and took Teresa and her father back with them in the car to the hospital. I waited by the window until they returned.

'Who would do that to our Gerard, Cora?' Teresa looked as if she had been punched between the eyes. 'He hasn't an enemy in the world so he hasn't. He didn't see them, he says, they came up behind him.' That could not be true: they would have met face to face as he came along the path. And Rosie would have screamed, called their names.

'Rosie–'

'What *about* Rosie? Was he with her, Cora? You know, recently I've had a funny feeling– He *was* with her, wasn't he?'

How could I deny it when she saw the answer in my face?

'So it was her uncles that did it! Well, I'm going to see that they pay for it! And that she pays for it and all too!'

'Don't, Teresa, please don't! Wait – you can't blame Rosie–'

'I hate her! Why couldn't she have left our Gerard alone? Any fool could have seen there'd be trouble.'

'He could have seen that too.'

But she was for her brother of course over Rosie who

was only her blood sister by smearing of their blood together. She fumed against Rosie and then she cried. I cried too.

'Ah, Cora,' she said, 'what will become of us?'

Everything would calm down, given time, I told her. We must give it time, we must stay calm. We must not say anything that would make the situation worse. I tried to speak unemotionally. I felt the tremor in my bottom lip.

'I'll need to talk to Gerard about it,' said Teresa.

Gerard did not want charges brought against anyone and he did not want Rosie to be involved.

'He made me promise to keep his secret. He loves her, Cora.'

'I know.'

'But he says it's over now.'

My spirit lifted, just a little. He might love me yet, might come to realize that with Rosie it had only been physical infatuation. I had to comfort myself in whatever way I could.

'It galls me to see those McGills getting away with it!' cried Teresa, as we watched Billy McGill go up the street with a jaunty step, a dark bruise flowering on his right cheek.

But Mr Lavery and his sons were not for letting the matter drop. They had their suspicions, perhaps not about Rosie, but about her uncles. 'Who else in the street would lift a hand to us?' said Mr Lavery. 'Sure everyone else was as decent as anything when my poor wife died.' Brian spat in the McGills' driveway when he passed, Peter and Paul chanted, 'Murderers, murderers!' and Anthony threw a stone that cracked the front room window. He danced with glee on the pavement.

'Hallions, the lot of youse!' cried Granny McGill. 'We'll have the polis on you.' But even they were not so cool that they could do that. Mr Lavery and his brother, with a drink or two in them, called on Uncle Sam at his shop. They bolted the door behind them as they went in and pulled down the blind.

'You bloody blackmouth! You near killed my son didn't you?'

Uncle Sam, by his account, tried to reason with them and tell them they'd got the wrong man. Mr Lavery, by his, said that Sam McGill had admitted his guilt straight-away and told them it was because his son was fucking their niece that they'd done it. Mr Lavery and his brother wrecked the shop hurling shoes, leather, tools, polishes, in every direction, and gave Uncle Sam two black eyes that shone for a week or more in the street afterwards.

So that was it then: tit for tat, an eye for an eye, or almost. The score was not quite levelled. Both sides retired, in the meantime, cursing.

'By God, we'll send those Fenians back to where they belong before we're done,' said Billy McGill. 'Or somewhere else they'll like even less!'

'We'll get those fuckers yet,' said Brian Lavery.

'Enough,' said Mr Lavery wearily.

His eldest son did not want to come home; he went to convalesce with an aunt on the Falls Road. He lost his job. Mr Brady was regretful but business was business and couldn't wait for anybody.

'It's not fair,' cried Teresa. 'None of it.'

On the gable end wall of the McGills' house somebody wrote with yellow chalk: *Rosie Meneely is a blackmouth hoor.*

A letter came postmarked Ballymena.

Dearest Cora, wrote Rosie, *you are the best and only friend I've got – I suppose I can't count Teresa now though I wish I could? How I wish you were here so that I could talk to you: I am so lonely and so unhappy.*

We are staying with two ghastly great-aunts. I am tempted to run away but where could I run to? I know you and your mother (how kind she is!) would have me but that would hardly do. Your house is too close for comfort.

How is Gerard? Please write to me poste restante . . .

I tried to write but could not. It was as if my hand were paralysed.

It would not work when I was at my desk in the dark

poky office either. I sat staring at my fingers clenching the pen and at the opened ledger in front of me. The lines wriggled and jiggled before my eyes like writhing snakes. I shrank back from them. I dropped the pen.

The elderly woman said I should see a doctor. The elderly man said he was sorry but he could not employ someone who could not write.

Another letter came, with an envelope enclosed. *Please would you give this to Gerard for me? I go to the post office every day hoping to hear from you . . .*

I held the letter in my hand, tempted to destroy it, but my conscience could take no more and so I passed it to Teresa. She, too, suffered in making her decision; she kept the letter for a day and a night guarding it closely and then burnt it.

'It's for the best, Cora.' She was miserable. 'They couldn't start all that up again. What would become of us if they did?'

The burned letter rested on her conscience weighing her down – she justified the burning of it to me for hours – but at least she could go to Father Flynn and confess and receive absolution. He might not even think it was a sin, might praise her for her good sense.

'I envy you being able to go to confession.'

'You're joking! You've always said you couldn't stomach it.'

'Maybe I didn't have any real sins to bother about then,' I said, as if I were making a joke.

We saw each other every spare minute that we had; we sat in my bedroom with the door closed and talked about Rosie and about Gerard, together and separately, and when Teresa was busy I followed her about her house helping, still talking all the time. She helped preserve my sanity for a limited time.

Father Flynn came in when I was ironing Mr Lavery's shirts. He praised my industry, said it was nice to see me being so neighbourly. He lit his pipe and settled himself in the only chair that had any springs left.

'Father,' I began tentatively and then went on in a rush

for Teresa would be back in once she'd hung up the clothes, 'if you repent of a sin is that enough to clear you?'

'Depends on what you mean, Cora, by being cleared?'

'Forgiven.' The word seemed to stick half way up my throat.

'By whom? Yourself? Or God?'

'Oh God,' I answered quickly. I could never hope to forgive myself.

'Well, that's not so easy now. In our faith you'd have to come to a priest–'

'But I'm not of your faith.'

'Quite so. I daresay though that if you pray with your whole heart and ask forgiveness then the good Lord would forgive you. He is a compassionate God, moved by love.' He spoke with ease. Of course he believed.

'You would have to believe in God first though wouldn't you?'

'That goes without saying. And you would have to promise not to commit the sin again.'

'Oh I never would!'

'You know, in the end though, Cora, it's a matter for your own conscience.'

That saddened me.

Father Flynn said quietly, 'You can tell me what's on your mind if you want, child. As a priest I would never divulge it.'

'Oh no, I couldn't!'

'Well, remember if you ever do–'

Teresa came in pushing the door open with her hip; against the other she carried the empty zinc bath. Through the open door I saw the clothes fluttering, caught by a good drying wind. They made a flapping noise which seemed to be trapped inside my head. To drown it out I began to sing a song. *The maid was in the garden hanging out the clothes when down came a blackbird . . .*

'Sing a song of sixpence eh, Cora?' said Father Flynn. I stopped. I had not meant to sing aloud. He said to Teresa, 'Aren't you a grand wee mother now? I wish all the women in the parish were as hard-working and efficient as you.'

'Get away with you, Father! You're just wanting a cup of tea.'

He laughed.

I got up to put the kettle on.

Polly put the kettle on . . .

'What is that you're singing, dear?'

Polly put the kettle on . . .

'Yes, we could do with a cup of tea. We can have some of my cherry cake with it. Mrs Hastings-Smith said she would drop in. That will be nice won't it?'

Sukey take it off again . . .

'You used to sing that song when you were small! But I was thinking, Cora, that you ought to look for another job. Mr MacAndrew – you remember him at church? – he was saying that *he* might–'

Sukey take it off again . . .

'You need to take up some of your interests again, dear. You hardly even read these days – that's not like you!'

They've all gone away . . .

I caught the bus in the city centre. Funny really to say caught for it didn't run away from me, it just sat there beside the City Hall looking like any other Belfast bus. I watched the driver wind the name plate through all the city destinations until FALLS ROAD came up and then I jumped on to the running board.

'Where to, love?'

I wasn't sure. The conductor said with a grin that I must be going somewhere. 'Oh yes,' I agreed, 'I am,' and added: 'Half way up'll do.' *The grand old Duke of York he had ten thousand men and when he was up he was up and when he was down he was down and when he was only half way up he was neither up nor down.*

The bus lumbered on, entering territory unknown to me. Snatches of song came into my head. *And on the Twelfth I'll always wear the Sash my Father wore.* People seemed to be quiet around me, the woman in front was looking over her shoulder. I slid down in my seat trying to make myself as small as possible. A priest got on and sat on the other half of my seat, the edge of his black skirt brushing my leg. I jumped, not because of his clothes touching me but because for a moment I thought he was Father Flynn. 'Sorry,' I muttered.

'That's all right,' he said comfortably and moved the skirt off my leg.

I looked out of the window.

If you were the only boy in the world and I was the only girl . . .

FALLS ROAD. The words leapt out at me from a brick wall. I sprang up. 'Excuse me,' I said clambering across the priest's black knee. 'This isn't half way up yet,' objected the conductor, pulling the cord. It was far enough, I said, and made a dive for the pavement without waiting for the bus to come to a full halt. I landed awkwardly just missing an old woman pushing a pramful of washing.

'I'm sorry, I'm so sorry.' I clutched at the edge of the pram setting it rocking.

'Want to kill yerself?'

'Maybe.'

Steering the pram well away from me she continued up the street. She looked back once or twice.

I was a stranger in a strange land. The names on the shops were Catholic names: Flynn, O'Brien, Murphy, Quin; the scrawled slogans told different tales to those on the walls of East Belfast: GOD BLESS THE POPE, UP THE IRA, REMEMBER 1916.

If I'd a penny do you know what I'd do?
I'd buy a rope –

Was I singing aloud again? I clamped my hand over my mouth.

I went into a shop, a small corner one that sold everything from milk to firelighters. The woman was sorting the evening papers. A spiral of smoke rose from the corner of her mouth. Would she know a Mrs Doyle by any chance? Mrs Doyle? She didn't take the cigarette from her mouth. There were dozens of Doyles in these parts. What was her Christian name?

'Mary.'

Mary, Mary, quite contrary,
How does your garden grow?

She shook her head spraying ash across the newsprint.

I wandered on, up one narrow street and down another. They all looked alike with the houses on either side terraced, brick, back-to-back, opening straight on to the pavement. Children were playing, jumping chalk marks, kicking tin cans, swinging ropes. *One, two, three a-leerie* . . . They eyed me. They knew I was an intruder.

On a corner stood a priest. I waved to him, called. He turned. It might have been the one from the bus. 'Could you help me please?' Only too pleased: that was what he said. When I told him I was looking for a Mrs Mary Doyle he smiled and said of course he knew her, she had three children, one grown up, was that the one? I believed so. 'Has she a nephew called Gerard who's come lately to stay with her?'

'Indeed she has.' He sighed. 'That was a bad business.'

I agreed: a very bad business.

'Nice lad too.'

He gave me directions, told me to take the first left, the second right, and set me on my way holding his arm and finger out at right angles like a signpost. I took the first left and then I stopped for on the opposite side of the road, with his head bandaged and his arm in a sling, stood Gerard Lavery talking to a boy. I had not visualized him bandaged, a wounded man. I saw a black boot kicking him in the head. I saw him lying on the railway path in a pool of blood. I heard him groaning. I covered my ears with my hands. I backed away, keeping close to the brick wall.

Once I had rounded the corner I began to run and came full tilt into the priest again. He caught me in his arms, held me against his black chest. 'Steady there!' He laughed. 'You're going in the wrong direction.'

But I was going in no direction at all.

Here we go round the mulberry bush, the mulberry bush . . .

The priest drove me home in his stuffy wee car that smelt of incense and tobacco smoke. I had to roll down the window. 'Aye, do that,' he said, 'take a breath of air to yourself, it'll do you a power of good, we'll have you home in no time. Ballyhackamore did you say?'

As we turned into the street we passed Uncle Sam and Uncle Billy stepping out in their navy-blue church-going Lodge-going suits. Uncle Billy's eyes bulged like a frog's when he saw me. I waved.

Do you think that I would ever let
A dirty Fenian cat . . .

'Now it's all right, lass. Just keep hold of yourself. What number is it? Seven? That's a grand number – a holy number. Ah, this looks like your mother herself.'

Before we left Belfast, my mother wrote to Rosie. She left the letter lying on the table while she went to pay the insurance man. *. . . I know Cora would want to write to you but she is not quite herself at the moment. There is nothing to worry about however. She is just in need of a change. As you know I have for a long time had it in my mind to go and live with my sister Belle in London. I feel sure that once there she will pick up quickly.*

I hope you are back to your old self and feeling happier. It would not have been possible, you know, for you to have made a life with Gerard Lavery. Too much stood against it. And he has his faith while you have yours. We think of you often, dear child, and pray for your happiness. You must come to visit us whenever you see the way clear to do so . . .

'Thanks very much, Mr Taylor,' said my mother. 'No, we won't be here next week.'

Now is the hour
That we must say goodbye . . .

'That's a silly song,' said my mother brightly, as she

came back into the room holding the Insurance book. The tips of her fingers curled round biting into the faded green cover. 'I never did care much for Gracie Fields.'

THIRTEEN

It took six months for me to come through the worst stage. Afterwards, my mother laughingly said that she didn't want to hear another song, popular or Orange, for the rest of her life. They were my chief means of communication during that time, if they could be called that. Tunes and jingles ran through my head incessantly, driving me mad.

I've got you under my skin . . .

'Try to substitute other thoughts for them, dear.'

What about there is no sin, disease or death? I could get no further than sin.

I'm wild again, beguiled again,
A simpering, whimpering child again,
Bewitched . . .

'Know thyself,' said my mother, reading from the Bible, 'and God will supply the wisdom and occasion for a victory over evil.'

I did know myself, very well, too well, wished that I knew myself less so that I need not sing so much to drown the knowledge out, but God – wherever he was or whatever else he was doing – did not supply me with any victories. Nor did I expect him to since I no longer believed in his existence.

'There is no God,' I told my mother.

She worked and prayed for me, as did Mrs Hastings-Smith back in her bungalow in Cherryvalley. They corresponded regularly and my mother read aloud her letters, or the parts she thought I might find interesting. She tried everything to take my mind off myself.

Bertrand seems to be settling in his new country. He says it is a land of opportunity. He sends me postcards of wild animals. I do hope he is not hunting them.

I am having a conservatory built on to the back of my bungalow modelled on the one at Hastings Court. Rather large the man said – it would take up half the garden. Who cares about that? I shall be creating a garden inside. So nice to be amongst plants I always think.

Tell Cora that God is watching over her and not to despair . . .

I had no hope for anything so there seemed no reason to despair.

It was my mother and Aunt Belle who despaired more. I saw it in their faces when I came into the room surprising them. They would stop in mid-sentence and look at me with pain that I had to turn and go out again.

I spent much time outside. Singing my songs, I tramped the streets of London. I walked with my head down, not stopping to look into glittering shop windows, or stare at some fine building which was vaguely familiar. Everything seemed vague except the songs in my head. I sang of the old Orange flute and the sash whose colours they were fine, of buying a paper doll that I could call my own, of the bluebirds that would soon be over the white cliffs of Dover, of the mountains of Mourne that sweep down to the sea, of the last rose of summer.

'Would you mind, dear?'

I had come into a church – how I had got there I did not know. I did not remember leaving the street, climbing the steps. But, suddenly, I became aware of candles flickering and choir boys singing. Their high sweet voices soared up to the roof, to heaven itself. Perhaps this *was* heaven. Perhaps I had passed on. Died. For I believed in death.

But no, it would not be heaven – there would be no place there for me.

It only happens when I dance with you . . .

'Shush!' said another voice.

'Can I not sing too?'

'Best to stay quiet and listen,' said the first voice, which had been gentler than the second.

Not trusting myself, I stuffed a handkerchief into my mouth. I did not trust myself in any place or with any person.

After two months Belle said, 'We can't go on like this, Eileen. Why don't we try a psychiatrist? It's not a case of taking medicine. He works on the principle that it's all in the mind, which is what you believe in too, in a different sort of way.'

Belle took me to a man with a bald head. The sun shone on it making the skin look polished.

'Would you like to sing something for me?' he asked.

I shook my head. Why should I sing for him?

'For yourself then?'

I could sing inside my head.

I wonder who's kissing her now.
I wonder who's showing her how . . .

He waited. He knew how to wait. I knew how to sing inside my head. Someone talked in another room making a burble of sound. Between songs I yawned.

'Your aunt tells me that you often sing songs about King Billy?'

I leant across his desk and asked, 'Who's the good man?'

'I don't know. You tell me.'

'King Billy.'

'Ah.'

'What does King Billy ride? You don't know do you?'

'No, I'm afraid I don't.'

'A white horse. Where's the white horse kept?'

'Where?'

'In the Orange Hall. And where's the Orange Hall?'

'Well?'

'Up Sandy Row! And who's the bad man?'

He waited.

'The Pope!'

'Ah-hah! So you're a fan of King Billy's are you?'

'No, I hate him!'

'And the Pope?'

I shuffled my feet.

'Well, let us talk about King Billy then. I'm not very clued up on history, but he was William of Orange wasn't he, married to Mary? And he fought at the Boyne?'

> *'Here am I a loyal Orangeman, just come*
> *across the sea . . .'*

I sang the song right through, tapping my foot in time to the rhythm.

'That's a very stirring song. Who taught you that, Cora?'

'Uncle Billy.'

'So there is an *Uncle* Billy too? Married to your Aunt Belle?'

'No, he's Rosie's uncle.'

'And who is Rosie?'

Who is Rosie? What is she?

I told him. 'And then there's Teresa. Now *she* blesses the Pope.'

'Rosie and Teresa–'

'And me.'

'And where do you come in?'

'Pig in the middle.'

I drew a map on his blotting paper of our street showing where each of our houses were and marked our shed with a cross.

'Tell me.'

He listened carefully to all that I had to say, nodding his shiny head, but otherwise remaining very still. His hands rested on either side of his blotting pad.

In the course of two months we progressed through my life and then when we came to the year that Gerard Lavery went to live at Hastings Court, I stopped dead.

He was no fool, he knew that we had reached the crucial part. 'Gerard Lavery,' he said, 'brother of Teresa.' He made a steeple with his hands. I made one too, with my hands.

This is the church and this the steeple, turn them inside out and you have the people.

'Quite so. Cora, do you know what your problem is?'
'Yes.'
'Then tell me.'
I told him.
'Why didn't you tell me before?'
'You didn't ask.'
'Why haven't you told anyone before? Your mother? Your aunt?'
I covered my face with my hands, not wanting it to be seen.
'Look at me, Cora! Uncover your face.'
I uncovered a patch round one eye so that I could see him. The shine on his head dazzled my eyes and my head ached.
'You must forgive yourself,' he said.
When I left him I went into a café and sat in a dark corner to drink a cup of coffee. I felt drained. I did not feel like singing.
On my next visit he said, 'You underestimate yourself. And on the other hand, you expect too much. You cannot expect to behave like a saint. You must realize that to sin is normal.'
That made me smile a little.
'What else troubles you, Cora?'
'Got a year to spare?'
'Yes, if necessary, I have.'
I began to pick up, as my mother called it, with the psychiatrist's help, and perhaps too through her prayers and those of Mrs Hastings-Smith. I would not discount them.
I made friends with an anthropology student who rented a room at the top of our house. She gave me books to read and we talked, often until late into the night. I began to go to the library, I visited museums and art galleries, I went with my mother and aunt to the theatre. 'So nice to see you taking an interest again,' said my mother.
But I still needed the man whose head shone in the sun. My weekly visit was like an oasis that I kept my eyes fixed on up ahead. Every Wednesday at three. The confessional

hour. Eventually I told him about the man on Cave Hill. He did not have to drag the incident up from the depths of my sub-conscious; it had remained very much in my conscious mind, haunting me, making me feel tainted. Unclean. He told me of course that I did not need to feel that – and I had known that he would – since it was *I* who had been wronged.

'But I was so stupid!'

'Try to stop punishing yourself, Cora. Be kind to yourself. Work at it.'

'Habits die hard,' I said and he smiled and said he didn't think he had much to tell me.

'You seem to be almost your old self again, Cora,' said Belle. 'Perhaps you'll be able to stop your treatment soon.'

Panic caught me like a hand at the throat. I protested.

'We wouldn't like you to become dependent.'

'And there's the question of money too,' said my mother gently. 'We were just talking, Belle and I, about the possibility of you going to university.'

I went to say goodbye to him.

'You'll be all right,' he said. 'I have faith in you. Now just try to have faith in yourself.'

'I find faith difficult.'

'I know. You need to believe.'

I felt desolate as I walked home. I had lost another friend.

When I got home I wrote to Teresa telling her that I was applying to go to London University the following year to read anthropology. *I feel it would bring a number of strands together that I'm interested in. And it will give me a chance to travel. You know I've always wanted that.* I wrote a similar letter to Rosie. I wrote regularly to them both, external sorts of letters about London and Aunt Belle's house, revealing nothing of my inner life. I did not mention the man whose head shone in the sun.

They both wrote back regularly. Teresa's letters were filled with family news which was all she had to write about. She couldn't indulge herself as I did, walking miles through the city, sitting for hours in libraries absorbed by adolescent behaviour patterns in the South Seas.

Bridie was engaged and saving to be married, Mary (now thirteen) was proving a splendid help in the house (being told by Father Flynn that she'd make a grand wee mother?), the boys were in and out of trouble, as usual. Teresa was resigned about that. *I get a note home every other day from the school. And the police were here yesterday. Anthony was caught climbing over the back wall behind the butcher's shop. I doubt if he was going to pinch a leg of lamb! Just don't get into anything* serious, *I tell them.* Mr Lavery seemed to be home less and less. Teresa was vague – late hours at the shop. (And in the pub no doubt.) Gerard had found a job in another solicitor's office and was attending night school. And the headaches which had plagued him since his attack were getting better. Teresa said little about herself except to tell me what book she was reading or that she'd bought wool to knit herself a jumper.

'Poor girl,' said Belle. 'It's not much of a life.'

'I wouldn't say she was unhappy though,' said my mother.

And neither would I. Teresa didn't seem to be cut out for unhappiness, in spite of the hardship and sorrow in her life, but I didn't attribute it to her faith, not totally anyway, for many Catholics are unhappy.

Rosie's letters were, predictably, much less domestic and contained more drama. I opened each one quickly, often ripping the envelope in two with my clumsy fingers.

Not long after we came to London she left Ballymena and returned to Belfast, though not to her family home. *It was out of the question to go back* there! *To live with* them. *You'd have to be joking! I'd go to Purdysburn first. (The mental hospital – then so-called.) I've got a room above a greengrocer's shop off the Antrim Road. It smells of rotting cabbages and diseased spuds, the linoleum's disgusting and the walls look like porridge spew but it's* mine *and I can do what I want and* they *can't stop me.*

What would she want to do?

'She's a survivor is Rosie,' said my mother.

I've got a job serving in a baby linen shop. Can you imagine me selling matinee jackets and bootees? No, neither can I. I'm going to go and see the bank manager to have me back.

He did of course. He sent her to be trained on the latest calculating machines and afterwards she was put to work in the ledger department which she liked less than walking the streets of Belfast carrying statements. But inside the bank she ran less risk of bumping into Gerard. Did she want to see him? She didn't say. She avoided mentioning his name directly, referred only once to *all that business*, as if it were over and done with. And I didn't mention his name in my letters either. She did write about Teresa, saying that she would like to see her but realised that it might be better not, at least until everyone had settled down and the wounds closed up a bit. *If they ever will.* I stared at the words until they danced on the page. *But send me word of Teresa, Cora, please. I want to know how she is.* And so I became a clearing house for news and that way they stayed in touch.

'It's good to keep in touch with old friends,' said Belle who seemed not to have kept in touch with any of hers. She and my mother went everywhere together, except church. 'I have nothing against Christian Science,' said Belle, 'but I cannot quite believe in it.' Anyway, she was partial to lying in bed on Sunday mornings.

Sunday mornings, wrote Rosie, *are the worst time. The whole God-damned place goes to church – as you well know. And afterwards everybody comes home for their roast lunch which lays them flat and then the place is dead. As a door-nail. It's like walking through a graveyard. Sometimes I stay in bed all day and eat Black Magic and read Georgette Heyer. Does that strike you as wicked? It doesn't strike me as wicked enough, that's the trouble.*

'She'll make new friends soon enough,' said my mother. 'As you will, once you go to university.'

University life suited me.

'You were always a bookworm of course,' said my mother, exchanging a look of satisfaction with Belle.

I made several acquaintances and one good friend, Imelda. She was Southern Irish. Her family had a country house in Wicklow and a flat in Dublin. They were rich. And Catholic. We became friends quickly and easily; there was no reason why we should not, and we had much in common. We talked about religion. I told her about my Protestant friend who had gone out with a Catholic boy.

'God, the fuss they make about it in the North! You wouldn't find that in the South.'

'Your parents wouldn't mind if you married a Prod?'

'Not as long as he turned.' She laughed. She showed even white teeth when she laughed and her dark eyes flashed with amusement. I seldom saw Imelda look dejected. Her life had been a straightforward, comfortable affair and after she graduated she went back to Dublin where she married a wealthy business man (Catholic of course), lived in a fine country house outside the city, had two children (none of that business about being anti-contraceptives, they could be bought on visits to London), and played the harp at private concerts.

I told Rosie about Imelda when I wrote but she showed no interest when she replied, any more than I did in the girls she was friendly with at the bank. She had moved to a better room near the university. This one was odourless, or almost. She thought it likely that all rented rooms smelt. Her mother came occasionally to see her, usually to beseech her to return home and all would be forgiven. *I don't want to be forgiven. Why the hell should I?*

One day Uncle Sam arrived asking to be forgiven. *I wasn't going to let him in to begin with, I just stood there staring at him and then he broke down. It was awful. He was blubbering like a baby. I had to take him in to get him off the street and away from Mrs Poke-Pry's eyes. 'Do you know the gentleman, Miss Meneely?' she asked, trying to speak ever so genteel. Old bitch was dragged up in the gutter – it's stamped on her. God, landladies! 'Never set eyes on him,' I told her and linking arms took him up to my room.*

Rosie forgave Uncle Sam, perhaps not completely, but enough to ease him. *What else could I do, Cora? There we were weeping tears by the bucketful together. He said he hadn't wanted to do anything to Gerard except tell him off for going with me, no more. In fact, he didn't do any more than that. It was my sweet Uncle William who beat Gerard up. Uncle Sam just stood by and watched.*

Just. That was a crime in itself, and Rosie knew it.

'She did right to forgive him, though,' said my mother.

'You'd even forgive Billy wouldn't you?'

'Not unless he repented.'

Shortly after Rosie wrote that letter Tom Thorburn sought her out. *He's nice, Cora. I always liked him. I may even marry him.*

They were married, quietly, with only his parents present, in the autumn of 1954, when Rosie was twenty.

FOURTEEN

The following year Teresa married in Dublin. I went over for the wedding. I travelled with Imelda and we spent a few days first at her parents' house in Wicklow. The country house was substantial and plush (no tarnished silver here, no wet rot in the west wing, no buckets strategically placed to catch persistent drips), the lawns were smooth and emerald green, the maids red-cheeked and country-born. Imelda's parents were lovers of horses and whisky. They were relaxed and easy to be with. They made me welcome but were not really interested in me. Those low-keyed days helped me to steady myself for the wedding of Teresa.

'I can't get used to the idea of her marrying,' I said to Imelda as we walked in the Garden of Ireland with two glossy red setters. I had forgotten grass could be so green and so soft underfoot – my eyes had adjusted to grey city streets, my feet to hard pavements. Teresa would be leaving our street in Belfast, the last of the three of us to go. The Laverys had sold their house, were moving back to the Falls.

'Not getting married is not on,' said Imelda. 'Well, I mean to say – who wants to be labelled a spinster? What an image that conjures up! Interlock knickers and mothballs. There are a few of them round here and what lives they lead! The odd ones out at parties unless poor old Jack or Toby who is a hundred-and-two and missing a leg can be raked up. Everybody's sorry for you. I've no intention of letting that happen to me.' She called the dogs to heel.

I reflected that it was four years since I had seen Teresa. 'And her brother,' I added, trying to speak lightly.

Imelda came up to Dublin with me, to the Georgian

flat her parents owned in a quiet square. They came there but seldom, only when absolutely necessary.

She drove me to the church. Dark-suited men with artificial flowers in their lapels and feathered and crimplened women were climbing the steep steps. The church was raised on high. I remembered the one near Hastings Court and the smell of that early morning. I remembered Marcellina's thick red legs. I remembered running. 'I wish you were coming with me, Imelda.' She revved up the engine and told me not to be a coward. 'On you go now, Cora! Just watch the person next to you and get down on your knees when they do. You'll be all right.' I wished I had not come at all. *Please come,* Teresa had written. *Most of the people there will be Kevin's friends and relations. I need somebody apart from my own family. I need you, Cora.*

I stepped out on to the pavement and Imelda droved away.

On my way up the steps I dropped my gloves and had to grovel about to retrieve them and so got in the way of a whole family on its way in to the ceremony, father, mother, sleek-haired boys, girls with bows and gleaming socks. 'Sorry, sorry . . .' 'That's all right, miss. Can I help?' 'Come on now, Dermot, or we'll not get a good seat.' They swept on and up and in. As the door opened the music of the organ billowed out. I hurried after the whole family.

They were already swarming up the aisle going as far as they could looking for good seats. The last little girl was dipping her fingers in the holy water font, genuflecting towards the high altar, the ribbons at the end of her tight pigtails bouncing.

Panic seized me. The ushers were waiting for me too to cross myself and bend my knee before the altar. Could I put my fingers into that cloudy pool of water? Would it be sacrilege? Then one of the ushers – Brian Lavery – recognized me and came forward saying my name. He led me up the aisle.

'This'll do,' I whispered after we had gone a few steps. I was not seeking a good seat.

I sat. Most of the members of the congregation were on

their knees, heads tilted forward, eyes closed, lips moving silently. I stuck out like a sore thumb. A Protestant sore thumb, an outsider who did not belong in this secret community. But I was here for the wedding, I reminded myself, I was an invited guest and the bride was one of my best friends. She was my blood sister. I lifted my head and hoped that I did not look too foolish in Imelda's navy straw boater with a red rose pinned to the brim. Through a gap in the rows of heads I saw one that I would have known anywhere. He sat in the second row from the front.

The music swelled into *Here Comes The Bride*. We rose. And here came the bride, not sixty inches wide as we used to sing when we were children, but slender and beautiful, as all brides should be. She rested lightly on the arm of her proud father whose breast appeared to puff out with every step they took. She wore a white veil which filmed her face and she carried a bouquet of roses the colour of the one in my hat. She looked pure. Tears pricked my eyelids and my throat tightened.

As they drew level with our row the bride looked sideways and saw me. Her veil rippled as she smiled beneath it and she almost spoke my name aloud – I saw it.

They moved on, followed by Mary, tall as Teresa, glowing in pink satin. Would it be on her that the mantle of motherhood would now fall? Her smile was demure.

I was at ease now, could sit back and look at the plaster saints set in their niches, at the candles flickering, at the grilled confessionals, at the stained glass windows, at the large solid gold cross above the altar. It was a church in a working-class area – on the way here we had passed some of the worst slums I had ever seen as well as better-kept houses and flats – but it was large, ornate and well-endowed. I heard Granny McGill's voice in my ear. 'The priests fleece them so they do, they'd take the last penny out of their hands and let their children starve so that they can fancy up their churches.' Granny McGill and Uncle Billy. No, don't let them intrude in here today!

Teresa and Kevin were joined in holy matrimony. Afterwards, the congregation went up to the altar rail to receive communion. I stayed where I was, with my hands folded on my lap. It seemed that I was the only non-Catholic at the wedding.

On the steps outside the usual photographs were taken and then Teresa was free to come to me. 'Cora, I'm so pleased to see you!' We hugged one another tight with a fierceness remembered from childhood. 'You'll crush your dress.' 'Who cares about that?' We separated so that she could introduce me to her husband. He looked a nice young man, open-faced; he was a plumber to trade, and a good dancer, for this Teresa had told me in a letter after she had met him at a dance in Bangor in County Down, and he was obviously fond of his bride, one could see that from the way he watched her face. He said he had heard a lot about me. I said I was looking forward to getting to know him though I suspected that I never would, not really know, and I suspected too that he would not care for my intimacy with Teresa, would feel uneasy when faced with it. She was his now, his wife, and would in a short time become the mother of his children.

'You remember Gerard, don't you?' said Teresa. 'What a silly thing to say! I think the day is making me foolish.'

Now Gerard stood in front of me wearing, like the other men, a dark suit, somewhat shiny, but the carnation in his buttonhole was real. He had broadened out, matured. He took my hand, saying it was great that I'd been able to come and they'd all been looking forward to seeing me again.

The crowd was moving towards the cars and buses. He put his hand under my elbow and guided me down the steps. If I were capable of wafting I would have done it then, as if in a dream. 'Are you remembering I'm accident prone?' We laughed. 'I remember picking you off the railway line.'

I went with him in the same car to the reception which was held in a dingy hall a few blocks away. Tables had been joined together into three long lines and covered with stiff white cloths. We sat together. He placed me on his left side. 'My good side.' That stung. But as we talked I pushed the remark to the back of my mind. I could not afford to think about such things now, not here at the wedding of Teresa.

'You'll never guess?' said Gerard. 'I'm going to Queen's in October!'

'Fantastic! To read law?'

'No.'

At that point we were asked to be upstanding to drink the health of the bride and groom so I had to wait until the speeches were over and the tables cleared away and the cloths packed up before I could ask, 'To do what then?'

'Medicine.'

'What made you change your mind again?'

The band was warming up.

'I can't talk about it here, I'll tell you after.'

I was content to wait knowing that there would be an 'after' which would carry us beyond the dancing here tonight. The bridal couple was taking the floor to the cheers of the guests.

'Come on!' said Gerard.

'I'm not much of a dancer.'

'Sure neither am I. I don't get much practice.'

We danced, and after the first round of the floor when he told me to relax and stop frowning so fiercely and I did, I felt that my feet would glide if only I would let them. I danced all evening and into the night, with Gerard and Brian and Kevin and Mr Lavery and Donny the husband of Bridie and Uncle Tom Cobleigh and all, but most of all with Gerard. When no other partner appeared he was there waiting to claim me. It seemed the most natural thing in the world to give my hand into his.

I had little time to talk to Teresa before she left for her four-day honeymoon but we promised we would see one another when she came back. I was planning to stay in Dublin for a week.

'I went to see Rosie before I left Belfast,' said Teresa. 'And guess what – she's expecting!'

'Come on, love.' Kevin eased her away.

'Wait till I come back,' she said over her shoulder.

She tried to throw her bouquet to me but at the last

moment a girl with saucy black eyes stepped out and caught it. The girl's mouth opened wide on a full-throated laugh.

'That means it'll be you next, Nancy,' someone called out.

We threw confetti over the heads of the departing bride and groom and tied an old shoe to the back of Kevin's beaten-up van.

'Weddings are great, aren't they?' said Mary.

'For girls,' said Anthony and made us laugh.

The party was not yet over: there was still much singing and dancing and drinking to be done.

I danced the last waltz with Gerard – the last waltz! – and then he said he'd leave me home if I didn't mind walking. How could I mind, when I was with him?

He took my hand. The streets were quiet after the clamour of the party, we saw only an occasional drunk, a policeman on his beat. We stopped on a bridge and leaned over the parapet to watch the dark, strong-flowing Liffey. I felt the magic of the city again, its promise of excitement, as I had when I had first come there as a child with my mother and Aunt Belle.

'So what about this change of direction of yours?' I asked.

'Back to medicine you mean? Ah well you see . . .' I heard the change in his voice and regretted at once that I had asked the question and changed the mood. 'It was after what happened – with Rosie.' My spirits dropped like a falling bird. I felt the wound in my breast. Why couldn't I have left well alone, let the Dublin night hold us in its spell? Why could I not learn to take the moment and what it offered?

He was telling me that he had gone off the idea of law and history. I knew that he'd always had the thought of going into politics in the back of his mind. 'But when I was lying in hospital I decided I wanted to have nothing to do with any of it. I wanted to be a doctor and heal the sick.' That was simpler and cleaner. We watched the ripple of a street light in the water. He had had to go to evening classes to study chemistry and physics. 'But I've made it, Cora – or I'm about to! I'm twenty-three, but no matter.'

No matter, I agreed: the thing was to make it.

We moved on and came at last into Imelda's Georgian Square. 'You must have posh friends these days.' 'Only one.' Would he ask to see me again? It was the only thought in my head now. We stopped outside the door, dropped hands, stood awkwardly, shuffling our feet. And then he said,

'Could I see you tomorrow maybe?'

I nodded.

'Say twelve?'

'Noon?'

'Hardly midnight.'

Our laughter rang out. We were both nervous.

'Goodnight, Cora, it's been great seeing you again.' He took a step back then came forward again and seizing my shoulders, kissed me, not at all awkwardly, but quite firmly, keeping his lips against mine for longer than was necessary for a polite goodnight kiss. It was not at all like playing Postman's Knock.

I ran up the stairs, switched on the lights, wakened Imelda. 'I've had the most wonderful evening of my whole life!'

'That's good,' she said, poking her head out and then squinting at the clock, 'Holy Mother of God, do you know the time? It's four o'clock in the morning!'

I went into the drawing room and cupping my arms to enfold my imaginary partner waltzed between the furniture making the chandelier tinkle.

We had three marvellous days together, Gerard and I, walking the streets of Dublin, riding in tramcars to Bray and Dun Laoghaire, drinking coffee in Bewleys, sharing half pints in Bartley Dunn's and Mooney's.

'It must be great to be in love,' said Imelda with a sigh.

It was, I said.

Was Gerard in love with me? He did not say and I did not ask. My happiness had lessened my need to question.

'Bring him up to the flat,' said Imelda, 'and I'll make

myself scarce. But you'll behave yourselves now won't you? You can have a bit of a cuddle and all that but sex before marriage isn't on, you know. You want to be a virgin when you get married. He won't respect you if you let him go too far.'

'He's a good Catholic.'

She snorted. 'That won't stop him. They'll all try anything on if they can get away with it.'

Going too far, trying things on, getting away with it. How did one cope with these concepts? How did one define them? How far *should* I let him go? As I waited, I wished I hadn't suggested he come up to the flat. I had made spaghetti bolognaise and bought a bottle of cheap red wine.

He brought another bottle with him. 'Rot gut probably.' He set it one the table. 'We don't have to drink the two.' But we did and got a little drunk and ended up in my bed and went too far, unable to stop ourselves and neither of us wanting to.

'Oh Cora!' he said, when he rolled off me. 'Will it be all right? I should have come out of you before–'

I reassured him: it was too early in the month, too soon to conceive. You can never be sure, he said. Of anything, I added, making him smile. Later, I often wished that I had conceived that evening and borne a child, his, ours, mine. We lay on our sides looking at one another. He stroked my face. 'Imagine, I never thought . . .' I knew he had not, had not come to try anything on, to seduce me, to get what he could whilst the going was good. He was an honourable man. Before he left we made love twice more. We asked was it good for you, are you happy, are you all right? We didn't speak of love. But we promised to write, to stay in touch, to meet again, somehow, somewhere. *Don't know how, don't know when, But we'll meet again, some sunny day...*

I lay on in bed after he had gone.

'Good God!' said Imelda when she came in. 'He'll never marry you now.'

FIFTEEN

Dear Cora, he wrote during the year that we had to wait to be together again, and at the foot of each letter he put, *Love Gerard*. Depending on my mood, I read everything and nothing into those beginnings and endings. The parts in between spoke not of love but of his family and studies but they spoke openly and brought me close to him. I wrote *Dear Gerard* and *Love Cora*, restraining myself from using other endearments, though I tried them out in my mind. *My dearest darling Gerard. Your ever-loving half-crazed Cora.*

I tried out much in my mind. What pleasure the sphere of the imagination gives – everything one wants! At times I thought I should like to stay there and give up this other world altogether. I imagined Gerard and myself married, living in Dublin (where else?), he a qualified doctor, sought out by both rich and poor, an acclaimed success (I wanted him to have it every way round), I working at Trinity College full-time or part-time, depending on whether we had started a family or not. For we would have children of course, two or three, no more. I could not give up my desire for a career nor could I see myself as a totally obsessed mother. That was a mistake, according to Imelda: I should be one thing or the other or else I would fall between two stools.

'I'll just have to learn to do a balancing act.' My confidence had never been so high. I knew what it meant to walk lightly. My feet skimmed the streets of London and if I sang I sang inside my head.

'You're looking great,' said Aunt Belle.

'Studying seems to be agreeing with you,' said my mother.

Imelda acted as my *poste restante*.

'Letters!' she said, handing them over. 'I don't know how they keep you going. Pieces of paper covered with writing!'

She went out with one man after another going only so far and no further and when they tried anything too much on she said goodbye. She seldom sighed. And she liked variety. 'Might as well have it while I can. Think of it – forty or fifty years of looking at the same man's face across the breakfast table every morning! Not that I will probably come down to breakfast *every* morning. But then there is the pillow . . . Now a bit of variety would do *you* good, Cora.'

But she was wrong: it would have done me no good at all, would have distressed me rather, caused me all sorts of anguish and worry. I wanted only one man and his letters kept me going very well indeed, easing me through my Finals year, nourishing my dreams and giving me something to look forward to. It might have been better if we had never met again, had just let the letters flow to and fro. For ever. But then nothing is for ever, so it is said.

I kept on writing, too, to Rosie and Teresa. Rosie gave birth to a girl, Emma, and Teresa to a boy, Liam, nine months after her wedding. Those were the main events of their year. Their children were beautiful, they were content.

'At least so far,' I said to Imelda.

'Your trouble is you expect too much.'

I was surprised by her saying that, having always thought I expected too little.

We graduated, and went to Dublin.

Make yourselves at home, said Imelda, regard the place as your own. She had put two bottles of champagne in the fridge for us and waited to meet Gerard, briefly, and to see that everything was all right. To see that I was all right.

Have a good time! she instructed us and then I went

with her to the door. 'No suffering now! Remember, Cora, that suffering is *verboten* in this flat!'

'Thanks, Imelda.' I kissed her smooth warm cheek. I wished that I could take life as uncomplicatedly as she did.

Gerard was standing in the middle of the drawing room floor looking as I had felt the night before when I'd been on the point of fleeing. The year between seemed suddenly to have been a long time, and the letters less substantial.

'Let's open the champagne shall we, Gerard?'

It was the first bottle of champagne he had opened. He had to wrestle with it and when the cork flew up in the air and hit the chandelier and set it tinkling we collapsed on to the floor with laughter. No harm was done though. The glass resettled itself and fell silent. We drank.

We finished the bottle – were we always going to have to drink a bottle? – and went to bed. And then the year between shrank and disappeared. I lay back, happy, satisfied, reassured.

He smiled too and fingered the fine linen sheets that smelled of fresh air and lavender. Sheets dried in the country, brought into the town. Talk about living in the lap of luxury! A little luxury would do us no harm, I said, not for ten days anyway. 'Nor for a lifetime either,' I added. He laughed, not expecting ever to have that.

On the wall opposite the bed the Virgin Mary stared modestly down into her lap, avoiding looking at us.

'Don't suppose she'd approve, do you?'

'Probably not.'

'Do you still believe in the Virgin birth?'

'Yes.'

'Life after death?'

'Why not?'

'Transubstantiation?'

'What is this, Cora? Your form of the catechism?' He was only half amused. He pulled himself up against the pillow. 'You know where I stand on these things.'

'I know where you used to stand.'

'I haven't changed.'

I found that surprising, for people *did* change, through

experience and age. *I* had changed. Well, he had not. But he was a man of science, going to be a doctor, did he not feel torn between conflicting evidence? It was not a case of evidence, he said: he believed. I had known he would say that. Belief was everything, so he would have me believe. And he had no intention of not believing. Had he? He shrugged.

Leave it! Cora, you have no idea when to hang back, let things lie. I pressed on. Weren't we accustomed, when we were younger, he and I, to talking freely about religion? Religion, politics, history. We'd seldom talked of anything else.

'Very Irish topics, eh – the three lumped together?' he said, trying to give the discussion a bantering tone.

'Does your religion make you happy?' I did want to know even though I asked semi-flippantly.

'It's got nothing to do with happiness. I just couldn't think of being without it. It's part of me. Part of what I am.'

Of course I had always known that.

'Why do Protestants ask so many questions?' He softened his question with a smile but the word 'Protestants' still had a harsh, grating sound to it. He saw me as one of *them*.

'Will you take me with you to Mass on Sunday?'

'Yes, of course, come if you want to.' Too smooth that, deadpan, revealing nothing of what he felt.

My second visit to a Roman Catholic church. There was no wedding today, no social reason to come, only the purely religious one. Blessed are the pure in heart. Or blessed are those who are at least striving to be pure in heart. I could not be numbered amongst them. My motive for being there was base. I wanted not God but the man I followed up the aisle. I walked with my face cast down, one hand clutching my headscarf so that it would not slide backwards and leave me bare-headed, my eyes fixed on the back of his black heels. We found seats in a pew and he went forward on to his knees to pray. I kept my back straight and locked my fingers together to stop them shaking.

The woman on my left rose up dusting off her knees and sat back beside me. She wore a hat shaped like a shovel and a small gold crucifix swung between the globes of her breasts. She glanced at me and I looked away. Gerard did not look at me at all when he surfaced, he appeared absorbed by his devotions.

I was in the midst of a devout congregation which ranged in age from the very young to the very old and in class from solid members of the Dublin bourgeoisie to black-shawled women. When they united in prayer I too went forward on to my knees and laced my fingers across my eyes. The murmuring around me was like the waves of the sea. I listened to its rise and fall and to the thin reedy voice of the priest in between. I liked the sound of the Latin.

When the time came for the congregation to take communion I turned in the opposite direction, fighting against the current to get outside. The queue forming at the altar rail was enormous, Gerard would be a while. I leant against the church wall blinking in the sunlight.

'There you are!' Gerard appeared in front of me.

'Didn't you take communion?'

'No. How could I?'

Of course: he was in a state of mortal sin. Because of me.

Did he *feel* guilty? I had to ask him. He said he hadn't really thought about it which couldn't have been true since he must have done when he was unable to go forward and take communion. Did it perturb him to know that he was committing a mortal sin in the eyes of the church, that his soul was in danger unless – or until – he repented? I wanted to probe, to force his confidence, to share his inner as well as his outer life.

We were sitting on the grass in St Stephen's Green. It was a perfect summer's day, almost cloudless, children playing, the smell of flowers, a priest dozing on a nearby bench. We had risen from Imelda's bed only an hour before, at one o'clock in the afternoon. 'Glory be, what a dissolute life we're leading!' he'd said and grinned and looked fourteen again. Now he sat with his face half turned away from me pulling up tufts of grass. The half of his face I could see was in shadow. He had a dark side to him and when it came over him he turned silent and withdrew into himself. Then he looked hard rather than vulnerable, like a man armoured. That side of him made me tremble but I did not love him less.

'Why does your church make such a fuss about sex?'

He shrugged, took a long blade of grass and put it between his teeth. I knew he did not want to answer because he would have had to use a word that had never been spoken between us. Marriage. Would we ever enter in the holy state of matrimony together? I wanted it more than anything else I could think of and was not afraid or ashamed to admit it to myself.

The priest on the bench jerked awake and consulted the watch that dangled over his rounded black stomach. Stretching, he got up and came towards us. Was he coming to scoop Gerard up and carry him back into the fold? His feet stopped beside us.

'Lovely day.'

'Yes, it is, Father,' said Gerard.

'On holiday are you?'

'We are.'

'From the North eh?'

'That's right.'

'Ah well see and have a lovely time. Dublin's a fair city.'

Where the girls are so pretty...I hummed the tune under my breath. The black feet moved away taking slightly staggery steps across the green. Under the influence? Granny McGill used to tell us that the Roman Catholic clergy was drunk more often than it was sober.

Gerard sank back on to his forearm and returned to munching the blade of grass.

I went back to my cross-questioning, knowing it was misguided, yet unable to stop myself.

'So you don't feel too disturbed?'

'About what?'

'Oh come on, you know what I'm talking about!'

'I can't be too disturbed now, can I? Or I wouldn't be here like this with you, would I?'

I should have asked him the questions in bed, where I could have touched him. He would not like me to touch him here, in this public place. He was a strange mixture of prudery and abandonment. A truly Irish mixture.

'Of course when you go back to Belfast you'll confess and get absolution, won't you?'

'I suppose so.'

'You know so.'

'All right, I know so.'

'Makes life easy doesn't it? Your sin will be taken away from you. No matter what you do.'

'*Only* if you repent. You talk as if that's easy. Look, Cora, you're making more fuss about sin than I am. It's just part of everyday life. Come on, let's go for a drink. I've a terrible thirst on me.'

A truly Irish escape route that was. I said so. He said I seemed to have everything taped, and labelled. We were on the brink of quarrelling.

'Let's stay and try to talk things out, Gerard.'

I was always wanting to talk things out, he said. And he was always wanting to let things slide, I retaliated. He said he didn't know the answer to a lot of things, he wished he did, but sometimes one had to be content to not-know, to let matters lie until the way forward seemed clear. To let them drift, was that not what he meant?

'What plans can you and I make, Cora?'

That stopped me dead for there were many plans that we could make, if we wanted to.

We went to Bartley Dunn's and talked of other things, extraneous matters that did not impinge on our personal lives. And then, mellowed by Guinness, we took a tram and went to visit Teresa.

'You're looking great the two of you.' She scrutinized our faces. I saw Gerard turn away to try to avoid being read. He lifted his young nephew from his pram and swung him up in the air until his mother, laughing, protested, and reached up for him herself. I, too, was glad to be relieved of her look. She had read us well though, I was sure.

After Kevin had come home and we'd had tea, the men went off to the pub. Liam was laid in his cot. He seemed a good baby.

'He's an angel.' Teresa closed the door on him and we sat ourselves down by the window of the living room. They lived in a narrow terraced house with a small front garden. 'It's great having that bit of garden to put Liam out in.' For a while we talked of her domestic life. In the street children playing with skipping ropes. We said do you remember when we . . . ? Then Teresa said, 'So what about yourself and Gerard? Is it serious between you like?' She frowned.

'Gerard can't really be serious yet can he?'

'That's what I'm thinking. You're staying at that girl's flat with him, aren't you? Cora, you shouldn't let him take advantage of you.'

Don't be silly, Teresa, I told her, he's not taking advantage, it's not like that, he cares for me.

She still looked troubled. 'But it's not right, Cora.'

'I suppose you were a virgin on your wedding night?'

'That was the way we both wanted it.'

'I am happy though, Teresa.'

'Ach well, pay no attention to me. It's none of my business, not really.'

I put my hand on her arm. 'Don't judge me, Teresa, please.'

'I'm sorry! I've no right to be judging you.'

But she had been of course. She had her standards, she couldn't help it, and also she *was* concerned, for both of us. For he might be her brother but I was her blood sister. She said again that she was sorry, she was being an eejit, and we laughed and kissed one another and reaffirmed the tie between us. We talked then of Rosie stopping in mid-sentence when the men came into view on the pavement in front of the window.

Gerard and I never talked of Rosie though at times other topics brought us close and we would see it in each other's eyes and quickly change the subject. I longed for us to be able to speak openly about her but feared my own exposure which would mean the end of Gerard and myself.

The days slipped past, the end of each one bringing us closer to that moment when we must say goodbye – *must say goodbye* – and many things we might have talked of remained undiscussed.

Now is the hour . . .

'What are you humming?'

I stopped at once.

'You know, Cora, next year we might try to go to Kerry or somewhere like together. I've never been to the west.'

'*Next* year?' I pounced. 'You don't expect to see me in between then?'

'It'd be difficult, wouldn't it?'

'Gerard–' I decided to be bold '–now that I've graduated I could come to Belfast and get a job, teaching maybe, and rent a flat. Then we could see one another regularly.'

He wasn't sure about that.

'Wouldn't you like to see me regularly.'

'Yes, I would but–'

'Not on your own territory?'

He sighed. He supposed we ought to talk, about us, and now that we had reached that point I wanted to back away, to say let's leave it, let's see . . . I was afraid to hear him spell out his position, define the limits of our relationship, for I suspected that it *was* going to be limited.

'Belfast is difficult for us. Well, there's Rosie for a start–' he'd said her name at last and I felt my heart palpitate '–and my family.'

'Would they mind about me?'

'No, I don't think so. But it's just that they take nearly all of me that's left over once I've done studying. I wouldn't have much time left for you.'

Should I say that I would not mind, or that I might mind but I would sit in my room and wait for the crumbs he could throw to me? That would be to give myself away cheap, offer myself up as a doormat and all the magazine articles I had ever read advised against that. On the other hand they ran features on how to keep your man happy. I was confused.

'What if I was to find work in Dublin, could you come and see me here sometimes?'

'That might be possible.'

'And when you graduate you could get a job here too.'

'But I want to work in Belfast when I qualify.'

'You can't be chained to your family all your life.'

'No. But I want to work for my own people in Belfast.'

'For Catholics you mean?'

'Yes.'

So he saw himself as a doctor for Catholics but not Protestants? I thought that discrimination of the worst kind.

'I wouldn't refuse to help a Protestant in need–'

'That's big of you.'

'Cora, you don't understand, you don't see things from my position – you can't. I'm not blaming you for heaven's sake. But the Catholic community in the North needs more help than the Protestant and I am a Catholic and I understand their problems.'

All right, I accepted that, but I would be willing to help too. I wanted to help. I wanted to help him, any time, anywhere.

'Are we talking about marriage now, Cora?'

I trembled. But I would not draw back. Why should I? Did I not have the right to say what I wanted too? Why should it always be left to the man to say what *he* wanted?

I faced him. Was there any reason why we shouldn't talk about marriage? It wasn't unknown for Catholics and Protestants to marry. And I was not even an ardent Protestant, it was a label I had attached to me by omission rather than commission. 'I love you, Gerard, I always have.' I gave him my hands. I did not see how he could resist such a simple declaration of love. His face had a troubled look on it similar to one I'd seen on Teresa's. 'You are fond of me, aren't you?'

'Very fond, Cora.'

'That's all right then! It doesn't matter if you don't love me.' I lied of course but was trying to talk myself into believing what I said. 'I know it's not the same as it was with Rosie–'

'I never think of Rosie. And it's not that at all. And it's not not loving you either for I do, only I'm not sure if it's the kind of love you're talking about, or maybe I'm not capable of that kind any more, not after all that . . .'

'What is it then?' I asked gently. I felt at peace. I felt that since he did care for me we could overcome whatever obstacles existed. My faith, however, was misplaced.

'Marriage must be difficult enough without making it more so. A divided family would be no good, Cora. And as a doctor working in a Catholic practice – Look, love, I've got to say this to you – when I marry I want to have a Catholic girl for my wife.'

'Did you argue about religion *all* the time?' asked Imelda.

'Of course not. Only now and then. Only occasionally.' When I had brought it up. When I had insisted. I began to weep afresh. If only I had been cleverer – love had nothing to do with cleverness did it, or did it? – and more restrained – or restraint either? – if only I could have let the arguing go then eventually we might have found a solution. Gerard might have changed his mind, was what I meant.

'If only is a blind alley,' said Imelda, putting her arms around me and letting me cry against her shoulder. She had a natural touch, she would make a good mother, would soothe her children when they tripped and fell or their pets died. She would stroke their hair as she was stroking mine quietening the disturbance in my body. How was it that I could see the pattern of everyone's life ahead but my own? 'Anyway, Cora,' she said, 'seeing him for summers just wouldn't have been that great.' It might not be great but it would have been no small thing either, not compared with not seeing him at all. But underneath my lamentations and protestations there was no surprise, no real outrage, even when I called him cruel, for in my heart – yes, there – I had anticipated no other outcome. I had not expected to find eternal love with Gerard Lavery: I knew I did not deserve it and that between us lay a deep secret which, if revealed, would shatter our relationship into smithereens. How would he be able to forgive me that? And how could I have lived with him without confessing sooner or later?

'I think we'd probably best not see one another again,' he'd said on the last morning. Very cold. Very formal. The darkness had come down over his face again.

We did not even kiss goodbye, we kept a distance between us. I felt myself shrinking back against the wall. At the door he turned and for one wild moment I thought he was going to put down his bag and come to me. Our eyes met. There was pain in his. To look at it was unbearable. When I looked again I saw the door closing. I heard his quick steps go along the corridor, the rap of his heels as he ran down the stairs. Quickly I crossed to the window. I watched him walk round the edge of the square. He kept his head down all the way. I thought he was crying.

'I love him, Imelda.'

'I know, lovey.' She rocked me to and fro. 'It sounds awful – but you'll get over it won't you, in time? You must think that way. I mean you're only twenty-two, that's not old. You couldn't have the biggest love of your life behind you could you?'

I didn't see why not: it was possible.

'Go and wash your face and I'll pour us a gin and tonic.'

When I looked in the bathroom mirror I saw that my face was swollen and my eyes looked like bloodshot poached eggs. My legs were weak. I sat down on the edge of the bath. I felt as if half of my life blood had been drained out of me.

'Come on,' cried Imelda, coming to the bathroom door waving two glasses as big as flower pots. I followed her back into the drawing room.

'Well, Cora, here's to–'

'What?'

'A new life.'

'Survival'll do.' I knew that it would not but I drank to it anyway. 'Perhaps I could come to believe in the Virgin birth?'

'There's more to it than the immaculate conception, dear,' said Imelda and made me laugh.

We got disgustingly drunk. I remembered Mrs Robinson coming home drunk with her fancy man, her breasts hanging out of the lilac taffeta dress, her ankles wobbling on their high white heels. I remembered Mrs Robinson after Mr Robinson had beaten her up.

'Perhaps I'm finished with men, Imelda. Except for casual encounters. Brief encounters on railway stations with the smoke swirling round us. Pity about diesels.'

'I haven't really begun yet – with men. Not properly. Imagine, I'm a virgin, pure as snow!'

'That's what Gerard's going to marry, one of those. You can be sure of that! A Catholic virgin. Like you, Imelda. Only not you. Because your family would have the vapours wouldn't it?'

She started to giggle and spilt her gin.

She put on a record and under the trembling chandelier we danced. And sang songs. I gave a rendering of *The Sash* and she of *The Wearing of the Green*. We collapsed on to the settee holding our sides in laughter.

Next morning I was wretchedly ill. I should have gone to say goodbye to Teresa but did not; I lay behind closed blinds reflecting on my first twenty-two years. Before I left on the following day I sent a letter to her saying that I'd been called to an interview for a job. I returned to London and the start of a new life.

SIXTEEN

Behind the drawn curtains the McGills were gathered, in the street the Lodge men waited. The cloying smell of massed flowers filled the house. Orange lilies and orange gladioli and mixed bouquets in red, white and blue. Sweet William in abundance. Oh the colours they were fine!

'He was a good man,' said Granny McGill.

'A fine man,' said Aunt Gertrude.

'Wouldn't have hurt a fly,' said Mrs Meneely.

'Cut down in his prime!' said Granny McGill and she wept.

Uncle Billy paced the floor between the coffin and the window in his church-going Lodge-going funeral-going suit, his hair slicked down with Brilliantine. As he turned he looked his niece in the face. 'You know what they say in the Bible about an eye for an eye?'

'That wouldn't do any good,' said Rosie uneasily. She looked very uneasy and exceedingly pale. No roses bloomed in her fair cheeks today. I kept looking at her trying to penetrate that outer shell and find within the Rosie that I used to know. For she must still be there, in spite of the extra flesh gathered over the years, and the darkening of her hair, and the paling of her skin. Her husband stood behind her with his hand on her shoulder. He was watchful, he was not going to let them hurt her.

'Haven't enough eyes been put out?' I said and then mumbled, under the blast of Uncle Billy's blue stare, 'Anyway, it'll be up to the police now won't it?'

'The police!' he snorted.

'Sure everybody loved him,' said Mrs Meneely, swivelling her eyes towards the coffin.

'The dear man,' said cousin Deanna whose hair was

fixed fast now in corrugated ridges and no longer bounced in ringlets.

'Only a monster'd do a thing like that,' said Aunt Gertrude.

'*Laverys*!' said Granny McGill and her tears ran dry.

'Those bastards are asking for it right enough,' said Uncle Billy and smacked his clenched fist against the palm of his other hand.

'Shall we get started then?' said the minister who had been clearing his throat for the past few minutes in an effort to break in. 'Dearly beloved . . .'

I said my own prayers. The minister gabbled his. He seemed anxious to get the coffin outside and on its way.

The Lodge was assembled in its full glory. The sun shone on the sashes making the orange and gold sparkle. We watched the procession move up the street and round the corner and then we retreated to the kitchen, we women, where we wept, each of us for different reasons, and Rosie, now that she no longer had the pressure of her husband's hand on her shoulder, turned to me, and we put our arms round one another and I felt her new soft plumpness against me.

After the tears we were calmer and dried our eyes and sliced the ham and tongue and cut the cake that was bursting with currants and filled the milk jugs and sugar basins.

'Sam'd have been pleased,' said Mrs Meneely, surveying the table. 'He loved his food.'

'Cora and I are going for a walk,' said Rosie. 'Just round the block. To get a breath of air.'

We linked arms, as we used to do, and fell into step. We passed my old house which looked much the same as it had always done and yet quite different since I knew that *we* no longer lived there, and the Laverys' which had a neat and tidy air about it with nothing left lying in the path or on the lawn. The Graceys had moved away to a better district so the street was now Protestant to a man. And woman. Like should stick to like, Granny McGill had often said: that way there would be less trouble. Not everything she said was wrong.

'I'm so glad you came, Cora.' Rosie squeezed my arm. She had a husband yet she needed me! In the midst of its misery my heart sang a small note.

And now we came to speak, as we must, of the killing of Uncle Sam.

'Why him, Rosie?'

'And not Uncle Billy, you mean? I suppose just because he happened to go to the door. They looked pretty much alike through the reeded glass.'

Was it chance then? No, we couldn't write the whole incident off to that, except in the small quirk at the end that the wrong man answered the door bell. If he was the wrong man. But we were fairly sure that he had been. Though, in fact, he had stood a greater chance than Billy of ending up a victim since he had always been more obliging about getting up to answer the door and the like. His good nature had not done him any good.

'So do you think the shooting was a reprisal, Rosie? For Gerard?' It grazed my throat to get his name out. Could it have been revenge after all this time? Memories were long in this country, Rosie reminded me, though she scarcely needed to, going back to 1921 and 1916 and 1798 and 1690. So what was seventeen years? What was it to us after all? We remembered everything didn't we, almost as if it was yesterday?

'But Anthony Lavery was only a child then,' I said. He had been four years old. And now he was twenty-one and being held in custody to await trial for the shooting of Sam McGill.

'Old enough to remember though. And I don't suppose his brothers let him forget. Oh, not Gerard, I wouldn't think . . .'

Had she seen him at all? 'Only once. Funny isn't it and we live in the same city. But our circles don't touch of course. I was in the car, he was walking up Royal Avenue. He looked up and saw me and then I had to drive on for the lights had changed and everybody was honking. He's married, you know that from Teresa, don't you? With kids and a busy practice.'

And what about Uncle Billy? Did she think that he–? I

could not finish the question. I felt as if my lungs were being squeezed together and denied air.

'Will take an eye in return? I don't know. A lot of his talk is hot air. I think.' Rosie sighed and said we must hope that he would not: that was all we could do. 'Are you all right, Cora? Funerals fairly knock the wind out of you don't they?' We had almost completed our circle of the block. She must see Teresa, she said, and asked me to arrange it.

I was staying with Rosie and Tom in their detached house up the Malone Road. After partaking of the funeral meats and tapping our feet in time to the funeral songs, we returned to it. 'It's so peaceful here,' said Rosie as we turned into their street. Tom touched her hand reassuringly. You will be safe with me, the touch said. Would that such safety could be so easily found! Rosie well knew that it could not.

Their street was tree-lined, the lawns behind the hedges smooth and close-cropped, the roses made a fine show and should bloom from May to September. There was no hint of menace here, not that one could see. It was an area that testified to law and order. Their children, Emma and Mark, aged fourteen and twelve respectively, were polite and well-mannered and lived well-regulated lives. Not like us at that age, I observed to Rosie who smiled and said perhaps it was just as well. Emma was kept busy with her homework and ballet and Mark was keen on rugby and model railways and was being taught golf by Tom. No time left for hanging about on corners or outside the chip shop, or for playing at weddings in the woods.

'Oh, *that*!' said Rosie. 'It was an odd time in our lives wasn't it. I've never even told Tom about it.'

'Do you ever see Deirdre Fish these days?'

'We have lunch in Cleavers once a month, Deirdre and Susan Orr and Angela Simpson and I, and catch up on all the gossip.'

Would that gossip include me? Poor Cora, it can't be easy for her, even though she does have a successful career and travels all over the place, but a career's not everything is it, not when it means missing out on having a home of your own and children? Children was what they all had in common. And husbands too of course. They were not the women that single parents are made of.

I did not think that Rosie would gossip about me, not in a derogatory way: she had always been loyal. Though who was I to talk about loyalty?

On the day after the funeral we sat in her garden under the spreading branches of an apple tree. It was the kind of garden we had always dreamed of having, with a wall and trees and a swing and a conservatory jutting out into it. The conservatory made me think of Mrs Hastings-Smith and I resolved to visit her. Since my mother's death five years previously our contact had lapsed except for a card at Christmas-time.

Rosie offered to drive me there. 'We could go now. Why not? I'm restless anyway.'

We drove across town to Mrs Hastings-Smith's bungalow in Cherryvalley. Rosie said she would not come in but would go for a walk, retrace her footsteps around old haunts.

Mrs Hastings-Smith did not seem at all surprised to see me. 'Come in, Cora,' she said, as if the years between had not existed, and led me through the house to the conservatory. Her back was a little stooped now. Perhaps she had bent her head when she moved into this low house. The ceilings had been high at Hastings Court. 'We'll sit in here if that's all the same with you? So much nicer to be amongst plants in summertime I always think.'

Most of them were tinged with brown or spotted. They crowded against the glass as if they were desperate to get out. The geraniums were doing well though, their blooms sizzling red and pink and coolly white. The sun beat in on us, the atmosphere was jungle-like. I had never been up the Amazon, in spite of my early ambitions, or perhaps because of them, had travelled eastward rather than west. 'So nice of you to come, dear. Shall we have some tea?'

Declining my offer of help, Mrs Hastings-Smith withdrew to the kitchenette where she remained for a long time. I sat in a daze of heat inhaling the smell of damp earth and the spicy scent of geraniums. My mind went into neutral.

'Here we are!' She returned with a silver tray and tea set. Tarnished of course. We drank tea in thin, cracked cups and ate crookedly cut cucumber sandwiches. The almond cakes were still thin and wafer-like, however.

'Baked by Marcellina. She has such a light hand.'

'How is she?'

'Just the same, grown a little stout and grey, but no different from what she ever was. She comes once a week to do for me. You are just the same too, you know, Cora.'

I could have denied that but chose not to, not having come to dispute anything. We talked of my mother. Mrs Hastings-Smith said she often thought of her. 'She was a good woman. You may rest assured that she has moved on to a better life.'

'And now, tell me about yourself, dear. You seem to go all over the place. Anthropology, is that you're doing? I would not have cared for such a life myself, I am too fond of my own home and my own things about me, but then we are all different, though, deep down, the same. We are God's children. Have your travels never taken you in Bertrand's direction?'

I had been working in India mainly, I told her, and Sri Lanka. 'Ceylon.'

'Ah yes. Tea. Thoese new names confuse me a little. One wonders if all that was quite necessary. Bertrand used to send me tea, do you recall? He sends nothing now except an occasional postcard. Wild animals, you know. He could scarcely *send* those! And I rather think he is growing tobacco which he is aware I would not welcome. And what about yourself and Christian Science, dear? Have you found your way back to it yet? I have never ceased to work for you.'

I said I was sorry even though I felt no need to apologize, having decided long since that one did not have to be apologetic for rejecting the ideals and beliefs of one's childhood since they had been bred in one unrequested. Nor did one have to be obliged to the people who had done the breeding merely because they had been doing it for one's own good. As they undoubtedly had. Though I did feel grateful to Mrs Hastings-Smith for the part that she had played in my life and before I left I was able to tell her so and she was pleased. She thought that it meant that I had not totally rejected her beliefs and indeed I had not, had simply taken a different path.

Rosie was leaning against the car. 'Well?'

'She hasn't changed. Which is immensely reassuring.' I laughed.

'Have *we* changed? Well, what do you think?'

I would have preferred to shrug the question off, was not ready yet to face it with her, but she was determined to probe, not only me, but herself. Uncle Sam's death had shaken the structure of her life, not enough to split it apart, as far as I could judge, but sufficiently to throw it off balance. 'We've compromised haven't we? Or at least I have. Oh I'm happy with Tom – he's a lovely man and he thinks the world of me – and I adore my children but–' She gazed up the street. 'Perhaps life's bound to seem a bit of an anti-climax after one's youth.'

'Depends on one's youth.'

'Yes, maybe. You're all right though, Cora – you're doing many of the things you dreamt of doing.'

'And missing out on others.'

'You're right. Who can have everything?'

I would have had a try at it, had I been given a chance.

We got back into the car. She did not want to go home. She drove around the city saying remember when we went here or there and did this or that. The city itself – though not our old neighbourhood – had changed much in my absence, new roads had been built linking and bypassing, obliterating landmarks, giving me a feeling of disorientation. There were armoured cars in the streets and soldiers on foot patrol wondering what they would find round the next corner.

'You'd think there was a war on,' said Rosie. 'Will you be all right going up the Falls on your own tomorrow?'

'I hardly think anyone's going to bother about me!' But her question had been serious and when she lent her car the next day she told me to take care and that if men jumped out into the road trying to commandeer the car I should put my foot on the accelerator and drive straight on.

The slogans were thicker on the walls since the last time I'd been up the Falls. UP THE IRA. PROVOS. BRITS OUT. FUCK KING BILLY. The sprayed letters leapt before my eyes. Men in battledress abounded. There had been an incident the night before. A car lay on its side burnt out. Women watched the vehicles go by. The children on the kerb stood poised for further excitement. I knew where to go, we had looked it up on a street map of the city: I turned right and left and left again with confidence. To hesitate might attract attention.

The Laverys lived in an end-terraced house. UP THE IRA, it said on its gable end wall. I parked, pulled on the brake. The half-drawn curtain moved at the front window.

After I had rung the bell nothing happened for a moment. I felt a stillness inside the house as if its occupants were listening. Even the traffic seemed to have died away. I hesitated to ring again, I did not want to be insistent. A woman came out of her house across the road and began to wash her door step. Slop! went the grey cloth over the grey stone. Her eyes never left me. I put out my hand and gave the bell another gentle press.

Footsteps. Slow ones. The door opened a crack. Through the slit I saw the puffy face of Mr Lavery.

'It's me – Cora.'

He could not quite take it in so I had to repeat my name and then he said, 'Cora? For dear sake!' He let the chain off the door.

And now that I was inside the house it was no longer quiet but filled with the ring of voices. All the Laverys were there but Gerard, and Anthony of course.

Teresa and I hugged one another tight. She was thinner, felt narrow against my chest after Rosie, and seemed darker too. She kept her arm linked to mine as we went through to the back kitchen.

Mary put the kettle on and set out soda scones and potato bread.

'I'll never get over this, Cora,' said Mr Lavery, who sat at the table with the palms of his hands placed face downwards on it, reminding me of the way he'd sat the night his wife died. The echoes of recognition were reaching me, one by one, demanding to be acknowledged, stirring up old memories, old emotions. 'Sure he was always a bit of devil but I never would have thought . . .' The tears came, coursing down the gouged out valleys in his cheeks.

'Take a cup of tea, Da.' Mary touched his shoulder.

'I'm flooded with tea,' he said but took the cup and drank.

'I think I'll go on out,' said Paul. At twenty-three he looked much as Gerard had at that age.

Mr Lavery lifted his head. 'I don't want any of youse in the streets.'

'I'm not going till stay in the street.'

'Or in the pubs neither.'

'For heavens sake, Da, we can't stick in here all the time.'

'We've got to face people sometime,' said Mary calmly.

'Face people?' Paul guffawed. 'There's a few think our Anthony's a hero.'

'Some hero,' said Mr Lavery.

'Well, I'm going.'

Paul went, taking Peter with him. Brian said he'd need to be getting home or Lindy'd be worried thinking something had happened to him. He was the father of five children. 'I'll need to be getting along too,' said Bridie, who was expecting her sixth. And Teresa had four. The Laverys were doing well keeping their line going. My own would peter out when I did.

Teresa and I took our tea into the front parlour. She shut the door and at once asked about Rosie.

'She wants to see you.'

Teresa nodded. 'I'll come tomorrow.'

We talked then about her children and my job. We did not speak of Gerard.

After an hour I got up to go. 'Come early tomorrow. We have a lot to talk about.'

I drove out of the Falls to Dunmurry on the edge of the city. From the map in the glove compartment I found my way to another street, quite different from the back-to-back terraced one where the houses opened straight on to the pavement and children scrawled slogans on the walls.

Gerard's suburb, like Rosie's, reflected professional and executive tastes: trees overhanging walls, well-kept gardens, well-kept houses, and well-kept lives too no doubt, on the surface at least. I parked the car and walked the last two blocks to the street where Gerard lived.

At this time of day he would be out on his rounds and if I were to bump into his wife she would not know me. When I was near the gate I stopped to adjust the strap of my shoe. The house was detached, had been built between the wars, with bits of black and white criss-crossing to make it look Mock-Tudor. How Rosie and I used to mock at Mock-Tudor! As we sauntered through the suburbs arm-in-arm, we would eye the houses picking out ones we fancied. This one looked undistinguished but comfortable. I could not imagine Gerard inside it.

A child was riding a tricycle up and down the path pursued by another who was screaming and trying to seize the handlebars whenever they came within tantalizing reach. Beside the porch stood a high pram whose occupant was wailing as if not to be left out of the protest. A woman, pregnant, younger than I, perhaps by about five years, came out of the front door and shoogled the pram to and fro. She seemed frazzled, as well she might. 'Michael,' she called to the screaming child, the pursuer of the tricycle, 'that'll do! You've wakened Lucy.' Then she looked in my direction and I saw what she must have seen: a strange woman loitering, spying on her privacy. She frowned. I straightened up, she came down the path towards the gate. She smoothed the dress over her swelling stomach. She was fair, and rather pretty, a pallid imitation of Rosie. The likeness struck me sharply.

'Can I help you?' she asked in a polite, well-modulated

voice that belonged in this street and not the Laverys' terraced one. I could not imagine her visiting there. But that was not true – I could have imagined it if I had wanted to, just as I could have imagined Gerard living inside that house. When it came to matters that affected my personal well-being I had trained my imagination not to go too far. It had only caused me trouble in the past. I seldom daydreamed now. I found life itself too absorbing.

'Are you looking for someone?' Her eyes were round and light blue, like the glass marbles we used to roll on the pavement.

It was all right, thank you, I mumbled, and moved on.

I found a telephone box and looked up Gerard's surgery number. When I dialled I was told that Dr Lavery was consulting between five and six that day. Then I rang Rosie and said I might be a little late back and not to worry. I drove out to the Antrim coast road and walked beside the sea and just before six was back in the city, in the district where Gerard worked. In all my travels I had not seen such desolation.

Into that urban wilderness, jagged with broken glass, barbed wire, corrugated iron and burnt-out vehicles, I moved cautiously, hand on the brake, eyes swivelling. Boarded-up windows added to the feeling of menace. The slogans said KILL FUCK KILL. Half-wild dogs ran in packs barking. Children swarmed. A stone grazed the back of the car.

The surgery, an ugly modern building covered with grey harling that looked like dried porridge, squatted in the middle of a piece of derelict ground. Red painted letters dripped down the side wall. PROVOS RULE OK. UP THE REPUBLIC. The receptionist had enough to do without being bothered with me. 'You're a visitor?' she said dubiously. 'Are you staying round here?' I gave the Laverys' address on the Falls which she seemed to think was good enough. The Malone Road would not have been. She cut short my stumbling excuses about a bad back and waved me into the waiting room. It was packed with bodies that gave off a thick, heavy smell. I squeezed into a corner. After the first few glances the occupants returned to staring apathetically across the room flickering into life each time the receptionist's voice came out of the small box above the door and called for the next patient.

I worked my way through the pile of tattered magazines, turning the limp pages, glancing but not reading, lifting my head in unison with everyone else when the tannoy crackled even though I knew it could not be my turn yet. It was going to be a long wait. The room's torpor invaded me. Slowly, the seats emptied. Only six people left, coughing and snuffling and sighing, then five, and two went in together, a mother and daughter, the one supporting the other, so now there were three. My courage was ebbing. Should I make a run for it whilst I could? Another two went in together, cheating, stealing my fast-disappearing time, and so now there was only one to go before me. The disembodied voice above the door summoned him. He went.

I stared round the room with slack eyes. Crumpled paper handkerchiefs lay on the floor, discarded sweet wrappers; the chairs were awry; the magazines lay in an untidy, teetering pile. With a deliberate act of will, I threw mine on top of the heap and walked towards the door.

The tannoy crackled. 'Miss Caldwell please.'

I went into the arms of the receptionist who was waiting to guide me to his room. I was trapped. Unless I wished to cause a stir. I went in, she closed the door behind me.

He stood at his filing cabinet with his back half turned. At first when he did look round and say 'Good evening' he did not recognize me.

'Have I changed that much?'

'Cora! Good God, it can't be–'

'It is.'

He came round to the front of his desk and took my hands between his. He looked older than his years and incredibly weary.

'Come on, sit down, let me give you a drink. You're my last patient and you're not really a patient, are you?' He kept whisky in a white cupboard behind a stack of folders. 'I'm not a secret drinker, you understand, but sometimes either my patients or myself have need of a drink to boost our morale.'

We drank to each other. He pulled up his chair close to mine, directly opposite, and looked into my face as he might with a patient he was trying to read. It would be a habit he had developed. It was not one he had had when younger; then he had tended to avoid eye contact. Except in bed.

'You haven't changed much at all,' he said abruptly. 'I should have known you.'

I would have known him anywhere. I half-turned my head, to avoid his eyes. Don't be so foolish, I told myself, you can't start all that up again, there *is* nothing to start up. There cannot be.

A tap on the door startled us both. The receptionist put her head into the room.

'Will there be anything else, Dr Lavery?'

His fingers trembled slightly as he ran them backwards through his hair. 'No, that's fine, thanks, Kathleen. You can get away now if you want. Just switch the phone through.'

'Thanks. Jim's working late and the kids'll be in on their own.'

She took another look at me and the bottle before she went.

'Don't worry about Kathleen.' Nobody would grudge him a drink with an old friend, he said. Not even his wife? I suspected he would not tell her.

He leant back in his chair a little. He asked me what I'd been doing, I asked him. We only half-listened to what the other said, we knew enough.

'We must seem dull to you here, Cora. You've travelled to all those exotic places and we've stayed put.'

'You didn't want to go anywhere though did you?'

He was a little embarrassed. He said, 'Well, maybe not,' and went on to say that they'd excitement enough on their hands now anyway. Excitement they could do without.

Outside, a commotion had erupted. Kids were yelling, doors slamming. Gerard got up and went to the window to look between the slats of the venetian blinds. 'The army has arrived. The days of wine and roses are over. This time last year they were all drinking tea together. Thank God my kids don't live round here,' he said, self-mockingly, yet meaning it too of course. 'They're going to have a better chance in life!' He dropped the blind and came back to his seat.

'And why not, Gerard? You've worked for it.'

'But I'd the brains to see how to improve my lot. Not everybody can be as smart as I was, can they?'

'That wasn't why you took up medicine, you know it wasn't!'

'Do I? Remind me.'

'It's not the reason you're doing it now. You wouldn't be sitting in this surgery if it were. There are easier ways of improving your lot.'

'I've missed you, you know, Cora.'

The telephone on his desk rang.

'Hello, Dr Lavery here. Oh, Denise. No, I won't, I'll be quite late, I'm afraid. I'm delayed at the surgery and I've a half dozen calls to make afterwards.

'Now don't worry and don't wait up. Goodbye, dear.'

'I should go, Gerard, you're busy.'

'Please don't. It's great to be talking to you again, it really is. I don't talk to anyone very much these days, not really talk.' He refilled our glasses. *Out*, *out*, *out*! the kids were chanting in the street. He said, towards the window, 'Away home and watch the telly for a bit!' He sighed. 'I wonder if the patterns will ever be broken.'

'You broke out of yours.'

'Yes, I did, didn't I? So do you think there's some hope for us here then?'

I couldn't imagine him giving up hope. He smiled briefly. Maybe not. He'd have a hell of a nerve if he did when he saw so many people struggling against the odds and not surrendering. 'I just wish they'd find some other way to promote their cause.'

'*Their* cause? So it's not yours any longer?'

'Oh, I'd still like to see a united Ireland – if we could start from scratch anyway and have a new concept which wasn't built on the idea of *us* joining *them* or *them* joining *us* – but I don't know what I'm prepared to do about it. Probably nothing. It takes me all my time to live.'

'And work.'

'The two are the same.'

The telephone rang again. As he spoke he made notes on the pad in front of him. 'Don't worry, I'll be there . . .' He turned back to me. 'She calls every night. Lost her husband last week. Pub bombing.'

'Gerard, about Anthony and Sam McGill–?'

'I don't know. I didn't know Anthony all that well, you see, I never gave enough time to him, I was too busy studying. And *he* had nothing much else to do but hang around street corners waiting for something to happen until, in the end, he made it happen himself.'

We were silent for a moment, then Gerard said, 'Anthony came to my house after the shooting. That pleased me. It was there that he was arrested.'

'The police followed him?'

'No, they came a couple of hours later. But they knew he was in the house all right, they had it surrounded. It was almost as if they'd been tipped off.'

I had a vision of his wife, fresh-faced, her hands smoothing the dress over her swelling stomach. She might have done it. The more I thought of it the more convinced I became. It was like having a flash of insight when one knows something to be true without having to have it confirmed. I could not blame her though, for she would have done it to try to preserve what she had and to protect her children. And in spite of that comfortable house, her life could not be easy.

It was not a life I could have lived.

'And how is Rosie?' At last he had got round to asking. Well, I told him. Happy? I thought so. 'Good.' He did not want to know any more about her or her life.

Finally, we talked about ourselves in Dublin.

'I treated you badly, Cora. I just didn't know how to handle it. And I was miserable as sin.'

'You were right though, weren't you?'

I got up to go.

'Take care,' he said.

'And you!'

We kissed affectionately and then we parted. As I got into Rosie's car I saw him watching me through the slats of the blinds. I waved.

The next morning Teresa came to Rosie's house.

'A good story this would make,' said Rosie as we gathered round her kitchen table at the back of the house. She tugged the curtains half across, then bent to take scones from the oven. 'I'm going to fatten you up, Teresa Lavery. Four children and you look like a rake. How have you got away with it anyway? Just four? They don't sell contraceptives down there do they?'

'There are ways.'

'Interrupting pleasure, I suppose, or something equally unpleasant. You Catholics really like to revel in your suffering.'

'I wouldn't say that,' said I, taking a warm, sweet-smelling scone. Rosie's domesticity bemused me. Who ever would have thought it? She'd never been known to do a hand's turn when she lived with her mother and grandmother. 'No, I wouldn't agree at all.'

'What would you know about it?'

'I converted two years ago.'

'You've *turned*? You haven't, Cora!' Rosie sat down hard on the chair which Teresa had pulled out for her. 'You couldn't, could you?' Her voice faded. She looked at Teresa. 'Did you know?' Teresa nodded. That wounded Rosie, I knew, but it had been only natural that I would tell Teresa before her. She looked back at me. 'Do you actually believe in all that now?'

All that. I saw, processing before her eyes, plaster saints in blue and gold, crowns of thorns, a twisted body hanging from a wooden cross, rosary beads swinging against black skirts. The external trappings of the church and not its creed. I understood the workings of her mind, when it came to religion.

'Not all. But enough. Not as much as Teresa here. On some issues I'm still sceptical. But I decided that what I couldn't believe in I'd have faith in. Or else not worry about it.' I smiled. 'You see – I *have* changed.'

'But how did it come about?'

'I couldn't answer that in a few minutes, Rosie. It took years.'

She was quiet.

Teresa poured the coffee, handed a cup to Rosie who took it as if in a dream. 'I hope your mother won't drop in?'

'My mother? Oh. No, she won't. I told her I'd be out all day. She'd have a heart attack if she was to walk in and see me consorting with the enemy and if she was to hear that Cora–'

'Conversion's not all *that* unusual.'

'Oh, I know. The church works at it, doesn't it?'

'It didn't work on me. Rather the other way round.'

'Well, I hope you'll be happy.'

I burst out laughing then and so did Rosie and Teresa and Rosie apologized and said she'd just been taken aback.

When the telephone rang she got up, swearing, to answer. 'Hell's bells! That bloody thing would annoy you so it would, but I'm not capable of ignoring it in case one of the kids has broken their heads and been rushed to hospital.' Her voice was changing, I noticed; coming back into it were traces of her childhood accent which had been smoothed out by her life with Tom in this suburb. She went into the hall. 'Uncle Billy?' She made a face through the open doorway. 'Yes, I am going out. In the next five minutes. I have my coat on.' She returned saying, 'Let's get the hell out of here! We'll get no peace otherwise. They'll never leave us alone.'

'Let's go to Portrush!' said Teresa.

As we were leaving the telephone started ringing again. Rosie hesitated then said, 'Oh dash it, let it ring!' She shut the door.

It was only after our return from Portrush that we would hear the news: a bomb had gone off in Gerard's surgery. He was not there at the time but Kathleen, his receptionist, was. She lost a leg and was blinded in both eyes.

The season had not properly begun, there were few people on the beach. The day was bright and windy, white caps stippled the green sea. Linking arms, with Rosie in the middle, we strolled along the promenade. We had the wind behind us propelling us along whipping our skirts around our legs.

'It's great isn't it?' said Rosie.

We went to the Northern Counties Hotel for lunch. Teresa was like a child out on a treat. Her eyes shone and the tightness in her face eased. She was looking younger. We all were, we knew it, we were moving backwards in time, growing closer and closer to the selves we had been when we were blood sisters. We wanted it, we were pushing time back with every tactic we could muster.

'What next?' asked Teresa.

We went down to the sea, on to the smooth, damp sand, and this time we walked into the wind. This time too we walked separately, straggling a little, one or other of us going close to the edge of the waves and retreating again and then another following suit. Behind us in the sand we left trails of zigzagging footprints.

We rounded a headland and found ourselves in a calmer stretch.

'Wait!' I said. 'I have something to tell you.'

We turned inward to one another forming a triangle.

'What is it now?' demanded Rosie. 'Have you joined the IRA or something? Nothing would surprise me, Cora Caldwell!'

'You're not getting married?' said Teresa.

'No.'

'Wouldn't you like to?' said Rosie.

'Not particularly. Well, not especially. I might if I met someone who would fit in with *my* life.'

'A tall order that.'

'Yes.'

'So, what is it then?'

'It's not about the present at all.'

That quietened them.

'I have a confession to make.' I knew it sounded melodramatic but needed to use the words.

'Shouldn't you keep that for the priest?' said Rosie uneasily. 'I mean you do have a priest for that kind of thing now.'

'I've already made that kind of confession.'

'Are you sure it's something you want to tell us, Cora?' said Teresa.

'Quite sure. I've had long enough to think about it.' I faced Rosie. 'It was I who betrayed you and Gerard. I told your Uncle Billy.'

After a moment she said, 'But *why*, Cora?'

'She loved him.' Teresa put her hand on my arm.

'Did you?' Rosie frowned. 'I never realized. How did I not? We were so close . . . What a self-centred little brat I must have been! You must have hated me.'

I admitted that there were times when I had. And Teresa said, 'I hated you too for a while, Rosie. I burnt the letter you wrote to Gerard from Ballymena. I've always had it on my conscience.'

'You needn't have. I wrote to him again care of the hospital and he replied. He said we shouldn't see each other again.'

I told them then about Gerard and myself in Dublin and his final rejection of me.

'And here you are a Catholic now,' said Rosie.

'Yes, here I am. Rosie, do you forgive me?' *Say it, Rosie! For God's sake say it!*

'Do you think I wouldn't after all this time? What an eejit you are!' She came to me and tucked her hand into the crook of my arm and then Teresa did the same on the other side. I felt the heat of their bodies giving warmth to mine.

'Do you know,' said Teresa, 'I always suspected?'

No, I had not known that. Dark-horse Teresa! Good at keeping secrets. Closes her mouth in a little smile.

'Shall I surprise you even more?' said Rosie. 'I *knew*.'

'You *knew*?'

'Uncle Billy told me when I came back from Ballymena.'

So she had known all these years. She had kept her secret, too, Rosie of the big mouth who had told about

Mrs Robinson. How little and how much I knew her! I would have to reread her letters in the light of this new knowledge, think back over her occasional visits to London. How the past kept shifting and changing! The concept was not at all new to me. I recalled how those visits of Rosie's had been a little strained and we had not been able to refind the intimacy of our youth. At the time I had attributed it to Tom being there, to our paths having separated, to my own uneasy conscience.

'Now that we've come clean do you think we could be considered to be in a state of grace?' said Rosie, making us laugh.

States of grace could only be transient, we all knew that, regardless of our religious beliefs. The knowledge though did not deject us, for we were not thinking about transience or eternity at that moment: we were on the beach, and together, and that was enough.